*The stillest hour of the night had come, the hour before dawn,
when the world seems to hold its breath. The moon hung low,
and had turned from silver to copper in the sleeping sky* (page 54).

THE
AWAKENING

✦

THE
$\mathscr{A}$WAKENING

Kate Chopin

✦

Introduction by Carol Shields

Illustrations by John Collier

SUI MON WU, EDITOR

BARNES
&NOBLE
BOOKS
NEW YORK

◆

The text of the Barnes & Noble Deluxe Edition of Kate Chopin's
The Awakening follows the text in *The Complete Works of Kate Chopin*
(Louisiana State University Press, 1969), edited by Per Seyersted.

Illustrations copyright © 1997 by John Collier
"A Woman Like Any Other . . ." copyright © 1997 by Carol Shields
"Kate Chopin: Spanning a Lifetime" copyright © 1997 by Susie Mee

Acknowledgments for all other copyrighted material appear at the opening
of each individual essay or work.

Page references for quotations from *The Awakening* that appear in
the essays originally published elsewhere reflect their location in the Barnes
& Noble edition. The quotations themselves have been
left as they originally appeared.

This edition published by Barnes & Noble, Inc.

1997 Barnes & Noble Books

ISBN 0-7607-0590-9, *Deluxe Edition*
ISBN 0-7607-0815-0, *Limited Edition*

PRODUCTION & DESIGN
Book design by Charles Ziga, Ziga Design
Senior Production Editor, Catherine Schurdak
Production Consultant, Laura Livingston, Max Graphics

Printed and bound in the United States of America

97 98 99 00 01 MD 9 8 7 6 5 4 3 2 1
97 98 99 00 01 ML 9 8 7 6 5 4 3 2 1
QH

Contents

◆

$\mathcal{A}$PPENDIX $\mathcal{B}$
Perspectives on Kate Chopin

Color Plates

✦

A WOMAN
LIKE ANY OTHER...

◆

Reading Kate Chopin's *The Awakening* for the first time—I must have been in my late twenties—left me exhilarated, for here was a voice that spoke to the middle of my heart: a human journey, and a woman's story that was familiar in its rhythms and direct in its expression—yet emanated from the distant past.

Imagine my surprise when I discovered that the book in my hands had been first published in 1899, three years before my mother was born, and yet it presumed to address a modern readership on the subject of the self and personal liberty. Its concerns circled and touched the historical validation many of us yearned for.

At the same time, *The Awakening* confronted me with a number of troubling questions, both personal and literary. The period was the late 1960s. The distinctions and prohibitions of gender framed an explosive issue: Where do we go from here? We'd already read Simone de Beauvoir's *The Second Sex* and were trying to make sense of it, and we'd absorbed Betty Friedan's *The Feminine Mystique,* which told women, among other things, to stop having babies and to claim their own lives. Yes, we said—or at least that is what a good many of us said—but what else is there?

Books, especially novels, were a consolation to us during

this difficult time, a precious resource in a society that was not quite ready to discuss the vague, amorphous sense of unease we'd stumbled into. Were we crazy, stupid, or just ungrateful? Could we possibly be feminists, and, if so, what did that mean? We groped for examples. How had women coped in the past? It was at this point that *The Awakening* found its modern audience.

We had seen in our traditional fiction very little evidence of the angry woman, the sad woman, or the frustrated mother. This curious absence suggested a monumental censorship, conscious or unconscious. The surprise was that we should be moved, and informed, by a novel written back at the fusty, dusty end of the nineteenth century, that heavily-upholstered, lace-curtainy epoch we associated with our grandmothers, for heaven's sake, their high starched collars and towering hats and stern, expressionless faces, their fearful rectitude and asexual stare.

The author of *The Awakening* was Kate Chopin, a brand-new name to most of us, but a name that shimmered with seductive resonance—Hepburn? Frédéric François? Chopin's short and baffling novel was in the bookstores all of a sudden, wrapped in a bright, fresh book jacket, speaking boldly to *us*—after lying sixty-some years at the bottom of the literary deep freeze. There was something of an affront about this republication, and we welcomed it.

The book's heroine—but we were learning to distrust that term—is one Edna Pontellier of New Orleans. (Those of us who knew a little French sniffed a kernel of authorly intention in the choice of name: Pontellier, bridger, one who bridges, yes—of course!) Edna is under thirty, the mother of two children, the adored wife of a wealthy businessman. She possesses a minor talent for drawing and painting, and a major talent for unhappiness. It was the nature of her unhappiness, as well as its attendant confusion, that so many contemporary readers recognized and were drawn to.

With her bustling air of entitlement, Edna is not particularly likeable. Nor is she politically sensitive. Her black servants flutter in the background, mere ciphers, and she wastes not one minute considering their degradation. Her refusal to attend her sister's wedding appears petulant, and her attentions to her children are loving but sporadic. She is monumentally self-absorbed, operating out of a kind of aesthetic peevishness. Always ready to inconvenience others, she asks more of her friends than she gives. A selfish woman, then, and disturbingly childish.

But she wakes up to the self within her, which is why readers in the second half of our century pricked up their ears. Who was this woman? What did she have to say to us?

I remember, even on first reading, that I believed absolutely in Edna's awakening. Within the brief space of this novel, a period of several months, Kate Chopin manages to bring her heroine gradually, organically, to life. Edna's transition from sleepy girl to passionate woman evolves through countless sensory visitations and hundreds of cultural moments observed and secured. This accretion, this slowly-turning spindle, is the engine that drives the novel and makes Edna's destiny inevitable.

First to wake is her body, her pleasure in physical sensation, a sort of autoeroticism assaulting her as she appraises the roundness of her own lovely arms. She smells the sea and is seduced by its "whispering, clamoring, murmuring" (p. 24). Listening to music, she finds herself weeping, trembling, and surrendering to a number of extraordinary images: a naked man standing beside a rock on the shore, a woman stroking a cat. What can this mean? She grows greedy for food and drink. The world is pouring its offerings before Mrs. Pontellier, and she is snatching them up.

Half the time she doesn't know what's hit her. Or, rather, she knows and she doesn't know. Her heightened sensuality is in fierce debate with the workings of her mind. A moment of clarity dissolves into anarchy. Confusion coils itself around each new revelation. She sleeps; she wakes. The reader turns the pages, mesmerized. This ambivalence is all too pressingly real.

The moments of insight arrive intermittently, a series of cool, authorly asides: "Mrs. Pontellier was beginning to realize her position in the universe as a human being, and to recognize her relations as an individual to the world within and about her" (p. 23). But just as often a cloud of incomprehension makes itself felt: "She could not have told why she was crying" (p. 12), "An indescribable oppression" came over her (p. 12). She endured a "vague anguish" (p. 12) and "all sense of reality had gone out of her life" (p. 173). She felt as though she were walking through a green meadow, "idly, aimlessly, unthinking and unguided" (p. 29). "She wanted something to happen—something, anything" (p. 126).

Edna's bewilderment was for many readers her seal of authenticity. It felt genuine, it had the citrus bite of the *real,* and it matched perfectly the contagion of doubt that colored our own society in the 1950s and '60s. This was the age of ambiguity, and we trusted Edna Pontellier's vague stirrings more than we did the certainty of scientific pronouncements.

Contemporary readings have advanced our understanding of Edna's self-doubts. But the pages of Kate Chopin's 1899 masterpiece stubbornly refuse to give way to the kind of sober, scholarly point-by-point analysis we love to impose on our major novels. *She did this because . . . She suddenly realized that . . . She was moved finally to the understanding that her life had become . . .*

Instead Edna Pontellier moves through a series of scenes,

each of them gesturing toward revelation and growth. She learns to swim, and this new skill is both immediate and emblematic. She allows the sun to fall directly on her skin, so that her husband scolds her, telling her she is "burnt beyond recognition," (p. 5) meaning that her worth has been devalued, and that he is unable to recognize the person she is becoming.

One night she refuses to go to bed, lingering stubbornly in an outdoor hammock instead, exasperating her husband, who insists on sitting beside her, battering her with his coercive brand of love. She goes to visit the eccentric and independent Mademoiselle Reisz, an unmarried, ill-tempered woman, an artist who lives alone in a crowded yet airy apartment, and she continues her friendship with Madame Ratignolle, who is, to use the French expression, a woman happy in her skin. Madame Ratignolle has found fulfillment in obeying convention, but this is exactly what Edna seems unable to do.

Her experiments in independence grow more dramatic. She moves to a smaller house of her own, gives herself a rather foolish coming-of-age party, and, finally, forms a loveless sexual liaison with a man-about-town, Alcée Arobin, and a blindly romantic attachment to Robert Lebrun, a man hopelessly unable to return her ardor.

Disillusion accompanies each of these acts; it is the banner she carries. Her passion for Robert never feels to the reader anything more than a sentimental diversion; her devotion to her drawing lacks convincing passion. Having no sanctioned vessel in which to place her newfound understanding, she suffers a splintering of the soul, even as she is discovering her self. By the final chapter she is both shockingly sane and grievously lost.

How are we to understand the extraordinary climax of the novel? It's easy enough to say that she was born at the wrong time, that her imagination was mismatched with historical possibility. She was a woman in a world where women's behaviour was codified, when members of her sex were infantilized by their male protectors, where few choices were offered and only a limited voice was permitted. But a single act of self-assertion *was* available to her, and she took it. Perhaps it was the revenge of the powerless, perhaps a mistake born of bewilderment, perhaps the realization that there is something finally numbing and monotonous about the state of ecstasy. Whether Edna's decision was a victory or a defeat will depend on the sensibility of her readers, but most will see that the two interpretations exist side by side.

It is this complexity of thought and of human response that makes *The Awakening* an important and enduring book. This is no crude manifesto, no parable, no fable for children, no morality play. Edna Pontellier is not our instructor in the matter of the self, but rather a woman like any other woman, feeling her way in a tantalizing but withholding world.

We read it today from a different slant and for different reasons than did its shocked 1899 audience, and differently again than the hungry, desperate sixties generation. For one thing, we feel the force of the book's almost cinematic immediacy and appreciate its literary innovations. And at the end of the twentieth century we are perhaps able to understand with greater clarity and sympathy what it is that women want, even while continuing to struggle with the old problems of personal freedom and social responsibility. Such multiple readings are the mark of a classic, and *The Awakening* continues, at the end of our century, to awaken us to a new apprehension of the world and our place in it.

—Carol Shields
May 1997

THE
AWAKENING

✦

I

◆

A green and yellow parrot, which hung in a cage outside the door, kept repeating over and over:

"*Allez vous-en! Allez vous-en! Sapristi!* That's all right!"

He could speak a little Spanish, and also a language which
nobody understood, unless it was the mocking-bird that
hung on the other side of the door, whistling his fluty notes
out upon the breeze with maddening persistence.

Mr. Pontellier, unable to read his newspaper with any degree of comfort, arose with an expression and an exclama-
tion of disgust. He walked down the gallery and across the
narrow "bridges" which connected the Lebrun cottages one
with the other. He had been seated before the door of the
main house. The parrot and the mocking-bird were the
property of Madame Lebrun, and they had the right to
make all the noise they wished. Mr. Pontellier had the privilege of quitting their society when they ceased to be entertaining.

He stopped before the door of his own cottage, which
was the fourth one from the main building and next to the
last. Seating himself in a wicker rocker which was there, he

once more applied himself to the task of reading the news-paper. The day was Sunday; the paper was a day old. The Sunday papers had not yet reached Grand Isle. He was al-ready acquainted with the market reports, and he glanced restlessly over the editorials and bits of news which he had not had time to read before quitting New Orleans the day before.

Mr. Pontellier wore eye-glasses. He was a man of forty, of medium height and rather slender build; he stooped a little. His hair was brown and straight, parted on one side. His beard was neatly and closely trimmed.

Once in a while he withdrew his glance from the news-paper and looked about him. There was more noise than ever over at the house. The main building was called "the house," to distinguish it from the cottages. The chattering and whistling birds were still at it. Two young girls, the Farival twins, were playing a duet from "Zampa" upon the piano. Madame Lebrun was bustling in and out, giving or-ders in a high key to a yard-boy whenever she got inside the house, and directions in an equally high voice to a dining-room servant whenever she got outside. She was a fresh, pretty woman, clad always in white with elbow sleeves. Her starched skirts crinkled as she came and went. Farther down, before one of the cottages, a lady in black was walk-ing demurely up and down, telling her beads. A good many persons of the *pension* had gone over to the *Chênière Cami-nada* in Beaudelet's lugger to hear mass. Some young peo-ple were out under the water-oaks playing croquet. Mr. Pontellier's two children were there—sturdy little fellows of four and five. A quadroon nurse followed them about with a far-away, meditative air.

Mr. Pontellier finally lit a cigar and began to smoke, let-ting the paper drag idly from his hand. He fixed his gaze upon a white sunshade that was advancing at snail's pace from the beach. He could see it plainly between the gaunt trunks of the water-oaks and across the stretch of yellow camomile. The gulf looked far away, melting hazily into the blue of the horizon. The sunshade continued to approach slowly. Beneath its pink-lined shelter were his wife, Mrs. Pontellier, and young Robert Lebrun. When they reached the cottage, the two seated themselves with some appearance of fatigue upon the upper step of the porch, facing each other, each leaning against a supporting post.

"What folly! to bathe at such an hour in such heat!" exclaimed Mr. Pontellier. He himself had taken a plunge at daylight. That was why the morning seemed long to him.

"You are burnt beyond recognition," he added, looking at his wife as one looks at a valuable piece of personal property which has suffered some damage. She held up her hands, strong, shapely hands, and surveyed them critically, drawing up her lawn sleeves above the wrists. Looking at them reminded her of her rings, which she had given to her husband before leaving for the beach. She silently reached out to him, and he, understanding, took the rings from his vest pocket and dropped them into her open palm. She slipped them upon her fingers; then clasping her knees, she looked across at Robert and began to laugh. The rings sparkled upon her fingers. He sent back an answering smile.

"What is it?" asked Pontellier, looking lazily and amused from one to the other. It was some utter nonsense; some adventure out there in the water, and they both tried to relate it at once. It did not seem half so amusing when told. They realized this, and so did Mr. Pontellier. He yawned and stretched himself. Then he got up, saying he had half a mind to go over to Klein's hotel and play a game of billiards.

"Come go along, Lebrun," he proposed to Robert. But

Robert admitted quite frankly that he preferred to stay where he was and talk to Mrs. Pontellier.

"Well, send him about his business when he bores you, Edna," instructed her husband as he prepared to leave.

"Here, take the umbrella," she exclaimed, holding it out to him. He accepted the sunshade, and lifting it over his head descended the steps and walked away.

"Coming back to dinner?" his wife called after him. He halted a moment and shrugged his shoulders. He felt in his vest pocket; there was a ten-dollar bill there. He did not know; perhaps he would return for the early dinner and perhaps he would not. It all depended upon the company which he found over at Klein's and the size of "the game." He did not say this, but she understood it, and laughed, nodding good-by to him.

Both children wanted to follow their father when they saw him starting out. He kissed them and promised to bring them back bonbons and peanuts.

II

✦

*M*rs. Pontellier's eyes were quick and bright; they were a yellowish brown, about the color of her hair. She had a way of turning them swiftly upon an object and holding them there as if lost in some inward maze of contemplation or thought.

Her eyebrows were a shade darker than her hair. They were thick and almost horizontal, emphasizing the depth of her eyes. She was rather handsome than beautiful. Her face was captivating by reason of a certain frankness of expression and a contradictory subtle play of features. Her manner was engaging.

Robert rolled a cigarette. He smoked cigarettes because he could not afford cigars, he said. He had a cigar in his pocket which Mr. Pontellier had presented him with, and he was saving it for his after-dinner smoke.

This seemed quite proper and natural on his part. In coloring he was not unlike his companion. A clean-shaved face made the resemblance more pronounced than it would otherwise have been. There rested no shadow of care upon his open countenance. His eyes gathered in and reflected the light and languor of the summer day.

Mrs. Pontellier reached over for a palm-leaf fan that lay on the porch and began to fan herself, while Robert sent between his lips light puffs from his cigarette. They chatted incessantly: about the things around them; their amusing adventure out in the water—it had again assumed its entertaining aspect; about the wind, the trees, the people who had gone to the *Chênière;* about the children playing croquet under the oaks, and the Farival twins, who were now performing the overture to "The Poet and the Peasant."

Robert talked a good deal about himself. He was very young, and did not know any better. Mrs. Pontellier talked a little about herself for the same reason. Each was interested in what the other said. Robert spoke of his intention to go to Mexico in the autumn, where fortune awaited him. He was always intending to go to Mexico, but some way never got there. Meanwhile he held on to his modest position in a mercantile house in New Orleans, where an equal familiarity with English, French and Spanish gave him no small value as a clerk and correspondent.

He was spending his summer vacation, as he always did, with his mother at Grand Isle. In former times, before Robert could remember, "the house" had been a summer luxury of the Lebruns. Now, flanked by its dozen or more cottages, which were always filled with exclusive visitors from the *"Quartier Français,"* it enabled Madame Lebrun to maintain the easy and comfortable existence which appeared to be her birthright.

Mrs. Pontellier talked about her father's Mississippi plantation and her girlhood home in the old Kentucky bluegrass country. She was an American woman, with a small infusion of French which seemed to have been lost in dilution. She read a letter from her sister, who was away in the

East, and who had engaged herself to be married. Robert was interested, and wanted to know what manner of girls the sisters were, what the father was like, and how long the mother had been dead.

When Mrs. Pontellier folded the letter it was time for her to dress for the early dinner.

"I see Léonce isn't coming back," she said, with a glance in the direction whence her husband had disappeared. Robert supposed he was not, as there were a good many New Orleans club men over at Klein's.

When Mrs. Pontellier left him to enter her room, the young man descended the steps and strolled over toward the croquet players, where, during the half-hour before dinner, he amused himself with the little Pontellier children, who were very fond of him.

III

✦

*I*t was eleven o'clock that night when Mr. Pontellier returned from Klein's hotel. He was in an excellent humor, in high spirits, and very talkative. His entrance awoke his wife, who was in bed and fast asleep when he came in. He talked to her while he undressed, telling her anecdotes and bits of news and gossip that he had gathered during the day. From his trousers pockets he took a fistful of crumpled bank notes and a good deal of silver coin, which he piled on the bureau indiscriminately with keys, knife, handkerchief, and whatever else happened to be in his pockets. She was overcome with sleep, and answered him with little half utterances.

He thought it very discouraging that his wife, who was the sole object of his existence, evinced so little interest in things which concerned him, and valued so little his conversation.

Mr. Pontellier had forgotten the bonbons and peanuts for the boys. Notwithstanding he loved them very much, and went into the adjoining room where they slept to take a look at them and make sure that they were resting com-

fortably. The result of his investigation was far from satis-
factory. He turned and shifted the youngsters about in bed.
One of them began to kick and talk about a basket full of
crabs.

Mr. Pontellier returned to his wife with the information
that Raoul had a high fever and needed looking after. Then he
lit a cigar and went and sat near the open door to smoke it.

Mrs. Pontellier was quite sure Raoul had no fever. He had
gone to bed perfectly well, she said, and nothing had ailed
him all day. Mr. Pontellier was too well acquainted with
fever symptoms to be mistaken. He assured her the child
was consuming at that moment in the next room.

He reproached his wife with her inattention, her habitual
neglect of the children. If it was not a mother's place to
look after children, whose on earth was it? He himself had
his hands full with his brokerage business. He could not be
in two places at once; making a living for his family on the
street, and staying at home to see that no harm befell them.
He talked in a monotonous, insistent way.

Mrs. Pontellier sprang out of bed and went into the next
room. She soon came back and sat on the edge of the bed,
leaning her head down on the pillow. She said nothing, and
refused to answer her husband when he questioned her.
When his cigar was smoked out he went to bed, and in half
a minute he was fast asleep.

Mrs. Pontellier was by that time thoroughly awake. She
began to cry a little, and wiped her eyes on the sleeve of her
peignoir. Blowing out the candle, which her husband had left
burning, she slipped her bare feet into a pair of satin *mules*
at the foot of the bed and went out on the porch, where she
sat down in the wicker chair and began to rock gently to
and fro.

It was then past midnight. The cottages were all dark. A
single faint light gleamed out from the hallway of the house.

There was no sound abroad except the hooting of an old owl in the top of a water-oak, and the everlasting voice of the sea, that was not uplifted at that soft hour. It broke like a mournful lullaby upon the night.

The tears came so fast to Mrs. Pontellier's eyes that the damp sleeve of her *peignoir* no longer served to dry them. She was holding the back of her chair with one hand; her loose sleeve had slipped almost to the shoulder of her up-lifted arm. Turning, she thrust her face, steaming and wet, into the bend of her arm, and she went on crying there, not caring any longer to dry her face, her eyes, her arms. She could not have told why she was crying. Such experiences as the foregoing were not uncommon in her married life. They seemed never before to have weighed much against the abundance of her husband's kindness and a uniform de-votion which had come to be tacit and self-understood.

An indescribable oppression, which seemed to generate in some unfamiliar part of her consciousness, filled her whole being with a vague anguish. It was like a shadow, like a mist passing across her soul's summer day. It was strange and unfamiliar; it was a mood. She did not sit there in-wardly upbraiding her husband, lamenting at Fate, which had directed her footsteps to the path which they had taken. She was just having a good cry all to herself. The mosqui-toes made merry over her, biting her firm, round arms and nipping at her bare insteps.

The little stinging, buzzing imps succeeded in dispelling a mood which might have held her there in the darkness half a night longer.

The following morning Mr. Pontellier was up in good time to take the rockaway which was to convey him to the steamer at the wharf. He was returning to the city to his business, and they would not see him again at the Island till the coming Saturday. He had regained his composure, which seemed to have been somewhat impaired the night before. He was eager to be gone, as he looked forward to a lively week in Carondelet Street.

Mr. Pontellier gave his wife half of the money which he had brought away from Klein's hotel the evening before. She liked money as well as most women, and accepted it with no little satisfaction.

"It will buy a handsome wedding present for Sister Janet!" she exclaimed, smoothing out the bills as she counted them one by one.

"Oh! we'll treat Sister Janet better than that, my dear," he laughed, as he prepared to kiss her good-by.

The boys were tumbling about, clinging to his legs, imploring that numerous things be brought back to them. Mr. Pontellier was a great favorite, and ladies, men, children, even nurses, were always on hand to say good-by to him. His wife stood smiling and waving, the boys shouting, as he disappeared in the old rockaway down the sandy road.

A few days later a box arrived for Mrs. Pontellier from New Orleans. It was from her husband. It was filled with *friandises,* with luscious and toothsome bits—the finest of fruits, *patés,* a rare bottle or two, delicious syrups, and bonbons in abundance.

Mrs. Pontellier was always very generous with the contents of such a box; she was quite used to receiving them when away from home. The *patés* and fruit were brought to the dining-room; the bonbons were passed around. And the ladies, selecting with dainty and discriminating fingers and a little greedily, all declared that Mr. Pontellier was the best husband in the world. Mrs. Pontellier was forced to admit that she knew of none better.

IV

✦

*I*t would have been a difficult matter for Mr. Pontellier to define to his own satisfaction or any one else's wherein his wife failed in her duty toward their children. It was something which he felt rather than perceived, and he never voiced the feeling without subsequent regret and ample atonement.

If one of the little Pontellier boys took a tumble whilst at play, he was not apt to rush crying to his mother's arms for comfort; he would more likely pick himself up, wipe the water out of his eyes and the sand out of his mouth, and go on playing. Tots as they were, they pulled together and stood their ground in childish battles with doubled fists and uplifted voices, which usually prevailed against the other mother-tots. The quadroon nurse was looked upon as a huge encumbrance, only good to button up waists and panties and to brush and part hair; since it seemed to be a law of society that hair must be parted and brushed.

In short, Mrs. Pontellier was not a mother-woman. The mother-women seemed to prevail that summer at Grand Isle. It was easy to know them, fluttering about with extended, protecting wings when any harm, real or imaginary, threatened their precious brood. They were women who idolized their children, worshiped their husbands, and esteemed it a holy privilege to efface themselves as individuals and grow wings as ministering angels.

Many of them were delicious in the rôle; one of them was the embodiment of every womanly grace and charm. If her husband did not adore her, he was a brute, deserving of death by slow torture. Her name was Adèle Ratignolle. There are no words to describe her save the old ones that have served so often to picture the bygone heroine of romance and the fair lady of our dreams. There was nothing subtle or hidden about her charms; her beauty was all there, flaming and apparent: the spun-gold hair that comb nor confining pin could restrain; the blue eyes that were like nothing but sapphires; two lips that pouted, that were so red one could only think of cherries or some other delicious crimson fruit in looking at them. She was growing a little stout, but it did not seem to detract an iota from the grace of every step, pose, gesture. One would not have wanted her white neck a mite less full or her beautiful arms more slender. Never were hands more exquisite than hers, and it was a joy to look at them when she threaded her needle or adjusted her gold thimble to her taper middle finger as she sewed away on the little night-drawers or fashioned a bodice or a bib.

Madame Ratignolle was very fond of Mrs. Pontellier, and often she took her sewing and went over to sit with her in the afternoons. She was sitting there the afternoon of the day the box arrived from New Orleans. She had possession of the rocker, and she was busily engaged in sewing upon a diminutive pair of night-drawers.

She had brought the pattern of the drawers for Mrs. Pontellier to cut out—a marvel of construction, fashioned to enclose a baby's body so effectually that only two small eyes might look out from the garment, like an Eskimo's. They were designed for winter wear, when treacherous drafts came down chimneys and insidious currents of deadly cold found their way through key-holes.

Mrs. Pontellier's mind was quite at rest concerning the present material needs of her children, and she could not see the use of anticipating and making winter night garments the subject of her summer meditations. But she did not want to appear unamiable and uninterested, so she had brought forth newspapers, which she spread upon the floor of the gallery, and under Madame Ratignolle's directions she had cut a pattern of the impervious garment.

Robert was there, seated as he had been the Sunday before, and Mrs. Pontellier also occupied her former position on the upper step, leaning listlessly against the post. Beside her was a box of bonbons, which she held out at intervals to Madame Ratignolle.

That lady seemed at a loss to make a selection, but finally settled upon a stick of nougat, wondering if it were not too rich; whether it could possibly hurt her. Madame Ratignolle had been married seven years. About every two years she had a baby. At that time she had three babies, and was beginning to think of a fourth one. She was always talking about her "condition." Her "condition" was in no way apparent, and no one would have known a thing about it but for her persistence in making it the subject of conversation.

Robert started to reassure her, asserting that he had known a lady who had subsisted upon nougat during the entire—but seeing the color mount into Mrs. Pontellier's face he checked himself and changed the subject.

Mrs. Pontellier, though she had married a Creole, was not thoroughly at home in the society of Creoles; never before had she been thrown so intimately among them. There were only Creoles that summer at Lebrun's. They all knew each other, and felt like one large family, among whom existed the most amicable relations. A characteristic which distinguished them and which impressed Mrs. Pontellier most forcibly was their entire absence of prudery. Their freedom of expression was at first incomprehensible to her, though she had no difficulty in reconciling it with a lofty chastity which in the Creole woman seems to be inborn and unmistakable.

Never would Edna Pontellier forget the shock with which she heard Madame Ratignolle relating to old Monsieur Farival the harrowing story of one of her *accouchements,* withholding no intimate detail. She was growing accustomed to like shocks, but she could not keep the mounting color back from her cheeks. Oftener than once her coming had interrupted the droll story with which Robert was entertaining some amused group of married women.

A book had gone the rounds of the *pension.* When it came her turn to read it, she did so with profound astonishment. She felt moved to read the book in secret and solitude, though none of the others had done so—to hide it from view at the sound of approaching footsteps. It was openly criticised and freely discussed at table. Mrs. Pontellier gave over being astonished, and concluded that wonders would never cease.

V

✦

*T*hey formed a congenial group sitting there that summer afternoon—Madame Ratignolle sewing away, often stopping to relate a story or incident with much expressive gesture of her perfect hands; Robert and Mrs. Pontellier sitting idle, exchanging occasional words, glances or smiles which indicated a certain advanced stage of intimacy and *camaraderie.*

He had lived in her shadow during the past month. No one thought anything of it. Many had predicted that Robert would devote himself to Mrs. Pontellier when he arrived. Since the age of fifteen, which was eleven years before, Robert each summer at Grand Isle had constituted himself the devoted attendant of some fair dame or damsel. Sometimes it was a young girl, again a widow; but as often as not it was some interesting married woman.

For two consecutive seasons he lived in the sunlight of Mademoiselle Duvigné's presence. But she died between summers; then Robert posed as an inconsolable, prostrating himself at the feet of Madame Ratignolle for whatever

The two women had no intention of bathing; they had just strolled down to the beach for a walk and to be alone and near the water (page 27).

crumbs of sympathy and comfort she might be pleased to vouchsafe.

Mrs. Pontellier liked to sit and gaze at her fair companion as she might look upon a faultless Madonna.

"Could any one fathom the cruelty beneath that fair exterior?" murmured Robert. "She knew that I adored her once, and she let me adore her. It was 'Robert, come; go; stand up; sit down; do this; do that; see if the baby sleeps; my thimble, please, that I left God knows where. Come and read Daudet to me while I sew.' "

"*Par exemple!* I never had to ask. You were always there under my feet, like a troublesome cat."

"You mean like an adoring dog. And just as soon as Ratignolle appeared on the scene, then it *was* like a dog. '*Passez! Adieu! Allez vous-en!*' "

"Perhaps I feared to make Alphonse jealous," she interjoined, with excessive naïveté. That made them all laugh. The right hand jealous of the left! The heart jealous of the soul! But for that matter, the Creole husband is never jealous; with him the gangrene passion is one which has become dwarfed by disuse.

Meanwhile Robert, addressing Mrs. Pontellier, continued to tell of his one time hopeless passion for Madame Ratignolle; of sleepless nights, of consuming flames till the very sea sizzled when he took his daily plunge. While the lady at the needle kept up a little running, contemptuous comment:

"*Blagueur—farceur—gros bête, va!*"

He never assumed this serio-comic tone when alone with Mrs. Pontellier. She never knew precisely what to make of it; at that moment it was impossible for her to guess how much of it was jest and what proportion was earnest. It was understood that he had often spoken words of love to Madame Ratignolle, without any thought of being taken seriously. Mrs. Pontellier was glad he had not assumed a similar rôle toward herself. It would have been unacceptable and annoying.

Mrs. Pontellier had brought her sketching materials, which she sometimes dabbled with in an unprofessional way. She liked the dabbling. She felt in it satisfaction of a kind which no other employment afforded her.

She had long wished to try herself on Madame Ratignolle. Never had that lady seemed a more tempting subject than at that moment, seated there like some sensuous Madonna, with the gleam of the fading day enriching her splendid color.

Robert crossed over and seated himself upon the step below Mrs. Pontellier, that he might watch her work. She handled her brushes with a certain ease and freedom which came, not from long and close acquaintance with them, but from a natural aptitude. Robert followed her work with close attention, giving forth little ejaculatory expressions of appreciation in French, which he addressed to Madame Ratignolle.

"Mais ce n'est pas mal! Elle s'y connait, elle a de la force, oui."

During his oblivious attention he once quietly rested his head against Mrs. Pontellier's arm. As gently she repulsed him. Once again he repeated the offense. She could not but believe it to be thoughtlessness on his part; yet that was no reason she should submit to it. She did not remonstrate, except again to repulse him quietly but firmly. He offered no apology.

The picture completed bore no resemblance to Madame Ratignolle. She was greatly disappointed to find that it did not look like her. But it was a fair enough piece of work, and in many respects satisfying.

Mrs. Pontellier evidently did not think so. After surveying the sketch critically she drew a broad smudge of paint across its surface, and crumpled the paper between her hands.

The youngsters came tumbling up the steps, the quadroon following at the respectful distance which they required her to observe. Mrs. Pontellier made them carry her paints and things into the house. She sought to detain them for a little talk and some pleasantry. But they were greatly in earnest. They had only come to investigate the contents of the bonbon box. They accepted without murmuring what she chose to give them, each holding out two chubby hands scoop-like, in the vain hope that they might be filled; and then away they went.

The sun was low in the west, and the breeze soft and languorous that came up from the south, charged with the seductive odor of the sea. Children, freshly befurbelowed, were gathering for their games under the oaks. Their voices were high and penetrating.

Madame Ratignolle folded her sewing, placing thimble, scissors and thread all neatly together in the roll, which she pinned securely. She complained of faintness. Mrs. Pontellier flew for the cologne water and a fan. She bathed Madame Ratignolle's face with cologne, while Robert plied the fan with unnecessary vigor.

The spell was soon over, and Mrs. Pontellier could not help wondering if there were not a little imagination responsible for its origin, for the rose tint had never faded from her friend's face.

She stood watching the fair woman walk down the long line of galleries with the grace and majesty which queens are sometimes supposed to possess. Her little ones ran to meet her. Two of them clung about her white skirts, the third she took from its nurse and with a thousand endearments bore it along in her own fond, encircling arms.

Though, as everybody well knew, the doctor had forbidden her to lift so much as a pin!

"Are you going bathing?" asked Robert of Mrs. Pontellier. It was not so much a question as a reminder.

"Oh, no," she answered, with a tone of indecision. "I'm tired; I think not." Her glance wandered from his face away toward the Gulf, whose sonorous murmur reached her like a loving but imperative entreaty.

"Oh, come!" he insisted. "You mustn't miss your bath. Come on. The water must be delicious; it will not hurt you. Come."

He reached up for her big, rough straw hat that hung on a peg outside the door, and put it on her head. They descended the steps, and walked away together toward the beach. The sun was low in the west and the breeze was soft and warm.

VI

$\blacklozenge$

$\mathcal{E}$dna Pontellier could not have told why, wishing to go to the beach with Robert, she should in the first place have declined, and in the second place have followed in obedience to one of the two contradictory impulses which impelled her.

A certain light was beginning to dawn dimly within her,—the light which, showing the way, forbids it.

At that early period it served but to bewilder her. It moved her to dreams, to thoughtfulness, to the shadowy anguish which had overcome her the midnight when she had abandoned herself to tears.

In short, Mrs. Pontellier was beginning to realize her position in the universe as a human being, and to recognize her relations as an individual to the world within and about her. This may seem like a ponderous weight of wisdom to descend upon the soul of a young woman of twenty-eight—perhaps more wisdom than the Holy Ghost is usually pleased to vouchsafe to any woman.

But the beginning of things, of a world especially, is necessarily vague, tangled, chaotic, and exceedingly disturbing.

How few of us ever emerge from such beginning! How many souls perish in its tumult!

The voice of the sea is seductive; never ceasing, whispering, clamoring, murmuring, inviting the soul to wander for a spell in abysses of solitude; to lose itself in mazes of inward contemplation.

The voice of the sea speaks to the soul. The touch of the sea is sensuous, enfolding the body in its soft, close embrace.

VII

✦

*M*rs. Pontellier was not a woman given to confidences, a characteristic hitherto contrary to her nature. Even as a child she had lived her own small life all within herself. At a very early period she had apprehended instinctively the dual life—that outward existence which conforms, the inward life which questions.

That summer at Grand Isle she began to loosen a little the mantle of reserve that had always enveloped her. There may have been—there must have been—influences, both subtle and apparent, working in their several ways to induce her to do this; but the most obvious was the influence of Adèle Ratignolle. The excessive physical charm of the Creole had first attracted her, for Edna had a sensuous susceptibility to beauty. Then the candor of the woman's whole existence, which every one might read, and which formed so striking a contrast to her own habitual reserve—this might have furnished a link. Who can tell what metals the gods use in forging the subtle bond which we call sympathy, which we might as well call love.

The two women went away one morning to the beach together, arm in arm, under the huge white sunshade. Edna had prevailed upon Madame Ratignolle to leave the children behind, though she could not induce her to relinquish a diminutive roll of needlework, which Adèle begged to be allowed to slip into the depths of her pocket. In some unaccountable way they had escaped from Robert.

The walk to the beach was no inconsiderable one, consisting as it did of a long, sandy path, upon which a sporadic and tangled growth that bordered it on either side made frequent and unexpected inroads. There were acres of yellow camomile reaching out on either hand. Further away still, vegetable gardens abounded, with frequent small plantations of orange or lemon trees intervening. The dark green clusters glistened from afar in the sun.

The women were both of goodly height, Madame Ratignolle possessing the more feminine and matronly figure. The charm of Edna Pontellier's physique stole insensibly upon you. The lines of her body were long, clean and symmetrical; it was a body which occasionally fell into splendid poses; there was no suggestion of the trim, stereotyped fashion-plate about it. A casual and indiscriminating observer, in passing, might not cast a second glance upon the figure. But with more feeling and discernment he would have recognized the noble beauty of its modeling, and the graceful severity of poise and movement, which made Edna Pontellier different from the crowd.

She wore a cool muslin that morning—white, with a waving vertical line of brown running through it; also a white linen collar and the big straw hat which she had taken from the peg outside the door. The hat rested any way on her yellow-brown hair, that waved a little, was heavy, and clung close to her head.

Madame Ratignolle, more careful of her complexion, had twined a gauze veil about her head. She wore dogskin gloves, with gauntlets that protected her wrists. She was dressed in pure white, with a fluffiness of ruffles that became her. The draperies and fluttering things which she wore suited her rich, luxuriant beauty as a greater severity of line could not have done.

There were a number of bath-houses along the beach, of rough but solid construction, built with small, protecting galleries facing the water. Each house consisted of two compartments, and each family at Lebrun's possessed a compartment for itself, fitted out with all the essential paraphernalia of the bath and whatever other conveniences the owners might desire. The two women had no intention of bathing; they had just strolled down to the beach for a walk and to be alone and near the water. The Pontellier and Ratignolle compartments adjoined one another under the same roof.

Mrs. Pontellier had brought down her key through force of habit. Unlocking the door of her bath-room she went inside, and soon emerged, bringing a rug, which she spread upon the floor of the gallery, and two huge hair pillows covered with crash, which she placed against the front of the building.

The two seated themselves there in the shade of the porch, side by side, with their backs against the pillows and their feet extended. Madame Ratignolle removed her veil, wiped her face with a rather delicate handkerchief, and fanned herself with the fan which she always carried suspended somewhere about her person by a long, narrow ribbon. Edna removed her collar and opened her dress at the throat. She took the fan from Madame Ratignolle and began to fan both herself and her companion. It was very warm, and for a while they did nothing but exchange remarks about the heat, the sun, the glare. But there was a breeze blowing, a choppy, stiff wind that whipped the water into froth. It fluttered the skirts of the two women and kept them for a while engaged in adjusting, readjusting, tucking in, securing hair-pins and hat-pins. A few persons were sporting some distance away in the water. The beach was very still of human sound at that hour. The lady in black was reading her morning devotions on the porch of a neighboring bath-house. Two young lovers were exchanging their hearts' yearnings beneath the children's tent, which they had found unoccupied.

Edna Pontellier, casting her eyes about, had finally kept them at rest upon the sea. The day was clear and carried the gaze out as far as the blue sky went; there were a few white clouds suspended idly over the horizon. A lateen sail was visible in the direction of Cat Island, and others to the south seemed almost motionless in the far distance.

"Of whom—of what are you thinking?" asked Adèle of her companion, whose countenance she had been watching with a little amused attention, arrested by the absorbed expression which seemed to have seized and fixed every feature into a statuesque repose.

"Nothing," returned Mrs. Pontellier, with a start, adding at once: "How stupid! But it seems to me it is the reply we make instinctively to such a question. Let me see," she went on, throwing back her head and narrowing her fine eyes till they shone like two vivid points of light. "Let me see. I was really not conscious of thinking of anything; but perhaps I can retrace my thoughts."

"Oh! never mind!" laughed Madame Ratignolle. "I am not quite so exacting. I will let you off this time. It is really too hot to think, especially to think about thinking."

"But for the fun of it," persisted Edna. "First of all, the sight of the water stretching so far away, those motionless sails against the blue sky, made a delicious picture that I just wanted to sit and look at. The hot wind beating in my face made me think—without any connection that I can trace—of a summer day in Kentucky, of a meadow that seemed as big as the ocean to the very little girl walking through the grass, which was higher than her waist. She threw out her arms as if swimming when she walked, beating the tall grass as one strikes out in the water. Oh, I see the connection now!"

"Where were you going that day in Kentucky, walking through the grass?"

"I don't remember now. I was just walking diagonally across a big field. My sun-bonnet obstructed the view. I could see only the stretch of green before me, and I felt as if I must walk on forever, without coming to the end of it. I don't remember whether I was frightened or pleased. I must have been entertained.

"Likely as not it was Sunday," she laughed; "and I was running away from prayers, from the Presbyterian service, read in a spirit of gloom by my father that chills me yet to think of."

"And have you been running away from prayers ever since, *ma chère?*" asked Madame Ratignolle, amused.

"No! oh, no!" Edna hastened to say. "I was a little unthinking child in those days, just following a misleading impulse without question. On the contrary, during one period of my life religion took a firm hold upon me; after I was twelve and until—until—why, I suppose until now, though I never thought much about it—just driven along by habit. But do you know," she broke off, turning her quick eyes upon Madame Ratignolle and leaning forward a little so as to bring her face quite close to that of her companion, "sometimes I feel this summer as if I were walking through the green meadow again; idly, aimlessly, unthinking and unguided."

Madame Ratignolle laid her hand over that of Mrs. Pontellier, which was near her. Seeing that the hand was not withdrawn, she clasped it firmly and warmly. She even stroked it a little, fondly, with the other hand, murmuring in an undertone, *"Pauvre chérie."*

The action was at first a little confusing to Edna, but she soon lent herself readily to the Creole's gentle caress. She was not accustomed to an outward and spoken expression of affection, either in herself or in others. She and her younger sister, Janet, had quarreled a good deal through force of unfortunate habit. Her older sister, Margaret, was matronly and dignified, probably from having assumed matronly and housewifely responsibilities too early in life, their mother having died when they were quite young. Margaret was not effusive; she was practical. Edna had had an occasional girl friend, but whether accidentally or not, they seemed to have been all of one type—the self-contained. She never realized that the reserve of her own character had much, perhaps everything, to do with this. Her most intimate friend at school had been one of rather exceptional intellectual gifts, who wrote fine-sounding essays, which Edna admired and strove to imitate; and with her she talked and glowed over the English classics, and sometimes held religious and political controversies.

Edna often wondered at one propensity which sometimes had inwardly disturbed her without causing any outward show or manifestation on her part. At a very early age— perhaps it was when she traversed the ocean of waving grass—she remembered that she had been passionately enamored of a dignified and sad-eyed cavalry officer who visited her father in Kentucky. She could not leave his presence when he was there, nor remove her eyes from his face, which was something like Napoleon's, with a lock of black hair falling across the forehead. But the cavalry officer melted imperceptibly out of her existence.

At another time her affections were deeply engaged by a young gentleman who visited a lady on a neighboring plantation. It was after they went to Mississippi to live. The young man was engaged to be married to the young lady, and they sometimes called upon Margaret, driving over of afternoons in a buggy. Edna was a little miss, just merging into her teens; and the realization that she herself was nothing, nothing, nothing to the engaged young man was a bitter affliction to her. But he, too, went the way of dreams.

She was a grown young woman when she was overtaken by what she supposed to be the climax of her fate. It was when the face and figure of a great tragedian began to haunt her imagination and stir her senses. The persistence of the infatuation lent it an aspect of genuineness. The hopelessness of it colored it with the lofty tones of a great passion.

The picture of the tragedian stood enframed upon her desk. Any one may possess the portrait of a tragedian without exciting suspicion or comment. (This was a sinister reflection which she cherished.) In the presence of others she expressed admiration for his exalted gifts, as she handed the photograph around and dwelt upon the fidelity of the likeness. When alone she sometimes picked it up and kissed the cold glass passionately.

Her marriage to Léonce Pontellier was purely an accident, in this respect resembling many other marriages which masquerade as the decrees of Fate. It was in the midst of her secret great passion that she met him. He fell in love, as men are in the habit of doing, and pressed his suit with an earnestness and an ardor which left nothing to be desired. He pleased her; his absolute devotion flattered her. She fancied there was a sympathy of thought and taste between them, in which fancy she was mistaken. Add to this the violent opposition of her father and her sister Margaret to her marriage with a Catholic, and we need seek no further for the motives which led her to accept Monsieur Pontellier for her husband.

The acme of bliss, which would have been a marriage with the tragedian, was not for her in this world. As the devoted wife of a man who worshiped her, she felt she would take her place with a certain dignity in the world of reality, closing the portals forever behind her upon the realm of romance and dreams.

But it was not long before the tragedian had gone to join the cavalry officer and the engaged young man and a few others; and Edna found herself face to face with the realities. She grew fond of her husband, realizing with some unaccountable satisfaction that no trace of passion or excessive and fictitious warmth colored her affection, thereby threatening its dissolution.

She was fond of her children in an uneven, impulsive way. She would sometimes gather them passionately to her heart; she would sometimes forget them. The year before they had spent part of the summer with their grandmother Pontellier in Iberville. Feeling secure regarding their happiness and welfare, she did not miss them except with an occasional intense longing. Their absence was a sort of relief, though she did not admit this, even to herself. It seemed to free her of a responsibility which she had blindly assumed and for which Fate had not fitted her.

Edna did not reveal so much as all this to Madame Ratignolle that summer day when they sat with faces turned to the sea. But a good part of it escaped her. She had put her head down on Madame Ratignolle's shoulder. She was flushed and felt intoxicated with the sound of her own voice and the unaccustomed taste of candor. It muddled her like wine, or like a first breath of freedom.

There was the sound of approaching voices. It was Robert, surrounded by a troop of children, searching for them. The two little Pontelliers were with him, and he carried Madame Ratignolle's little girl in his arms. There were other children beside, and two nurse-maids followed, looking disagreeable and resigned.

The women at once rose and began to shake out their draperies and relax their muscles. Mrs. Pontellier threw the cushions and rug into the bath-house. The children all scampered off to the awning, and they stood there in a line, gazing upon the intruding lovers, still exchanging their vows and sighs. The lovers got up, with only a silent protest, and walked slowly away somewhere else.

The children possessed themselves of the tent, and Mrs. Pontellier went over to join them.

Madame Ratignolle begged Robert to accompany her to the house; she complained of cramp in her limbs and stiffness of the joints. She leaned draggingly upon his arm as they walked.

VIII

✦

*D*o me a favor, Robert," spoke the pretty woman at his side, almost as soon as she and Robert had started on their slow, homeward way. She looked up in his face, leaning on his arm beneath the encircling shadow of the umbrella which he had lifted.

"Granted; as many as you like," he returned, glancing down into her eyes that were full of thoughtfulness and some speculation.

"I only ask for one; let Mrs. Pontellier alone."

"Tiens!" he exclaimed, with a sudden, boyish laugh. *"Voilà que Madame Ratignolle est jalouse!"*

"Nonsense! I'm in earnest; I mean what I say. Let Mrs. Pontellier alone."

"Why?" he asked; himself growing serious at his companion's solicitation.

"She is not one of us; she is not like us. She might make the unfortunate blunder of taking you seriously."

His face flushed with annoyance, and taking off his soft hat he began to beat it impatiently against his leg as he walked. "Why shouldn't she take me seriously?" he demanded sharply. "Am I a comedian, a clown, a jack-in-the-box? Why shouldn't she? You Creoles! I have no patience with you! Am I always to be regarded as a feature of an amusing programme? I hope Mrs. Pontellier does take me seriously. I hope she has discernment enough to find in me something besides the *blagueur.* If I thought there was any doubt—"

"Oh, enough, Robert!" she broke into his heated outburst. "You are not thinking of what you are saying. You speak with about as little reflection as we might expect from one of those children down there playing in the sand. If your attentions to any married women here were ever offered with any intention of being convincing, you would not be the gentleman we all know you to be, and you would be unfit to associate with the wives and daughters of the people who trust you."

Madame Ratignolle had spoken what she believed to be the law and the gospel. The young man shrugged his shoulders impatiently.

"Oh! well! That isn't it," slamming his hat down vehemently upon his head. "You ought to feel that such things are not flattering to say to a fellow."

"Should our whole intercourse consist of an exchange of compliments? *Ma foi!*"

"It isn't pleasant to have a woman tell you—" he went on, unheedingly, but breaking off suddenly: "Now if I were like Arobin—you remember Alcée Arobin and that story of the consul's wife at Biloxi?" And he related the story of Alcée Arobin and the consul's wife; and another about the tenor of the French Opera, who received letters which should never have been written; and still other stories, grave and gay, till Mrs. Pontellier and her possible propensity for taking young men seriously was apparently forgotten.

Madame Ratignolle, when they had regained her cottage, went in to take the hour's rest which she considered helpful. Before leaving her, Robert begged her pardon for the impatience—he called it rudeness—with which he had received her well-meant caution.

"You made one mistake, Adèle," he said, with a light smile; "there is no earthly possibility of Mrs. Pontellier ever taking me seriously. You should have warned me against taking myself seriously. Your advice might then have carried some weight and given me subject for some reflection. *Au revoir.* But you look tired," he added, solicitously. "Would you like a cup of bouillon? Shall I stir you a toddy? Let me mix you a toddy with a drop of Angostura."

She acceded to the suggestion of bouillon, which was grateful and acceptable. He went himself to the kitchen, which was a building apart from the cottages and lying to the rear of the house. And he himself brought her the golden-brown bouillon, in a dainty Sèvres cup, with a flaky cracker or two on the saucer.

She thrust a bare, white arm from the curtain which shielded her open door, and received the cup from his hands. She told him he was a *bon garçon,* and she meant it. Robert thanked her and turned away toward "the house."

The lovers were just entering the grounds of the *pension.* They were leaning toward each other as the water-oaks bent from the sea. There was not a particle of earth beneath their feet. Their heads might have been turned upside-down, so absolutely did they tread upon blue ether. The lady in black, creeping behind them, looked a trifle paler and more jaded than usual. There was no sign of Mrs. Pontellier and the children. Robert scanned the distance for any such apparition. They would doubtless remain away till the dinner hour. The young man ascended to his mother's room. It was situated at the top of the house, made up of odd angles and a queer, sloping ceiling. Two broad dormer windows looked out toward the Gulf, and as far across it as a man's eye might reach. The furnishings of the room were light, cool, and practical.

Madame Lebrun was busily engaged at the sewing-machine. A little black girl sat on the floor, and with her hands worked the treadle of the machine. The Creole woman does not take any chances which may be avoided of imperiling her health.

Robert went over and seated himself on the broad sill of one of the dormer windows. He took a book from his pocket and began energetically to read it, judging by the precision and frequency with which he turned the leaves. The sewing-machine made a resounding clatter in the room; it was of a ponderous, by-gone make. In the lulls, Robert and his mother exchanged bits of desultory conversation.

"Where is Mrs. Pontellier?"

"Down at the beach with the children."

"I promised to lend her the Goncourt. Don't forget to take it down when you go; it's there on the bookshelf over the small table." Clatter, clatter, clatter, bang! for the next five or eight minutes.

"Where is Victor going with the rockaway?"

"The rockaway? Victor?"

"Yes; down there in front. He seems to be getting ready to drive away somewhere."

"Call him." Clatter, clatter!

Robert uttered a shrill, piercing whistle which might have been heard back at the wharf.

"He won't look up."

Madame Lebrun flew to the window. She called "Victor!" She waved a handkerchief and called again. The young fellow below got into the vehicle and started the horse off at a gallop.

Madame Lebrun went back to the machine, crimson with

annoyance. Victor was the younger son and brother—a *tête montée,* with a temper which invited violence and a will which no ax could break.

"Whenever you say the word I'm ready to thrash any amount of reason into him that he's able to hold."

"If your father had only lived!" Clatter, clatter, clatter, clatter, bang! It was a fixed belief with Madame Lebrun that the conduct of the universe and all things pertaining thereto would have been manifestly of a more intelligent and higher order had not Monsieur Lebrun been removed to other spheres during the early years of their married life.

"What do you hear from Montel?" Montel was a middle-aged gentleman whose vain ambition and desire for the past twenty years had been to fill the void which Monsieur Lebrun's taking off had left in the Lebrun household. Clatter, clatter, bang, clatter!

"I have a letter somewhere," looking in the machine drawer and finding the letter in the bottom of the work-basket. "He says to tell you he will be in Vera Cruz the beginning of next month"—clatter, clatter!—"and if you still have the intention of joining him"—bang! clatter, clatter, bang!

"Why didn't you tell me so before, mother? You know I wanted—" Clatter, clatter, clatter!

"Do you see Mrs. Pontellier starting back with the children? She will be in late to luncheon again. She never starts to get ready for luncheon till the last minute." Clatter, clatter! "Where are you going?"

"Where did you say the Goncourt was?"

IX

✦

$\mathcal{E}$very light in the hall was ablaze; every lamp turned as high as it could be without smoking the chimney or threatening explosion. The lamps were fixed at intervals against the wall, encircling the whole room. Some one had gathered orange and lemon branches, and with these fashioned graceful festoons between. The dark green of the branches stood out and glistened against the white muslin curtains which draped the windows, and which puffed, floated, and flapped at the capricious will of a stiff breeze that swept up from the Gulf.

It was Saturday night a few weeks after the intimate conversation held between Robert and Madame Ratignolle on their way from the beach. An unusual number of husbands, fathers, and friends had come down to stay over Sunday; and they were being suitably entertained by their families, with the material help of Madame Lebrun. The dining tables had all been removed to one end of the hall, and the chairs ranged about in rows and in clusters. Each little family group had had its say and exchanged its domestic gossip earlier in the evening. There was now an apparent disposition to relax; to widen the circle of confidences and give a more general tone to the conversation.

Many of the children had been permitted to sit up beyond their usual bedtime. A small band of them were lying on their stomachs on the floor looking at the colored sheets of the comic papers which Mr. Pontellier had brought down. The little Pontellier boys were permitting them to do so, and making their authority felt.

Music, dancing, and a recitation or two were the entertainments furnished, or rather, offered. But there was nothing systematic about the programme, no appearance of prearrangement nor even premeditation.

At an early hour in the evening the Farival twins were prevailed upon to play the piano. They were girls of fourteen, always clad in the Virgin's colors, blue and white, having been dedicated to the Blessed Virgin at their baptism. They played a duet from "Zampa," and at the earnest solicitation of every one present followed it with the overture to "The Poet and the Peasant."

"Allez vous-en! Sapristi!" shrieked the parrot outside the door. He was the only being present who possessed sufficient candor to admit that he was not listening to these gracious performances for the first time that summer. Old Monsieur Farival, grandfather of the twins, grew indignant over the interruption, and insisted upon having the bird removed and consigned to regions of darkness. Victor Lebrun objected; and his decrees were as immutable as those of Fate. The parrot fortunately offered no further interruption to the entertainment, the whole venom of his nature apparently having been cherished up and hurled against the twins in that one impetuous outburst.

Later a young brother and sister gave recitations, which every one present had heard many times at winter evening entertainments in the city.

A little girl performed a skirt dance in the center of the floor. The mother played her accompaniments and at the same time watched her daughter with greedy admiration and nervous apprehension. She need have had no apprehension. The child was mistress of the situation. She had been properly dressed for the occasion in black tulle and black silk tights. Her little neck and arms were bare, and her hair, artificially crimped, stood out like fluffy black plumes over her head. Her poses were full of grace, and her little black-shod toes twinkled as they shot out and upward with a rapidity and suddenness which were bewildering.

But there was no reason why every one should not dance. Madame Ratignolle could not, so it was she who gaily consented to play for the others. She played very well, keeping excellent waltz time and infusing an expression into the strains which was indeed inspiring. She was keeping up her music on account of the children, she said; because she and her husband both considered it a means of brightening the home and making it attractive.

Almost every one danced but the twins, who could not be induced to separate during the brief period when one or the other should be whirling around the room in the arms of a man. They might have danced together, but they did not think of it.

The children were sent to bed. Some went submissively; others with shrieks and protests as they were dragged away. They had been permitted to sit up till after the ice-cream, which naturally marked the limit of human indulgence.

The ice-cream was passed around with cake—gold and silver cake arranged on platters in alternate slices; it had been made and frozen during the afternoon back of the kitchen by two black women, under the supervision of Victor. It was pronounced a great success—excellent if it had only contained a little less vanilla or a little more sugar, if it had been frozen a degree harder, and if the salt might have been kept out of portions of it. Victor was proud of his achievement, and went about recommending it and urging every one to partake of it to excess.

After Mrs. Pontellier had danced twice with her husband, once with Robert, and once with Monsieur Ratignolle, who was thin and tall and swayed like a reed in the wind when he danced, she went out on the gallery and seated herself on the low window-sill, where she commanded a view of all that went on in the hall and could look out toward the Gulf. There was a soft effulgence in the east. The moon was coming up, and its mystic shimmer was casting a million lights across the distant, restless water.

"Would you like to hear Mademoiselle Reisz play?" asked Robert, coming out on the porch where she was. Of course Edna would like to hear Mademoiselle Reisz play; but she feared it would be useless to entreat her.

"I'll ask her," he said. "I'll tell her that you want to hear her. She likes you. She will come." He turned and hurried away to one of the far cottages, where Mademoiselle Reisz was shuffling away. She was dragging a chair in and out of her room, and at intervals objecting to the crying of a baby, which a nurse in the adjoining cottage was endeavoring to put to sleep. She was a disagreeable little woman, no longer young, who had quarreled with almost every one, owing to a temper which was self-assertive and a disposition to trample upon the rights of others. Robert prevailed upon her without any too great difficulty.

She entered the hall with him during a lull in the dance. She made an awkward, imperious little bow as she went in. She was a homely woman, with a small weazened face and body and eyes that glowed. She had absolutely no taste in dress, and wore a batch of rusty black lace with a bunch of artificial violets pinned to the side of her hair.

"Ask Mrs. Pontellier what she would like to hear me play," she requested of Robert. She sat perfectly still before the piano, not touching the keys, while Robert carried her message to Edna at the window. A general air of surprise and genuine satisfaction fell upon every one as they saw the pianist enter. There was a settling down, and a prevailing air of expectancy everywhere. Edna was a trifle embarrassed at being thus signaled out for the imperious little woman's favor. She would not dare to choose, and begged that Mademoiselle Reisz would please herself in her selections.

Edna was what she herself called very fond of music. Musical strains, well rendered, had a way of evoking pictures in her mind. She sometimes liked to sit in the room of mornings when Madame Ratignolle played or practiced. One piece which that lady played Edna had entitled "Solitude." It was a short, plaintive, minor strain. The name of the piece was something else, but she called it "Solitude." When she heard it there came before her imagination the figure of a man standing beside a desolate rock on the seashore. He was naked. His attitude was one of hopeless resignation as he looked toward a distant bird winging its flight away from him.

Another piece called to her mind a dainty young woman clad in an Empire gown, taking mincing dancing steps as she came down a long avenue between tall hedges. Again, another reminded her of children at play, and still another of nothing on earth but a demure lady stroking a cat.

The very first chords which Mademoiselle Reisz struck upon the piano sent a keen tremor down Mrs. Pontellier's spinal column. It was not the first time she had heard an artist at the piano. Perhaps it was the first time she was ready, perhaps the first time her being was tempered to take an impress of the abiding truth.

She waited for the material pictures which she thought

would gather and blaze before her imagination. She waited in vain. She saw no pictures of solitude, of hope, of longing, or of despair. But the very passions themselves were aroused within her soul, swaying it, lashing it, as the waves daily beat upon her splendid body. She trembled, she was choking, and the tears blinded her.

Mademoiselle had finished. She arose, and bowing her stiff, lofty bow, she went away, stopping for neither thanks nor applause. As she passed along the gallery she patted Edna upon the shoulder.

"Well, how did you like my music?" she asked. The young woman was unable to answer; she pressed the hand of the pianist convulsively. Mademoiselle Reisz perceived her agitation and even her tears. She patted her again upon the shoulder as she said:

"You are the only one worth playing for. Those others? Bah!" and she went shuffling and sidling on down the gallery toward her room.

But she was mistaken about "those others." Her playing had aroused a fever of enthusiasm. "What passion!" "What an artist!" "I have always said no one could play Chopin like Mademoiselle Reisz!" "That last prelude! Bon Dieu! It shakes a man!"

It was growing late, and there was a general disposition to disband. But some one, perhaps it was Robert, thought of a bath at that mystic hour and under that mystic moon.

X

✦

At all events Robert proposed it, and there was not a dissenting voice. There was not one but was ready to follow when he led the way. He did not lead the way, however, he directed the way; and he himself loitered behind with the lovers, who had betrayed a disposition to linger and hold themselves apart. He walked between them, whether with malicious or mischievous intent was not wholly clear, even to himself.

The Pontelliers and Ratignolles walked ahead; the women leaning upon the arms of their husbands. Edna could hear Robert's voice behind them, and could sometimes hear what he said. She wondered why he did not join them. It was unlike him not to. Of late he had sometimes held away from her for an entire day, redoubling his devotion upon the next and the next, as though to make up for hours that had been lost. She missed him the days when some pretext served to take him away from her, just as one misses the sun on a cloudy day without having thought much about the sun when it was shining.

The people walked in little groups toward the beach.

They talked and laughed; some of them sang. There was a band playing down at Klein's hotel, and the strains reached them faintly, tempered by the distance. There were strange, rare odors abroad—a tangle of the sea smell and of weeds and damp, new-plowed earth, mingled with the heavy perfume of a field of white blossoms somewhere near. But the night sat lightly upon the sea and the land. There was no weight of darkness; there were no shadows. The white light of the moon had fallen upon the world like the mystery and the softness of sleep.

Most of them walked into the water as though into a native element. The sea was quiet now, and swelled lazily in broad billows that melted into one another and did not break except upon the beach in little foamy crests that coiled back like slow, white serpents.

Edna had attempted all summer to learn to swim. She had received instructions from both the men and women; in some instances from the children. Robert had pursued a system of lessons almost daily; and he was nearly at the point of discouragement in realizing the futility of his efforts. A certain ungovernable dread hung about her when in the water, unless there was a hand near by that might reach out and reassure her.

But that night she was like the little tottering, stumbling, clutching child, who of a sudden realizes its powers, and walks for the first time alone, boldly and with over-confidence. She could have shouted for joy. She did shout for joy, as with a sweeping stroke or two she lifted her body to the surface of the water.

A feeling of exultation overtook her, as if some power of significant import had been given her to control the working of her body and her soul. She grew daring and reckless, overestimating her strength. She wanted to swim far out, where no woman had swum before.

Her unlooked-for achievement was the subject of wonder, applause, and admiration. Each one congratulated himself that his special teachings had accomplished this desired end.

"How easy it is!" she thought. "It is nothing," she said aloud; "why did I not discover before that it was nothing. Think of the time I have lost splashing about like a baby!" She would not join the groups in their sports and bouts, but intoxicated with her newly conquered power, she swam out alone.

She turned her face seaward to gather in an impression of space and solitude, which the vast expanse of water, meeting and melting with the moonlit sky, conveyed to her excited fancy. As she swam she seemed to be reaching out for the unlimited in which to lose herself.

Once she turned and looked toward the shore, toward the people she had left there. She had not gone any great distance—that is, what would have been a great distance for an experienced swimmer. But to her unaccustomed vision the stretch of water behind her assumed the aspect of a barrier which her unaided strength would never be able to overcome.

A quick vision of death smote her soul, and for a second of time appalled and enfeebled her senses. But by an effort she rallied her staggering faculties and managed to regain the land.

She made no mention of her encounter with death and her flash of terror, except to say to her husband, "I thought I should have perished out there alone."

"You were not so very far, my dear; I was watching you," he told her.

Edna went at once to the bath-house, and she had put on her dry clothes and was ready to return home before the others had left the water. She started to walk away alone.

They all called to her and shouted to her. She waved a dissenting hand, and went on, paying no further heed to their renewed cries which sought to detain her.

"Sometimes I am tempted to think that Mrs. Pontellier is capricious," said Madame Lebrun, who was amusing herself immensely and feared that Edna's abrupt departure might put an end to the pleasure.

"I know she is," assented Mr. Pontellier; "sometimes, not often."

Edna had not traversed a quarter of the distance on her way home before she was overtaken by Robert.

"Did you think I was afraid?" she asked him, without a shade of annoyance.

"No; I knew you weren't afraid."

"Then why did you come? Why didn't you stay out there with the others?"

"I never thought of it."

"Thought of what?"

"Of anything. What difference does it make?"

"I'm very tired," she uttered, complainingly.

"I know you are."

"You don't know anything about it. Why should you know? I never was so exhausted in my life. But it isn't unpleasant. A thousand emotions have swept through me to-night. I don't comprehend half of them. Don't mind what I'm saying; I am just thinking aloud. I wonder if I shall ever be stirred again as Mademoiselle Reisz's playing moved me to-night. I wonder if any night on earth will ever again be like this one. It is like a night in a dream. The people about me are like some uncanny, half-human beings. There must be spirits abroad to-night."

"There are," whispered Robert. "Didn't you know this was the twenty-eighth of August?"

"The twenty-eighth of August?"

"Yes. On the twenty-eighth of August, at the hour of midnight, and if the moon is shining—the moon must be shining—a spirit that has haunted these shores for ages rises up from the Gulf. With its own penetrating vision the spirit seeks some one mortal worthy to hold him company, worthy of being exalted for a few hours into realms of the semi-celestials. His search has always hitherto been fruitless, and he has sunk back, disheartened, into the sea. But to-night he found Mrs. Pontellier. Perhaps he will never wholly release her from the spell. Perhaps she will never again suffer a poor, unworthy earthling to walk in the shadow of her divine presence."

"Don't banter me," she said, wounded at what appeared to be his flippancy. He did not mind the entreaty, but the tone with its delicate note of pathos was like a reproach. He could not explain; he could not tell her that he had penetrated her mood and understood. He said nothing except to offer her his arm, for, by her own admission, she was exhausted. She had been walking alone with her arms hanging limp, letting her white skirts trail along the dewy path. She took his arm, but she did not lean upon it. She let her hand lie listlessly, as though her thoughts were elsewhere—somewhere in advance of her body, and she was striving to overtake them.

Robert assisted her into the hammock which swung from the post before her door out to the trunk of a tree.

"Will you stay out here and wait for Mr. Pontellier?" he asked.

"I'll stay out here. Good-night."

"Shall I get you a pillow?"

"There's one here," she said, feeling about, for they were in the shadow.

"It must be soiled; the children have been tumbling it about."

"No matter." And having discovered the pillow, she adjusted it beneath her head. She extended herself in the hammock with a deep breath of relief. She was not a supercilious or an over-dainty woman. She was not much given to reclining in the hammock, and when she did so it was with no cat-like suggestion of voluptuous ease, but with a beneficent repose which seemed to invade her whole body.

"Shall I stay with you till Mr. Pontellier comes?" asked Robert, seating himself on the outer edge of one of the steps and taking hold of the hammock rope which was fastened to the post.

"If you wish. Don't swing the hammock. Will you get my white shawl which I left on the window-sill over at the house?"

"Are you chilly?"

"No; but I shall be presently."

"Presently?" he laughed. "Do you know what time it is? How long are you going to stay out here?"

"I don't know. Will you get the shawl?"

"Of course I will," he said, rising. He went over to the house, walking along the grass. She watched his figure pass in and out of the strips of moonlight. It was past midnight. It was very quiet.

When he returned with the shawl she took it and kept it in her hand. She did not put it around her.

"Did you say I should stay till Mr. Pontellier came back?"

"I said you might if you wished to."

He seated himself again and rolled a cigarette, which he smoked in silence. Neither did Mrs. Pontellier speak. No multitude of words could have been more significant than those moments of silence, or more pregnant with the first-felt throbbings of desire.

When the voices of the bathers were heard approaching, Robert said good-night. She did not answer him. He thought she was asleep. Again she watched his figure pass in and out of the strips of moonlight as he walked away.

XI

✦

What are you doing out here, Edna? I thought I should find you in bed," said her husband, when he discovered her lying there. He had walked up with Madame Lebrun and left her at the house. His wife did not reply.

"Are you asleep?" he asked, bending down close to look at her.

"No." Her eyes gleamed bright and intense, with no sleepy shadows, as they looked into his.

"Do you know it is past one o'clock? Come on," and he mounted the steps and went into their room.

"Edna!" called Mr. Pontellier from within, after a few moments had gone by.

"Don't wait for me," she answered. He thrust his head through the door.

"You will take cold out there," he said, irritably. "What folly is this? Why don't you come in?"

"It isn't cold; I have my shawl."

"The mosquitoes will devour you."

"There are no mosquitoes."

She heard him moving about the room; every sound indicating impatience and irritation. Another time she would have gone in at his request. She would, through habit, have yielded to his desire; not with any sense of submission or obedience to his compelling wishes, but unthinkingly, as we walk, move, sit, stand, go through the daily treadmill of the life which has been portioned out to us.

"Edna, dear, are you not coming in soon?" he asked again, this time fondly, with a note of entreaty.

"No; I am going to stay out here."

"This is more than folly," he blurted out. "I can't permit you to stay out there all night. You must come in the house instantly."

With a writhing motion she settled herself more securely in the hammock. She perceived that her will had blazed up, stubborn and resistant. She could not at that moment have done other than denied and resisted. She wondered if her husband had ever spoken to her like that before, and if she had submitted to his command. Of course she had; she remembered that she had. But she could not realize why or how she should have yielded, feeling as she then did.

"Léonce, go to bed," she said. "I mean to stay out here. I don't wish to go in, and I don't intend to. Don't speak to me like that again; I shall not answer you."

Mr. Pontellier had prepared for bed, but he slipped on an extra garment. He opened a bottle of wine, of which he kept a small and select supply in a buffet of his own. He drank a glass of the wine and went out on the gallery and offered a glass to his wife. She did not wish any. He drew up the rocker, hoisted his slippered feet on the rail, and proceeded to smoke a cigar. He smoked two cigars; then he went inside and drank another glass of wine. Mrs. Pontellier again declined to accept a glass when it was offered to her. Mr. Pontellier once more seated himself with elevated feet, and after a reasonable interval of time smoked some more cigars.

Edna began to feel like one who awakens gradually out of a dream, a delicious, grotesque, impossible dream, to feel again the realities pressing into her soul. The physical need for sleep began to overtake her; the exuberance which had sustained and exalted her spirit left her helpless and yielding to the conditions which crowded her in.

The stillest hour of the night had come, the hour before dawn, when the world seems to hold its breath. The moon hung low, and had turned from silver to copper in the sleeping sky. The old owl no longer hooted, and the water-oaks had ceased to moan as they bent their heads.

Edna arose, cramped from lying so long and still in the hammock. She tottered up the steps, clutching feebly at the post before passing into the house.

"Are you coming in, Léonce?" she asked, turning her face toward her husband.

"Yes, dear," he answered, with a glance following a misty puff of smoke. "Just as soon as I have finished my cigar."

XII

✦

She slept but a few hours. They were troubled and feverish hours, disturbed with dreams that were intangible, that eluded her, leaving only an impression upon her half-awakened senses of something unattainable. She was up and dressed in the cool of the early morning. The air was invigorating and steadied somewhat her faculties. However, she was not seeking refreshment or help from any source, either external or from within. She was blindly following whatever impulse moved her, as if she had placed herself in alien hands for direction, and freed her soul of responsibility.

Most of the people at that early hour were still in bed and asleep. A few, who intended to go over to the *Chênière* for mass, were moving about. The lovers, who had laid their plans the night before, were already strolling toward the wharf. The lady in black, with her Sunday prayer-book, velvet and gold-clasped, and her Sunday silver beads, was following them at no great distance. Old Monsieur Farival was up, and was more than half inclined to do anything that suggested itself. He put on his big straw hat, and taking his umbrella from the stand in the hall, followed the lady in black, never overtaking her.

The little negro girl who worked Madame Lebrun's sewing-machine was sweeping the galleries with long, absent-minded strokes of the broom. Edna sent her up into the house to awaken Robert.

"Tell him I am going to the *Chênière*. The boat is ready; tell him to hurry."

He had soon joined her. She had never sent for him before. She had never asked for him. She had never seemed to want him before. She did not appear conscious that she had done anything unusual in commanding his presence. He was apparently equally unconscious of anything extraordinary in the situation. But his face was suffused with a quiet glow when he met her.

They went together back to the kitchen to drink coffee. There was no time to wait for any nicety of service. They stood outside the window and the cook passed them their coffee and a roll, which they drank and ate from the window-sill. Edna said it tasted good. She had not thought of coffee nor of anything. He told her he had often noticed that she lacked forethought.

"Wasn't it enough to think of going to the *Chênière* and waking you up?" she laughed. "Do I have to think of everything?—as Lèonce says when he's in a bad humor. I don't blame him; he'd never be in a bad humor if it weren't for me."

They took a short cut across the sands. At a distance they could see the curious procession moving toward the wharf—the lovers, shoulder to shoulder, creeping; the lady in black, gaining steadily upon them; old Monsieur Farival, losing ground inch by inch, and a young barefooted Spanish girl, with a red kerchief on her head and a basket on her arm, bringing up the rear.

Robert knew the girl, and he talked to her a little in the boat. No one present understood what they said. Her name was Mariequita. She had a round, sly, piquant face and pretty black eyes. Her hands were small, and she kept them folded over the handle of her basket. Her feet were broad and coarse. She did not strive to hide them. Edna looked at her feet, and noticed the sand and slime between her brown toes.

Beaudelet grumbled because Mariequita was there, taking up so much room. In reality he was annoyed at having old Monsieur Farival, who considered himself the better sailor of the two. But he would not quarrel with so old a man as Monsieur Farival, so he quarreled with Mariequita. The girl was deprecatory at one moment, appealing to Robert. She was saucy the next, moving her head up and down, making "eyes" at Robert and making "mouths" at Beaudelet.

The lovers were all alone. They saw nothing, they heard nothing. The lady in black was counting her beads for the third time. Old Monsieur Farival talked incessantly of what he knew about handling a boat, and of what Beaudelet did not know on the same subject.

Edna liked it all. She looked Mariequita up and down, from her ugly brown toes to her pretty black eyes, and back again.

"Why does she look at me like that?" inquired the girl of Robert.

"Maybe she thinks you are pretty. Shall I ask her?"

"No. Is she your sweetheart?"

"She's a married lady, and has two children."

"Oh! well! Francisco ran away with Sylvano's wife, who had four children. They took all his money and one of the children and stole his boat."

"Shut up!"

"Does she understand?"

"Oh, hush!"

"Are those two married over there—leaning on each other?"

"Of course not," laughed Robert.

"Of course not," echoed Mariequita, with a serious, confirmatory bob of the head.

The sun was high up and beginning to bite. The swift breeze seemed to Edna to bury the sting of it into the pores of her face and hands. Robert held his umbrella over her.

As they went cutting sidewise through the water, the sails bellied taut, with the wind filling and overflowing them. Old Monsieur Farival laughed sardonically at something as he looked at the sails, and Beaudelet swore at the old man under his breath.

Sailing across the bay to the *Chênière Caminada,* Edna felt as if she were being borne away from some anchorage which had held her fast, whose chains had been loosening—had snapped the night before when the mystic spirit was abroad, leaving her free to drift whithersoever she chose to set her sails. Robert spoke to her incessantly; he no longer noticed Mariequita. The girl had shrimps in her bamboo basket. They were covered with Spanish moss. She beat the moss down impatiently, and muttered to herself sullenly.

"Let us go to Grande Terre to-morrow?" said Robert in a low voice.

"What shall we do there?"

"Climb up the hill to the old fort and look at the little wriggling gold snakes, and watch the lizards sun themselves."

She gazed away toward Grande Terre and thought she would like to be alone there with Robert, in the sun, listening to the ocean's roar and watching the slimy lizards writhe in and out among the ruins of the old fort.

"And the next day or the next we can sail to the Bayou Brulow," he went on.

"What shall we do there?"

"Anything—cast bait for fish."

"No; we'll go back to Grande Terre. Let the fish alone."

"We'll go wherever you like," he said. "I'll have Tonie come over and help me patch and trim my boat. We shall not need Beaudelet nor any one. Are you afraid of the pirogue?"

"Oh, no."

"Then I'll take you some night in the pirogue when the moon shines. Maybe your Gulf spirit will whisper to you in which of these islands the treasures are hidden—direct you to the very spot, perhaps."

"And in a day we should be rich!" she laughed. "I'd give it all to you, the pirate gold and every bit of treasure we could dig up. I think you would know how to spend it. Pirate gold isn't a thing to be hoarded or utilized. It is something to squander and throw to the four winds, for the fun of seeing the golden specks fly."

"We'd share it, and scatter it together," he said. His face flushed.

They all went together up to the quaint little Gothic church of Our Lady of Lourdes, gleaming all brown and yellow with paint in the sun's glare.

Only Beaudelet remained behind, tinkering at his boat, and Mariequita walked away with her basket of shrimps, casting a look of childish ill-humor and reproach at Robert from the corner of her eye.

XIII

✦

$\mathcal{A}$ feeling of oppression and drowsiness overcame Edna during the service. Her head began to ache, and the lights on the altar swayed before her eyes. Another time she might have made an effort to regain her composure; but her one thought was to quit the stifling atmosphere of the church and reach the open air. She arose, climbing over Robert's feet with a muttered apology. Old Monsieur Farival, flurried, curious, stood up, but upon seeing that Robert had followed Mrs. Pontellier, he sank back into his seat. He whispered an anxious inquiry of the lady in black, who did not notice him or reply, but kept her eyes fastened upon the pages of her velvet prayer-book.

"I felt giddy and almost overcome," Edna said, lifting her hands instinctively to her head and pushing her straw hat up from her forehead. "I couldn't have stayed through the service." They were outside in the shadow of the church. Robert was full of solicitude.

"It was folly to have thought of going in the first place, let alone staying. Come over to Madame Antoine's; you can rest there." He took her arm and led her away, looking anxiously and continuously down into her face.

How still it was, with only the voice of the sea whispering through the reeds that grew in the salt-water pools! The long line of little gray, weather-beaten houses nestled peacefully among the orange trees. It must always have been God's day on that low, drowsy island, Edna thought. They stopped, leaning over a jagged fence made of sea-drift, to ask for water. A youth, a mild-faced Acadian, was drawing water from the cistern, which was nothing more than a rusty buoy, with an opening on one side, sunk in the ground. The water which the youth handed to them in a tin pail was not cold to taste, but it was cool to her heated face, and it greatly revived and refreshed her.

Madame Antoine's cot was at the far end of the village. She welcomed them with all the native hospitality, as she would have opened her door to let the sunlight in. She was fat, and walked heavily and clumsily across the floor. She could speak no English, but when Robert made her understand that the lady who accompanied him was ill and desired to rest, she was all eagerness to make Edna feel at home and to dispose of her comfortably.

The whole place was immaculately clean, and the big, four-posted bed, snow-white, invited one to repose. It stood in a small side room which looked out across a narrow grass plot toward the shed, where there was a disabled boat lying keel upward.

Madame Antoine had not gone to mass. Her son Tonie had, but she supposed he would soon be back, and she invited Robert to be seated and wait for him. But he went and sat outside the door and smoked. Madame Antoine busied herself in the large front room preparing dinner. She was boiling mullets over a few red coals in the huge fireplace.

Edna, left alone in the little side room, loosened her clothes, removing the greater part of them. She bathed her face, her neck and arms in the basin that stood between the windows. She took off her shoes and stockings and stretched herself in the very center of the high, white bed. How luxurious it felt to rest thus in a strange, quaint bed, with its sweet country odor of laurel lingering about the sheets and mattress! She stretched her strong limbs that ached a little. She ran her fingers through her loosened hair for a while. She looked at her round arms as she held them straight up and rubbed them one after the other, observing closely, as if it were something she saw for the first time, the fine, firm quality and texture of her flesh. She clasped her hands easily above her head, and it was thus she fell asleep.

She slept lightly at first, half awake and drowsily attentive to the things about her. She could hear Madame Antoine's heavy, scraping tread as she walked back and forth on the sanded floor. Some chickens were clucking outside the windows, scratching for bits of gravel in the grass. Later she half heard the voices of Robert and Tonie talking under the shed. She did not stir. Even her eyelids rested numb and heavily over her sleepy eyes. The voices went on—Tonie's slow, Acadian drawl, Robert's quick, soft, smooth French. She understood French imperfectly unless directly addressed, and the voices were only part of the other drowsy, muffled sounds lulling her senses.

When Edna awoke it was with the conviction that she had slept long and soundly. The voices were hushed under the shed. Madame Antoine's step was no longer to be heard in the adjoining room. Even the chickens had gone elsewhere to scratch and cluck. The mosquito bar was drawn over her; the old woman had come in while she slept and let down the bar. Edna arose quietly from the bed, and looking between the curtains of the window, she saw by the slanting rays of the sun that the afternoon was far advanced. Robert was out there under the shed, reclining in the shade against the sloping keel of the overturned boat. He was reading from a book. Tonie was no longer with him. She wondered what had become of the rest of the party. She peeped out at him two or three times as she stood washing herself in the little basin between the windows.

Madame Antoine had laid some coarse, clean towels upon a chair, and had placed a box of *poudre de riz* within easy reach. Edna dabbed the powder upon her nose and cheeks as she looked at herself closely in the little distorted mirror which hung on the wall above the basin. Her eyes were bright and wide awake and her face glowed.

When she had completed her toilet she walked into the adjoining room. She was very hungry. No one was there. But there was a cloth spread upon the table that stood against the wall, and a cover was laid for one, with a crusty brown loaf and a bottle of wine beside the plate. Edna bit a piece from the brown loaf, tearing it with her strong, white teeth. She poured some of the wine into the glass and drank it down. Then she went softly out of doors, and plucking an orange from the low-hanging bough of a tree, threw it at Robert, who did not know she was awake and up.

An illumination broke over his whole face when he saw her and joined her under the orange tree.

"How many years have I slept?" she inquired. "The whole island seems changed. A new race of beings must have sprung up, leaving only you and me as past relics. How many ages ago did Madame Antoine and Tonie die? and when did our people from Grand Isle disappear from the earth?"

He familiarly adjusted a ruffle upon her shoulder.

"You have slept precisely one hundred years. I was left here to guard your slumbers; and for one hundred years I have been out under the shed reading a book. The only evil

I couldn't prevent was to keep a broiled fowl from drying up."

"If it has turned to stone, still will I eat it," said Edna, moving with him into the house. "But really, what has become of Monsieur Farival and the others?"

"Gone hours ago. When they found that you were sleeping they thought it best not to awake you. Any way, I wouldn't have let them. What was I here for?"

"I wonder if Léonce will be uneasy!" she speculated, as she seated herself at table.

"Of course not; he knows you are with me," Robert replied, as he busied himself among sundry pans and covered dishes which had been left standing on the hearth.

"Where are Madame Antoine and her son?" asked Edna.

"Gone to Vespers, and to visit some friends, I believe. I am to take you back in Tonie's boat whenever you are ready to go."

He stirred the smoldering ashes till the broiled fowl began to sizzle afresh. He served her with no mean repast, dripping the coffee anew and sharing it with her. Madame Antoine had cooked little else than the mullets, but while Edna slept Robert had foraged the island. He was childishly gratified to discover her appetite, and to see the relish with which she ate the food which he had procured for her.

"Shall we go right away?" she asked, after draining her glass and brushing together the crumbs of the crusty loaf.

"The sun isn't as low as it will be in two hours," he answered.

"The sun will be gone in two hours."

"Well, let it go; who cares!"

They waited a good while under the orange trees, till Madame Antoine came back, panting, waddling, with a thousand apologies to explain her absence. Tonie did not dare to return. He was shy, and would not willingly face any woman except his mother.

It was very pleasant to stay there under the orange trees, while the sun dipped lower and lower, turning the western sky to flaming copper and gold. The shadows lengthened and crept out like stealthy, grotesque monsters across the grass.

Edna and Robert both sat upon the ground—that is, he lay upon the ground beside her, occasionally picking at the hem of her muslin gown.

Madame Antoine seated her fat body, broad and squat, upon a bench beside the door. She had been talking all the afternoon, and had wound herself up to the story-telling pitch.

And what stories she told them! But twice in her life she had left the *Chênière Caminada,* and then for the briefest span. All her years she had squatted and waddled there upon the island, gathering legends of the Baratarians and the sea. The night came on, with the moon to lighten it. Edna could hear the whispering voices of dead men and the click of muffled gold.

When she and Robert stepped into Tonie's boat, with the red lateen sail, misty spirit forms were prowling in the shadows and among the reeds, and upon the water were phantom ships, speeding to cover.

XIV

✦

*T*he youngest boy, Etienne, had been very naughty, Madame Ratignolle said, as she delivered him into the hands of his mother. He had been unwilling to go to bed and had made a scene; whereupon she had taken charge of him and pacified him as well as she could. Raoul had been in bed and asleep for two hours.

The youngster was in his long white nightgown, that kept tripping him up as Madame Ratignolle led him along by the hand. With the other chubby fist he rubbed his eyes, which were heavy with sleep and ill humor. Edna took him in her arms, and seating herself in the rocker, began to coddle and caress him, calling him all manner of tender names, soothing him to sleep.

It was not more than nine o'clock. No one had yet gone to bed but the children.

Léonce had been very uneasy at first, Madame Ratignolle said, and had wanted to start at once for the *Chênière*. But Monsieur Farival had assured him that his wife was only overcome with sleep and fatigue, that Tonie would bring her safely back later in the day; and he had thus been dissuaded from crossing the bay. He had gone over to Klein's, looking up some cotton broker whom he wished to see in regard to securities, exchanges, stocks, bonds, or something of the sort, Madame Ratignolle did not remember what. He said he would not remain away late. She herself was suffering from heat and oppression, she said. She carried a bottle of salts and a large fan. She would not consent to remain with Edna, for Monsieur Ratignolle was alone, and he detested above all things to be left alone.

When Etienne had fallen asleep Edna bore him into the back room, and Robert went and lifted the mosquito bar that she might lay the child comfortably in his bed. The quadroon had vanished. When they emerged from the cottage Robert bade Edna good-night.

"Do you know we have been together the whole livelong day, Robert—since early this morning?" she said at parting.

"All but the hundred years when you were sleeping. Good-night."

He pressed her hand and went away in the direction of the beach. He did not join any of the others, but walked alone toward the Gulf.

Edna stayed outside, awaiting her husband's return. She had no desire to sleep or to retire; nor did she feel like going over to sit with the Ratignolles, or to join Madame Lebrun and a group whose animated voices reached her as they sat in conversation before the house. She let her mind wander back over her stay at Grand Isle; and she tried to discover wherein this summer had been different from any and every other summer of her life. She could only realize that she herself—her present self—was in some way different from the other self. That she was seeing with different eyes and making the acquaintance of new conditions in herself that colored and changed her environment, she did not yet suspect.

She wondered why Robert had gone away and left her. It did not occur to her to think he might have grown tired of being with her the livelong day. She was not tired, and she felt that he was not. She regretted that he had gone. It was so much more natural to have him stay when he was not absolutely required to leave her.

As Edna waited for her husband she sang low a little song that Robert had sung as they crossed the bay. It began with "Ah! *Si tu savais*," and every verse ended with *"si tu savais."*

Robert's voice was not pretentious. It was musical and true. The voice, the notes, the whole refrain haunted her memory.

XV

✦

When Edna entered the dining-room one evening a little late, as was her habit, an unusually animated conversation seemed to be going on. Several persons were talking at once, and Victor's voice was predominating, even over that of his mother. Edna had returned late from her bath, had dressed in some haste, and her face was flushed. Her head, set off by her dainty white gown, suggested a rich, rare blossom. She took her seat at table between old Monsieur Farival and Madame Ratignolle.

As she seated herself and was about to begin to eat her soup, which had been served when she entered the room, several persons informed her simultaneously that Robert was going to Mexico. She laid her spoon down and looked about her bewildered. He had been with her, reading to her all the morning, and had never even mentioned such a place as Mexico. She had not seen him during the afternoon; she had heard some one say he was at the house, upstairs with his mother. This she had thought nothing of, though she was surprised when he did not join her later in the afternoon, when she went down to the beach.

She looked across at him, where he sat beside Madame Lebrun, who presided. Edna's face was a blank picture of bewilderment, which she never thought of disguising. He lifted his eyebrows with the pretext of a smile as he returned her glance. He looked embarrassed and uneasy.

"When is he going?" she asked of everybody in general, as if Robert were not there to answer for himself.

"To-night!" "This very evening!" "Did you ever!" "What possesses him!" were some of the replies she gathered, uttered simultaneously in French and English.

"Impossible!" she exclaimed. "How can a person start off from Grand Isle to Mexico at a moment's notice, as if he were going over to Klein's or to the wharf or down to the beach?"

"I said all along I was going to Mexico; I've been saying so for years!" cried Robert, in an excited and irritable tone, with the air of a man defending himself against a swarm of stinging insects.

Madame Lebrun knocked on the table with her knife handle.

"Please let Robert explain why he is going, and why he is going to-night," she called out. "Really, this table is getting to be more and more like Bedlam every day, with everybody talking at once. Sometimes—I hope God will forgive me—but positively, sometimes I wish Victor would lose the power of speech."

Victor laughed sardonically as he thanked his mother for her holy wish, of which he failed to see the benefit to anybody, except that it might afford her a more ample opportunity and license to talk herself.

Monsieur Farival thought that Victor should have been taken out in mid-ocean in his earliest youth and drowned. Victor thought there would be more logic in thus disposing of old people with an established claim for making themselves universally obnoxious. Madame Lebrun grew a trifle hysterical; Robert called his brother some sharp, hard names.

"There's nothing much to explain, mother," he said; though he explained, nevertheless—looking chiefly at Edna—that he could only meet the gentleman whom he intended to join at Vera Cruz by taking such and such a steamer, which left New Orleans on such a day; that Beaudelet was going out with his lugger-load of vegetables that night, which gave him an opportunity of reaching the city and making his vessel in time.

"But when did you make up your mind to all this?" demanded Monsieur Farival.

"This afternoon," returned Robert, with a shade of annoyance.

"At what time this afternoon?" persisted the old gentleman, with nagging determination, as if he were cross-questioning a criminal in a court of justice.

"At four o'clock this afternoon, Monsieur Farival," Robert replied, in a high voice and with a lofty air, which reminded Edna of some gentleman on the stage.

She had forced herself to eat most of her soup, and now she was picking the flaky bits of a *court bouillon* with her fork.

The lovers were profiting by the general conversation on Mexico to speak in whispers of matters which they rightly considered were interesting to no one but themselves. The lady in black had once received a pair of prayer-beads of curious workmanship from Mexico, with very special indulgence attached to them, but she had never been able to ascertain whether the indulgence extended outside the Mexican border. Father Fochel of the Cathedral had attempted to explain it; but he had not done so to her satisfaction. And she begged that Robert would interest himself, and discover, if possible, whether she was entitled to the indulgence accompanying the remarkably curious Mexican prayer-beads.

Madame Ratignolle hoped that Robert would exercise extreme caution in dealing with the Mexicans, who, she considered, were a treacherous people, unscrupulous and revengeful. She trusted she did them no injustice in thus condemning them as a race. She had known personally but one Mexican, who made and sold excellent tamales, and whom she would have trusted implicitly, so soft-spoken was he. One day he was arrested for stabbing his wife. She never knew whether he had been hanged or not.

Victor had grown hilarious, and was attempting to tell an anecdote about a Mexican girl who served chocolate one winter in a restaurant in Dauphine Street. No one would listen to him but old Monsieur Farival, who went into convulsions over the droll story.

Edna wondered if they had all gone mad, to be talking and clamoring at that rate. She herself could think of nothing to say about Mexico or the Mexicans.

"At what time do you leave?" she asked Robert.

"At ten," he told her. "Beaudelet wants to wait for the moon."

"Are you all ready to go?"

"Quite ready. I shall only take a hand-bag, and shall pack my trunk in the city."

He turned to answer some question put to him by his mother, and Edna, having finished her black coffee, left the table.

She went directly to her room. The little cottage was close and stuffy after leaving the outer air. But she did not mind; there appeared to be a hundred different things demanding her attention indoors. She began to set the toilet-stand to rights, grumbling at the negligence of the quadroon, who was in the adjoining room putting the children to bed. She gathered together stray garments that were hanging on the backs of chairs, and put each where it belonged in closet or bureau drawer. She changed her gown for a more comfortable and commodious wrapper. She rearranged her hair, combing and brushing it with unusual energy. Then she went in and assisted the quadroon in getting the boys to bed.

They were very playful and inclined to talk—to do anything but lie quiet and go to sleep. Edna sent the quadroon away to her supper and told her she need not return. Then she sat and told the children a story. Instead of soothing it excited them, and added to their wakefulness. She left them in heated argument, speculating about the conclusion of the tale which their mother promised to finish the following night.

The little black girl came in to say that Madame Lebrun would like to have Mrs. Pontellier go and sit with them over at the house till Mr. Robert went away. Edna returned answer that she had already undressed, that she did not feel quite well, but perhaps she would go over to the house later. She started to dress again, and got as far advanced as to remove her *peignoir*. But changing her mind once more she resumed the *peignoir,* and went outside and sat down before her door. She was overheated and irritable, and fanned herself energetically for a while. Madame Ratignolle came down to discover what was the matter.

"All that noise and confusion at the table must have upset me," replied Edna, "and moreover, I hate shocks and surprises. The idea of Robert starting off in such a ridiculously sudden and dramatic way! As if it were a matter of life and death! Never saying a word about it all morning when he was with me."

"Yes," agreed Madame Ratignolle. "I think it was show-ing us all—you especially—very little consideration. It wouldn't have surprised me in any of the others; those Le-bruns are all given to heroics. But I must say I should never have expected such a thing from Robert. Are you not com-ing down? Come on, dear; it doesn't look friendly."

"No," said Edna, a little sullenly. "I can't go to the trouble of dressing again; I don't feel like it."

"You needn't dress; you look all right; fasten a belt around your waist. Just look at me!"

"No," persisted Edna; "but you go on. Madame Lebrun might be offended if we both stayed away."

Madame Ratignolle kissed Edna good-night, and went away, being in truth rather desirous of joining in the general and animated conversation which was still in progress con-cerning Mexico and the Mexicans.

Somewhat later Robert came up, carrying his hand-bag.

"Aren't you feeling well?" he asked.

"Oh, well enough. Are you going right away?"

He lit a match and looked at his watch. "In twenty min-utes," he said. The sudden and brief flare of the match em-phasized the darkness for a while. He sat down upon a stool which the children had left out on the porch.

"Get a chair," said Edna.

"This will do," he replied. He put on his soft hat and ner-vously took it off again, and wiping his face with his hand-kerchief, complained of the heat.

"Take the fan," said Edna, offering it to him.

"Oh, no! Thank you. It does no good; you have to stop fanning some time, and feel all the more uncomfortable af-terward."

"That's one of the ridiculous things which men always say. I have never known one to speak otherwise of fanning. How long will you be gone?"

"Forever, perhaps. I don't know. It depends upon a good many things."

"Well, in case it shouldn't be forever, how long will it be?"

"I don't know."

"This seems to me perfectly preposterous and uncalled for. I don't like it. I don't understand your motive for silence and mystery, never saying a word to me about it this morning." He remained silent, not offering to defend himself. He only said, after a moment:

"Don't part from me in an ill-humor. I never knew you to be out of patience with me before."

"I don't want to part in any ill-humor," she said. "But can't you understand? I've grown used to seeing you, to having you with me all the time, and your action seems unfriendly, even unkind. You don't even offer an excuse for it. Why, I was planning to be together, thinking of how pleasant it would be to see you in the city next winter."

"So was I," he blurted. "Perhaps that's the——" He stood up suddenly and held out his hand. "Good-by, my dear Mrs. Pontellier; good-by. You won't——I hope you won't completely forget me." She clung to his hand, striving to detain him.

"Write to me when you get there, won't you, Robert?" she entreated.

"I will, thank you. Good-by."

How unlike Robert! The merest acquaintance would have said something more emphatic than "I will, thank you; good-by," to such a request.

He had evidently already taken leave of the people over at the house, for he descended the steps and went to join Beaudelet, who was out there with an oar across his shoulder waiting for Robert. They walked away in the darkness. She could only hear Beaudelet's voice; Robert had apparently not even spoken a word of greeting to his companion.

Edna bit her handkerchief convulsively, striving to hold back and to hide, even from herself as she would have hidden from another, the emotion which was troubling— tearing—her. Her eyes were brimming with tears.

For the first time she recognized anew the symptoms of infatuation which she had felt incipiently as a child, as a girl in her earliest teens, and later as a young woman. The recognition did not lessen the reality, the poignancy of the revelation by any suggestion or promise of instability. The past was nothing to her; offered no lesson which she was willing to heed. The future was a mystery which she never attempted to penetrate. The present alone was significant; was hers, to torture her as it was doing then with the biting conviction that she had lost that which she had held, that she had been denied that which her impassioned, newly awakened being demanded.

XVI

✦

"Do you miss your friend greatly?" asked Mademoiselle Reisz one morning as she came creeping up behind Edna, who had just left her cottage on her way to the beach. She spent much of her time in the water since she had acquired finally the art of swimming. As their stay at Grand Isle drew near its close, she felt that she could not give too much time to a diversion which afforded her the only real pleasurable moments that she knew. When Mademoiselle Reisz came and touched her upon the shoulder and spoke to her, the woman seemed to echo the thought which was ever in Edna's mind; or, better, the feeling which constantly possessed her.

Robert's going had some way taken the brightness, the color, the meaning out of everything. The conditions of her life were in no way changed, but her whole existence was dulled, like a faded garment which seems to be no longer worth wearing. She sought him everywhere—in others whom she induced to talk about him. She went up in the mornings to Madame Lebrun's room, braving the clatter of the old sewing-machine. She sat there and chatted at intervals as Robert had done. She gazed around the room at the pictures and photographs hanging upon the wall, and discovered in some corner an old family album, which she examined with the keenest interest, appealing to Madame Lebrun for enlightenment concerning the many figures and faces which she discovered between its pages.

There was a picture of Madame Lebrun with Robert as a baby, seated in her lap, a round-faced infant with a fist in his mouth. The eyes alone in the baby suggested the man. And that was he also in kilts, at the age of five, wearing long curls and holding a whip in his hand. It made Edna laugh, and she laughed, too, at the portrait in his first long trousers; while another interested her, taken when he left for college, looking thin, long-faced, with eyes full of fire, ambition and great intentions. But there was no recent picture, none which suggested the Robert who had gone away five days ago, leaving a void and wilderness behind him.

"Oh, Robert stopped having his pictures taken when he had to pay for them himself! He found wiser use for his money, he says," explained Madame Lebrun. She had a letter from him, written before he left New Orleans. Edna wished to see the letter, and Madame Lebrun told her to look for it either on the table or the dresser, or perhaps it was on the mantelpiece.

The letter was on the bookshelf. It possessed the greatest interest and attraction for Edna; the envelope, its size and shape, the post-mark, the handwriting. She examined every detail of the outside before opening it. There were only a few lines, setting forth that he would leave the city that afternoon, that he had packed his trunk in good shape, that he was well, and sent her his love and begged to be affectionately remembered to all. There was no special message to Edna except a postscript saying that if Mrs. Pontellier desired to finish the book which he had been reading to her, his mother would find it in his room, among other books there on the table. Edna experienced a pang of jealousy because he had written to his mother rather than to her.

Every one seemed to take for granted that she missed him. Even her husband, when he came down the Saturday following Robert's departure, expressed regret that he had gone.

"How do you get on without him, Edna?" he asked.

"It's very dull without him," she admitted. Mr. Pontellier had seen Robert in the city, and Edna asked him a dozen questions or more. Where had they met? On Carondelet Street, in the morning. They had gone "in" and had a drink and a cigar together. What had they talked about? Chiefly about his prospects in Mexico, which Mr. Pontellier thought were promising. How did he look? How did he seem—grave, or gay, or how? Quite cheerful, and wholly taken up with the idea of his trip, which Mr. Pontellier found altogether natural in a young fellow about to seek fortune and adventure in a strange, queer country.

Edna tapped her foot impatiently, and wondered why the children persisted in playing in the sun when they might be under the trees. She went down and led them out of the sun, scolding the quadroon for not being more attentive.

It did not strike her as in the least grotesque that she should be making of Robert the object of conversation and leading her husband to speak of him. The sentiment which she entertained for Robert in no way resembled that which she felt for her husband, or had ever felt, or ever expected to feel. She had all her life long been accustomed to harbor thoughts and emotions which never voiced themselves. They had never taken the form of struggles. They belonged to her and were her own, and she entertained the conviction that she had a right to them and that they concerned no one but herself. Edna had once told Madame Ratignolle that she would never sacrifice herself for her children, or for any one. Then had followed a rather heated argument; the two women did not appear to understand each other or to be talking the same language. Edna tried to appease her friend, to explain.

"I would give up the unessential; I would give my money, I would give my life for my children; but I wouldn't give myself. I can't make it more clear; it's only something which I am beginning to comprehend, which is revealing itself to me."

"I don't know what you would call the essential, or what you mean by the unessential," said Madame Ratignolle, cheerfully; "but a woman who would give her life for her children could do no more than that—your Bible tells you so. I'm sure I couldn't do more than that."

"Oh, yes you could!" laughed Edna.

She was not surprised at Mademoiselle Reisz's question the morning that lady, following her to the beach, tapped her on the shoulder and asked if she did not greatly miss her young friend.

"Oh, good morning, Mademoiselle; is it you? Why, of course I miss Robert. Are you going down to bathe?"

"Why should I go down to bathe at the very end of the season when I haven't been in the surf all summer," replied the woman, disagreeably.

"I beg your pardon," offered Edna, in some embarrassment, for she should have remembered that Mademoiselle Reisz's avoidance of the water had furnished a theme for much pleasantry. Some among them thought it was on account of her false hair, or the dread of getting the violets wet, while others attributed it to the natural aversion for water sometimes believed to accompany the artistic temperament. Mademoiselle offered Edna some chocolates in a paper bag, which she took from her pocket, by way of showing that she bore no ill feeling. She habitually ate chocolates for their sustaining quality; they contained much nutriment in small compass, she said. They saved her from starvation, as Madame Lebrun's table was utterly impossible; and no one save so impertinent a woman as Madame Lebrun could think of offering such food to people and requiring them to pay for it.

"She must feel very lonely without her son," said Edna, desiring to change the subject. "Her favorite son, too. It must have been quite hard to let him go."

Mademoiselle laughed maliciously.

"Her favorite son! Oh, dear! Who could have been imposing such a tale upon you? Aline Lebrun lives for Victor, and for Victor alone. She has spoiled him into the worthless creature he is. She worships him and the ground he walks on. Robert is very well in a way, to give up all the money he can earn to the family, and keep the barest pittance for himself. Favorite son, indeed! I miss the poor fellow myself, my dear. I liked to see him and to hear him about the place—the only Lebrun who is worth a pinch of salt. He comes to see me often in the city. I like to play to him. That Victor! hanging would be too good for him. It's a wonder Robert hasn't beaten him to death long ago."

"I thought he had great patience with his brother," offered Edna, glad to be talking about Robert, no matter what was said.

"Oh! he thrashed him well enough a year or two ago," said Mademoiselle. "It was about a Spanish girl, whom Victor considered that he had some sort of claim upon. He met Robert one day talking to the girl, or walking with her, or bathing with her, or carrying her basket—I don't remember what;—and he became so insulting and abusive that Robert gave him a thrashing on the spot that has kept him comparatively in order for a good while. It's about time he was getting another."

"Was her name Mariequita?" asked Edna.

"Mariequita—yes, that was it; Mariequita. I had forgotten. Oh, she's a sly one, and a bad one, that Mariequita!"

Edna looked down at Mademoiselle Reisz and wondered how she could have listened to her venom so long. For some reason she felt depressed, almost unhappy. She had not intended to go into the water; but she donned her bathing suit, and left Mademoiselle alone, seated under the shade of the children's tent. The water was growing cooler as the season advanced. Edna plunged and swam about with an abandon that thrilled and invigorated her. She remained a long time in the water, half hoping that Mademoiselle Reisz would not wait for her.

But Mademoiselle waited. She was very amiable during the walk back, and raved much over Edna's appearance in her bathing suit. She talked about music. She hoped that Edna would go to see her in the city, and wrote her address with the stub of a pencil on a piece of card which she found in her pocket.

"When do you leave?" asked Edna.

"Next Monday; and you?"

"The following week," answered Edna, adding, "It has been a pleasant summer, hasn't it, Mademoiselle?"

"Well," agreed Mademoiselle Reisz, with a shrug, "rather pleasant, if it hadn't been for the mosquitoes and the Farival twins."

Her name was Mariequita. She had a round, sly, piquant face and pretty black eyes (page 57).

XVII

✦

$\mathcal{T}$he Pontelliers possessed a very charming home on Esplanade Street in New Orleans. It was a large, double cottage, with a broad front veranda, whose round, fluted columns supported the sloping roof. The house was painted a dazzling white; the outside shutters, or jalousies, were green. In the yard, which was kept scrupulously neat, were flowers and plants of every description which flourishes in South Louisiana. Within doors the appointments were perfect after the conventional type. The softest carpets and rugs covered the floors; rich and tasteful draperies hung at doors and windows. There were paintings, selected with judgment and discrimination, upon the walls. The cut glass, the silver, the heavy damask which daily appeared upon the table were the envy of many women whose husbands were less generous than Mr. Pontellier.

Mr. Pontellier was very fond of walking about his house examining its various appointments and details, to see that nothing was amiss. He greatly valued his possessions, chiefly because they were his, and derived genuine pleasure from contemplating a painting, a statuette, a rare lace curtain—no matter what—after he had bought it and placed it among his household gods.

On Tuesday afternoons—Tuesday being Mrs. Pontellier's reception day—there was a constant stream of callers— women who came in carriages or in the street cars, or walked when the air was soft and distance permitted. A light-colored mulatto boy, in dress coat and bearing a diminutive silver tray for the reception of cards, admitted them. A maid, in white fluted cap, offered the callers liqueur, coffee, or chocolate, as they might desire. Mrs. Pontellier, attired in a handsome reception gown, remained in the drawing-room the entire afternoon receiving her visitors. Men sometimes called in the evening with their wives.

This had been the programme which Mrs. Pontellier had religiously followed since her marriage, six years before. Certain evenings during the week she and her husband attended the opera or sometimes the play.

Mr. Pontellier left his home in the mornings between nine and ten o'clock, and rarely returned before half-past six or seven in the evening—dinner being served at half-past seven.

He and his wife seated themselves at table one Tuesday evening, a few weeks after their return from Grand Isle. They were alone together. The boys were being put to bed; the patter of their bare, escaping feet could be heard occasionally, as well as the pursuing voice of the quadroon, lifted in mild protest and entreaty. Mrs. Pontellier did not wear her usual Tuesday reception gown; she was in ordinary house dress. Mr. Pontellier, who was observant about such things, noticed it, as he served the soup and handed it to the boy in waiting.

"Tired out, Edna? Whom did you have? Many callers?" he asked. He tasted his soup and began to season it with pepper, salt, vinegar, mustard—everything within reach.

"There were a good many," replied Edna, who was eating her soup with evident satisfaction. "I found their cards when I got home; I was out."

"Out!" exclaimed her husband, with something like genuine consternation in his voice as he laid down the vinegar cruet and looked at her through his glasses. "Why, what could have taken you out on Tuesday? What did you have to do?"

"Nothing. I simply felt like going out, and I went out."

"Well, I hope you left some suitable excuse," said her husband, somewhat appeased, as he added a dash of cayenne pepper to the soup.

"No, I left no excuse. I told Joe to say I was out, that was all."

"Why, my dear, I should think you'd understand by this time that people don't do such things; we've got to observe *les convenances* if we ever expect to get on and keep up with the procession. If you felt that you had to leave home this afternoon, you should have left some suitable explanation for your absence.

"This soup is really impossible; it's strange that woman hasn't learned yet to make a decent soup. Any free-lunch stand in town serves a better one. Was Mrs. Belthrop here?"

"Bring the tray with the cards, Joe. I don't remember who was here."

The boy retired and returned after a moment, bringing the tiny silver tray, which was covered with ladies' visiting cards. He handed it to Mrs. Pontellier.

"Give it to Mr. Pontellier," she said.

Joe offered the tray to Mr. Pontellier, and removed the soup.

Mr. Pontellier scanned the names of his wife's callers, reading some of them aloud, with comments as he read.

" 'The Misses Delasidas.' I worked a big deal in futures for their father this morning; nice girls; it's time they were getting married. 'Mrs. Belthrop.' I tell you what it is, Edna; you can't afford to snub Mrs. Belthrop. Why, Belthrop could buy and sell us ten times over. His business is worth a good, round sum to me. You'd better write her a note. 'Mrs. James Highcamp.' Hugh! the less you have to do with Mrs. Highcamp, the better. 'Madame Laforcé.' Came all the way from Carrolton, too, poor old soul. 'Miss Wiggs,' 'Mrs. Eleanor Boltons.' " He pushed the cards aside.

"Mercy!" exclaimed Edna, who had been fuming. "Why are you taking the thing so seriously and making such a fuss over it?"

"I'm not making any fuss over it. But it's just such seeming trifles that we've got to take seriously; such things count."

The fish was scorched. Mr. Pontellier would not touch it. Edna said she did not mind a little scorched taste. The roast was in some way not to his fancy, and he did not like the manner in which the vegetables were served.

"It seems to me," he said, "we spend money enough in this house to procure at least one meal a day which a man could eat and retain his self-respect."

"You used to think the cook was a treasure," returned Edna, indifferently.

"Perhaps she was when she first came; but cooks are only human. They need looking after, like any other class of persons that you employ. Suppose I didn't look after the clerks in my office, just let them run things their own way; they'd soon make a nice mess of me and my business."

"Where are you going?" asked Edna, seeing that her husband arose from table without having eaten a morsel except a taste of the highly-seasoned soup.

"I'm going to get my dinner at the club. Good-night." He

went into the hall, took his hat and stick from the stand, and left the house.

She was somewhat familiar with such scenes. They had often made her very unhappy. On a few previous occasions she had been completely deprived of any desire to finish her dinner. Sometimes she had gone into the kitchen to administer a tardy rebuke to the cook. Once she went to her room and studied the cookbook during an entire evening, finally writing out a menu for the week, which left her harassed with a feeling that, after all, she had accomplished no good that was worth the name.

But that evening Edna finished her dinner alone, with forced deliberation. Her face was flushed and her eyes flamed with some inward fire that lighted them. After finishing her dinner she went to her room, having instructed the boy to tell any other callers that she was indisposed.

It was a large, beautiful room, rich and picturesque in the soft, dim light which the maid had turned low. She went and stood at an open window and looked out upon the deep tangle of the garden below. All the mystery and witchery of the night seemed to have gathered there amid the perfumes and the dusky and tortuous outlines of flowers and foliage. She was seeking herself and finding herself in just such sweet, half-darkness which met her moods. But the voices were not soothing that came to her from the darkness and the sky above and the stars. They jeered and sounded mournful notes without promise, devoid even of hope. She turned back into the room and began to walk to and fro down its whole length, without stopping, without resting. She carried in her hands a thin handkerchief, which she tore into ribbons, rolled into a ball, and flung from her. Once she stopped, and taking off her wedding ring, flung it upon the carpet. When she saw it lying there, she stamped her heel upon it, striving to crush it. But her small boot heel did not make an indenture, not a mark upon the little glittering circlet.

In a sweeping passion she seized a glass vase from the table and flung it upon the tiles of the hearth. She wanted to destroy something. The crash and clatter were what she wanted to hear.

A maid, alarmed at the din of breaking glass, entered the room to discover what was the matter.

"A vase fell upon the hearth," said Edna. "Never mind; leave it till morning."

"Oh! you might get some of the glass in your feet, ma'am," insisted the young woman, picking up bits of the broken vase that were scattered upon the carpet. "And here's your ring, ma'am, under the chair."

Edna held out her hand, and taking the ring, slipped it upon her finger.

XVIII

✦

$\mathcal{T}$he following morning Mr. Pontellier, upon leaving for his office, asked Edna if she would not meet him in town in order to look at some new fixtures for the library.

"I hardly think we need new fixtures, Léonce. Don't let us get anything new; you are too extravagant. I don't believe you ever think of saving or putting by."

"The way to become rich is to make money, my dear Edna, not to save it," he said. He regretted that she did not feel inclined to go with him and select new fixtures. He kissed her good-by, and told her she was not looking well and must take care of herself. She was unusually pale and very quiet.

She stood on the front veranda as he quitted the house, and absently picked a few sprays of jessamine that grew upon a trellis near by. She inhaled the odor of the blossoms and thrust them into the bosom of her white morning gown. The boys were dragging along the banquette a small "express wagon," which they had filled with blocks and sticks. The quadroon was following them with little quick steps, having assumed a fictitious animation and alacrity for the occasion. A fruit vendor was crying his wares in the street.

Edna looked straight before her with a self-absorbed expression upon her face. She felt no interest in anything about her. The street, the children, the fruit vendor, the flowers growing there under her eyes, were all part and parcel of an alien world which had suddenly become antagonistic.

She went back into the house. She had thought of speaking to the cook concerning her blunders of the previous night; but Mr. Pontellier had saved her that disagreeable mission, for which she was so poorly fitted. Mr. Pontellier's arguments were usually convincing with those whom he employed. He left home feeling quite sure that he and Edna would sit down that evening, and possibly a few subsequent evenings, to a dinner deserving of the name.

Edna spent an hour or two in looking over some of her old sketches. She could see their shortcomings and defects, which were glaring in her eyes. She tried to work a little, but found she was not in the humor. Finally she gathered together a few of the sketches—those which she considered the least discreditable; and she carried them with her when, a little later, she dressed and left the house. She looked handsome and distinguished in her street gown. The tan of the seashore had left her face, and her forehead was smooth, white, and polished beneath her heavy, yellow-brown hair. There were a few freckles on her face, and a small, dark mole near the under lip and one on the temple, half-hidden in her hair.

As Edna walked along the street she was thinking of Robert. She was still under the spell of her infatuation. She had tried to forget him, realizing the inutility of remembering. But the thought of him was like an obsession, ever pressing itself upon her. It was not that she dwelt upon de-

tails of their acquaintance, or recalled in any special or peculiar way his personality; it was his being, his existence,
which dominated her thought, fading sometimes as if it
would melt into the mist of the forgotten, reviving again
with an intensity which filled her with an incomprehensible
longing.

Edna was on her way to Madame Ratignolle's. Their intimacy, begun at Grand Isle, had not declined, and they had
seen each other with some frequency since their return to
the city. The Ratignolles lived at no great distance from
Edna's home, on the corner of a side street, where Monsieur Ratignolle owned and conducted a drug store which
enjoyed a steady and prosperous trade. His father had been
in the business before him, and Monsieur Ratignolle stood
well in the community and bore an enviable reputation for
integrity and clear-headedness. His family lived in commodious apartments over the store, having an entrance on
the side within the *porte cochère.* There was something
which Edna thought very French, very foreign, about their
whole manner of living. In the large and pleasant salon
which extended across the width of the house, the Ratignolles entertained their friends once a fortnight with a *soirée
musicale,* sometimes diversified by card-playing. There was a
friend who played upon the 'cello. One brought his flute
and another his violin, while there were some who sang and
a number who performed upon the piano with various degrees of taste and agility. The Ratignolles' *soirées musicales*
were widely known, and it was considered a privilege to be
invited to them.

Edna found her friend engaged in assorting the clothes
which had returned that morning from the laundry. She at
once abandoned her occupation upon seeing Edna, who had
been ushered without ceremony into her presence.

" 'Cité can do it as well as I; it is really her business," she explained to Edna, who apologized for interrupting her. And she summoned a young black woman, whom she instructed, in French, to be very careful in checking off the list which she handed her. She told her to notice particularly if a fine linen handkerchief of Monsieur Ratignolle's, which was missing last week, had been returned; and to be sure to set to one side such pieces as required mending and darning.

Then placing an arm around Edna's waist, she led her to the front of the house, to the salon, where it was cool and sweet with the odor of great roses that stood upon the hearth in jars.

Madame Ratignolle looked more beautiful than ever there at home, in a negligé which left her arms almost wholly bare and exposed the rich, melting curves of her white throat.

"Perhaps I shall be able to paint your picture some day," said Edna with a smile when they were seated. She produced the roll of sketches and started to unfold them. "I believe I ought to work again. I feel as if I wanted to be doing something. What do you think of them? Do you think it worth while to take it up again and study some more? I might study for a while with Laidpore."

She knew that Madame Ratignolle's opinion in such a matter would be next to valueless, that she herself had not alone decided, but determined; but she sought the words of praise and encouragement that would help her to put heart into her venture.

"Your talent is immense, dear!"

"Nonsense!" protested Edna, well pleased.

"Immense, I tell you," persisted Madame Ratignolle, surveying the sketches one by one, at close range, then holding them at arm's length, narrowing her eyes, and dropping her head on one side. "Surely, this Bavarian peasant is worthy of framing; and this basket of apples! never have I seen any-thing more lifelike. One might almost be tempted to reach out a hand and take one."

Edna could not control a feeling which bordered upon complacency at her friend's praise, even realizing, as she did, its true worth. She retained a few of the sketches, and gave all the rest to Madame Ratignolle, who appreciated the gift far beyond its value and proudly exhibited the pictures to her husband when he came up from the store a little later for his midday dinner.

Mr. Ratignolle was one of those men who are called the salt of the earth. His cheerfulness was unbounded, and it was matched by his goodness of heart, his broad charity, and common sense. He and his wife spoke English with an accent which was only discernible through its un-English emphasis and a certain carefulness and deliberation. Edna's husband spoke English with no accent whatever. The Ratig-nolles understood each other perfectly. If ever the fusion of two human beings into one has been accomplished on this sphere it was surely in their union.

As Edna seated herself at table with them she thought, "Better a dinner of herbs," though it did not take her long to discover that it was no dinner of herbs, but a delicious repast, simple, choice, and in every way satisfying.

Monsieur Ratignolle was delighted to see her, though he found her looking not so well as at Grand Isle, and he ad-vised a tonic. He talked a good deal on various topics, a lit-tle politics, some city news and neighborhood gossip. He spoke with an animation and earnestness that gave an exag-gerated importance to every syllable he uttered. His wife was keenly interested in everything he said, laying down her fork the better to listen, chiming in, taking the words out of his mouth.

Edna felt depressed rather than soothed after leaving

them. The little glimpse of domestic harmony which had been offered her, gave her no regret, no longing. It was not a condition of life which fitted her, and she could see in it but an appalling and hopeless ennui. She was moved by a kind of commiseration for Madame Ratignolle,—a pity for that colorless existence which never uplifted its possessor beyond the region of blind contentment, in which no moment of anguish ever visited her soul, in which she would never have the taste of life's delirium. Edna vaguely wondered what she meant by "life's delirium." It had crossed her thought like some unsought, extraneous impression.

XIX

✦

$\mathcal{E}$dna could not help but think that it was very foolish, very childish, to have stamped upon her wedding ring and smashed the crystal vase upon the tiles. She was visited by no more outbursts, moving her to such futile expedients. She began to do as she liked and to feel as she liked. She completely abandoned her Tuesdays at home, and did not return the visits of those who had called upon her. She made no ineffectual efforts to conduct her household *en bonne ménagère,* going and coming as it suited her fancy, and, so far as she was able, lending herself to any passing caprice.

Mr. Pontellier had been a rather courteous husband so long as he met a certain tacit submissiveness in his wife. But her new and unexpected line of conduct completely bewildered him. It shocked him. Then her absolute disregard for her duties as a wife angered him. When Mr. Pontellier became rude, Edna grew insolent. She had resolved never to take another step backward.

"It seems to me the utmost folly for a woman at the head of a household, and the mother of children, to spend in an atelier days which would be better employed contriving for the comfort of her family."

"I feel like painting," answered Edna. "Perhaps I shan't always feel like it."

"Then in God's name paint! but don't let the family go to the devil. There's Madame Ratignolle; because she keeps up her music, she doesn't let everything else go to chaos. And she's more of a musician than you are a painter."

"She isn't a musician, and I'm not a painter. It isn't on account of painting that I let things go."

"On account of what, then?"

"Oh! I don't know. Let me alone; you bother me."

It sometimes entered Mr. Pontellier's mind to wonder if his wife were not growing a little unbalanced mentally. He could see plainly that she was not herself. That is, he could not see that she was becoming herself and daily casting aside that fictitious self which we assume like a garment with which to appear before the world.

Her husband let her alone as she requested, and went away to his office. Edna went up to her atelier—a bright room in the top of the house. She was working with great energy and interest, without accomplishing anything, however, which satisfied her even in the smallest degree. For a time she had the whole household enrolled in the service of art. The boys posed for her. They thought it amusing at first, but the occupation soon lost its attractiveness when they discovered that it was not a game arranged especially for their entertainment. The quadroon sat for hours before Edna's palette, patient as a savage, while the house-maid took charge of the children, and the drawing-room went undusted. But the house-maid, too, served her term as model when Edna perceived that the young woman's back and shoulders were molded on classic lines, and that her hair, loosened from its confining cap, became an inspiration. While Edna worked she sometimes sang low the little air, *"Ah! si tu savais!"*

It moved her with recollections. She could hear again the ripple of the water, the flapping sail. She could see the glint of the moon upon the bay, and could feel the soft, gusty beating of the hot south wind. A subtle current of desire passed through her body, weakening her hold upon the brushes and making her eyes burn.

There were days when she was very happy without knowing why. She was happy to be alive and breathing, when her whole being seemed to be one with the sunlight, the color, the odors, the luxuriant warmth of some perfect Southern day. She liked then to wander alone into strange and unfamiliar places. She discovered many a sunny, sleepy corner, fashioned to dream in. And she found it good to dream and to be alone and unmolested.

There were days when she was unhappy, she did not know why—when it did not seem worth while to be glad or sorry, to be alive or dead; when life appeared to her like a grotesque pandemonium and humanity like worms struggling blindly toward inevitable annihilation. She could not work on such a day, nor weave fancies to stir her pulses and warm her blood.

XX

✦

*I*t was during such a mood that Edna hunted up Mademoiselle Reisz. She had not forgotten the rather disagreeable impression left upon her by their last interview; but she nevertheless felt a desire to see her—above all, to listen while she played upon the piano. Quite early in the afternoon she started upon her quest for the pianist. Unfortunately she had mislaid or lost Mademoiselle Reisz's card, and looking up her address in the city directory, she found that the woman lived on Bienville Street, some distance away. The directory which fell into her hands was a year or more old, however, and upon reaching the number indicated, Edna discovered that the house was occupied by a respectable family of mulattoes who had *chambres garnies* to let. They had been living there for six months, and knew absolutely nothing of a Mademoiselle Reisz. In fact, they knew nothing of any of their neighbors; their lodgers were all people of the highest distinction, they assured Edna. She did not linger to discuss class distinctions with Madame Pouponne, but hastened to a neighboring grocery store, feeling sure that Mademoiselle would have left her address with the proprietor.

He knew Mademoiselle Reisz a good deal better than he wanted to know her, he informed his questioner. In truth, he did not want to know her at all, or anything concerning her—the most disagreeable and unpopular woman who ever lived in Bienville Street. He thanked heaven she had left the neighborhood, and was equally thankful that he did not know where she had gone.

Edna's desire to see Mademoiselle Reisz had increased tenfold since these unlooked-for obstacles had arisen to thwart it. She was wondering who could give her the information she sought, when it suddenly occurred to her that Madame Lebrun would be the one most likely to do so. She knew it was useless to ask Madame Ratignolle, who was on the most distant terms with the musician, and preferred to know nothing concerning her. She had once been almost as emphatic in expressing herself upon the subject as the corner grocer.

Edna knew that Madame Lebrun had returned to the city, for it was the middle of November. And she also knew where the Lebruns lived, on Chartres Street.

Their home from the outside looked like a prison, with iron bars before the door and lower windows. The iron bars were a relic of the old *régime,* and no one had ever thought of dislodging them. At the side was a high fence enclosing the garden. A gate or door opening upon the street was locked. Edna rang the bell at this side garden gate, and stood upon the banquette, waiting to be admitted.

It was Victor who opened the gate for her. A black woman, wiping her hands upon her apron, was close at his heels. Before she saw them Edna could hear them in altercation, the woman—plainly an anomaly—claiming the right to be allowed to perform her duties, one of which was to answer the bell.

Victor was surprised and delighted to see Mrs. Pontellier, and he made no attempt to conceal either his astonishment or his delight. He was a dark-browed, good-looking young-ster of nineteen, greatly resembling his mother, but with ten times her impetuosity. He instructed the black woman to go at once and inform Madame Lebrun that Mrs. Pontel-lier desired to see her. The woman grumbled a refusal to do part of her duty when she had not been permitted to do it all, and started back to her interrupted task of weeding the garden. Whereupon Victor administered a rebuke in the form of a volley of abuse, which, owing to its rapidity and incoherence, was all but incomprehensible to Edna. What-ever it was, the rebuke was convincing, for the woman dropped her hoe and went mumbling into the house.

Edna did not wish to enter. It was very pleasant there on the side porch, where there were chairs, a wicker lounge, and a small table. She seated herself, for she was tired from her long tramp; and she began to rock gently and smooth out the folds of her silk parasol. Victor drew up his chair beside her. He at once explained that the black woman's of-fensive conduct was all due to imperfect training, as he was not there to take her in hand. He had only come up from the island the morning before, and expected to return next day. He stayed all winter at the island; he lived there, and kept the place in order and got things ready for the summer visitors.

But a man needed occasional relaxation, he informed Mrs. Pontellier, and every now and again he drummed up a pretext to bring him to the city. My! but he had had a time of it the evening before! He wouldn't want his mother to know, and he began to talk in a whisper. He was scintillant with recollections. Of course, he couldn't think of telling

Mrs. Pontellier all about it, she being a woman and not comprehending such things. But it all began with a girl peeping and smiling at him through the shutters as he passed by. Oh! but she was a beauty! Certainly he smiled back, and went up and talked to her. Mrs. Pontellier did not know him if she supposed he was one to let an opportunity like that escape him. Despite herself, the youngster amused her. She must have betrayed in her look some degree of interest or entertainment. The boy grew more daring, and Mrs. Pontellier might have found herself, in a little while, listening to a highly colored story but for the timely appearance of Madame Lebrun.

That lady was still clad in white, according to her custom of the summer. Her eyes beamed an effusive welcome. Would not Mrs. Pontellier go inside? Would she partake of some refreshment? Why had she not been there before? How was that dear Mr. Pontellier and how were those sweet children? Had Mrs. Pontellier ever known such a warm November?

Victor went and reclined on the wicker lounge behind his mother's chair, where he commanded a view of Edna's face. He had taken her parasol from her hands while he spoke to her, and he now lifted it and twirled it above him as he lay on his back. When Madame Lebrun complained that it was *so* dull coming back to the city; that she saw *so* few people now; that even Victor, when he came up from the island for a day or two, had *so* much to occupy him and engage his time; then it was that the youth went into contortions on the lounge and winked mischievously at Edna. She somehow felt like a confederate in crime, and tried to look severe and disapproving.

There had been but two letters from Robert, with little in them, they told her. Victor said it was really not worth while to go inside for the letters, when his mother entreated him to go in search of them. He remembered the contents, which in truth he rattled off very glibly when put to the test.

One letter was written from Vera Cruz and the other from the City of Mexico. He had met Montel, who was doing everything toward his advancement. So far, the financial situation was no improvement over the one he had left in New Orleans, but of course the prospects were vastly better. He wrote of the City of Mexico, the buildings, the people and their habits, the conditions of life which he found there. He sent his love to the family. He inclosed a check to his mother, and hoped she would affectionately remember him to all his friends. That was about the substance of the two letters. Edna felt that if there had been a message for her, she would have received it. The despondent frame of mind in which she had left home began again to overtake her, and she remembered that she wished to find Mademoiselle Reisz.

Madame Lebrun knew where Mademoiselle Reisz lived. She gave Edna the address, regretting that she would not consent to stay and spend the remainder of the afternoon, and pay a visit to Mademoiselle Reisz some other day. The afternoon was already well advanced.

Victor escorted her out upon the banquette, lifted her parasol, and held it over her while he walked to the car with her. He entreated her to bear in mind that the disclosures of the afternoon were strictly confidential. She laughed and bantered him a little, remembering too late that she should have been dignified and reserved.

"How handsome Mrs. Pontellier looked!" said Madame Lebrun to her son.

"Ravishing!" he admitted. "The city atmosphere has improved her. Some way she doesn't seem like the same woman."

XXI

✦

Some people contended that the reason Mademoiselle Reisz always chose apartments up under the roof was to discourage the approach of beggars, peddlars and callers. There were plenty of windows in her little front room. They were for the most part dingy, but as they were nearly always open it did not make so much difference. They often admitted into the room a good deal of smoke and soot; but at the same time all the light and air that there was came through them. From her windows could be seen the crescent of the river, the masts of ships and the big chimneys of the Mississippi steamers. A magnificent piano crowded the apartment. In the next room she slept, and in the third and last she harbored a gasoline stove on which she cooked her meals when disinclined to descend to the neighboring restaurant. It was there also that she ate, keeping her belongings in a rare old buffet, dingy and battered from a hundred years of use.

When Edna knocked at Mademoiselle Reisz's front room door and entered, she discovered that person standing beside the window, engaged in mending or patching an old prunella gaiter. The little musician laughed all over when she saw Edna. Her laugh consisted of a contortion of the face and all the muscles of the body. She seemed strikingly homely, standing there in the afternoon light. She still wore the shabby lace and the artificial bunch of violets on the side of her head.

"So you remembered me at last," said Mademoiselle. "I had said to myself, 'Ah, bah! she will never come.' "

"Did you want me to come?" asked Edna with a smile.

"I had not thought much about it," answered Mademoiselle. The two had seated themselves on a little bumpy sofa which stood against the wall. "I am glad, however, that you came. I have the water boiling back there, and was just about to make some coffee. You will drink a cup with me. And how is *la belle dame?* Always handsome! always healthy! always contented!" She took Edna's hand between her strong wiry fingers, holding it loosely without warmth, and executing a sort of double theme upon the back and palm.

"Yes," she went on; "I sometimes thought: 'She will never come. She promised as those women in society always do, without meaning it. She will not come.' For I really don't believe you like me, Mrs. Pontellier."

"I don't know whether I like you or not," replied Edna, gazing down at the little woman with a quizzical look.

The candor of Mrs. Pontellier's admission greatly pleased Mademoiselle Reisz. She expressed her gratification by repairing forthwith to the region of the gasoline stove and rewarding her guest with the promised cup of coffee. The coffee and the biscuit accompanying it proved very acceptable to Edna, who had declined refreshment at Madame Lebrun's and was now beginning to feel hungry. Mademoiselle set the tray which she brought in upon a small table near at hand, and seated herself once again on the lumpy sofa.

"I have had a letter from your friend," she remarked, as she poured a little cream into Edna's cup and handed it to her.

"My friend?"

"Yes, your friend Robert. He wrote to me from the City of Mexico."

"Wrote to *you?*" repeated Edna in amazement, stirring her coffee absently.

"Yes, to me. Why not? Don't stir all the warmth out of your coffee; drink it. Though the letter might as well have been sent to you; it was nothing but Mrs. Pontellier from beginning to end."

"Let me see it," requested the young woman, entreatingly.

"No; a letter concerns no one but the person who writes it and the one to whom it is written."

"Haven't you just said it concerned me from beginning to end?"

"It was written about you, not to you. 'Have you seen Mrs. Pontellier? How is she looking?' he asks. 'As Mrs. Pontellier says,' or 'as Mrs. Pontellier once said.' 'If Mrs. Pontellier should call upon you, play for her that Impromptu of Chopin's, my favorite. I heard it here a day or two ago, but not as you play it. I should like to know how it affects her,' and so on, as if he supposed we were constantly in each other's society."

"Let me see the letter."

"Oh, no."

"Have you answered it?"

"No."

"Let me see the letter."

"No, and again, no."

"Then play the Impromptu for me."

"It is growing late; what time do you have to be home?"

"Time doesn't concern me. Your question seems a little rude. Play the Impromptu."

"But you have told me nothing of yourself. What are you doing?"

"Painting!" laughed Edna. "I am becoming an artist. Think of it!"

"Ah! an artist! You have pretensions, Madame."

"Why pretensions? Do you think I could not become an artist?"

"I do not know you well enough to say. I do not know your talent or your temperament. To be an artist includes much; one must possess many gifts—absolute gifts—which have not been acquired by one's own effort. And, moreover, to succeed, the artist must possess the courageous soul."

"What do you mean by the courageous soul?"

"Courageous, *ma foi!* The brave soul. The soul that dares and defies."

"Show me the letter and play for me the Impromptu. You see that I have persistence. Does that quality count for anything in art?"

"It counts with a foolish old woman whom you have captivated," replied Mademoiselle, with her wriggling laugh.

The letter was right there at hand in the drawer of the little table upon which Edna had just placed her coffee cup. Mademoiselle opened the drawer and drew forth the letter, the topmost one. She placed it in Edna's hands, and without further comment arose and went to the piano.

Mademoiselle played a soft interlude. It was an improvisation. She sat low at the instrument, and the lines of her body settled into ungraceful curves and angles that gave it an appearance of deformity. Gradually and imperceptibly the interlude melted into the soft opening minor chords of the Chopin Impromptu.

Edna did not know when the Impromptu began or ended. She sat in the sofa corner reading Robert's letter by the fading light. Mademoiselle had glided from the Chopin into the quivering love-notes of Isolde's song, and back again to the Impromptu with its soulful and poignant longing.

The shadows deepened in the little room. The music grew strange and fantastic—turbulent, insistent, plaintive and soft with entreaty. The shadows grew deeper. The music filled the room. It floated out upon the night, over the housetops, the crescent of the river, losing itself in the silence of the upper air.

Edna was sobbing, just as she had wept one midnight at Grand Isle when strange, new voices awoke in her. She arose in some agitation to take her departure. "May I come again, Mademoiselle?" she asked at the threshold.

"Come whenever you feel like it. Be careful; the stairs and landings are dark; don't stumble."

Mademoiselle reëntered and lit a candle. Robert's letter was on the floor. She stooped and picked it up. It was crumpled and damp with tears. Mademoiselle smoothed the letter out, restored it to the envelope, and replaced it in the table drawer.

XXII

✦

One morning on his way into town Mr. Pontellier stopped at the house of his old friend and family physician, Doctor Mandelet. The Doctor was a semi-retired physician, resting, as the saying is, upon his laurels. He bore a reputation for wisdom rather than skill—leaving the active practice of medicine to his assistants and younger contemporaries—and was much sought for in matters of consultation. A few families, united to him by bonds of friendship, he still attended when they required the services of a physician. The Pontelliers were among these.

Mr. Pontellier found the Doctor reading at the open window of his study. His house stood rather far back from the street, in the center of a delightful garden, so that it was quiet and peaceful at the old gentleman's study window. He was a great reader. He stared up disapprovingly over his eye-glasses as Mr. Pontellier entered, wondering who had the temerity to disturb him at that hour of the morning.

"Ah, Pontellier! Not sick, I hope. Come and have a seat. What news do you bring this morning?" He was quite portly, with a profusion of gray hair, and small blue eyes which age had robbed of much of their brightness but none of their penetration.

"Oh! I'm never sick, Doctor. You know that I come of tough fiber—of that old Creole race of Pontelliers that dry up and finally blow away. I came to consult—no, not precisely to consult—to talk to you about Edna. I don't know what ails her."

"Madame Pontellier not well?" marveled the Doctor. "Why, I saw her—I think it was a week ago—walking along Canal Street, the picture of health, it seemed to me."

"Yes, yes; she seems quite well," said Mr. Pontellier, leaning forward and whirling his stick between his two hands; "but she doesn't act well. She's odd, she's not like herself. I can't make her out, and I thought perhaps you'd help me."

"How does she act?" inquired the doctor.

"Well, it isn't easy to explain," said Mr. Pontellier, throwing himself back in his chair. "She lets the housekeeping go to the dickens."

"Well, well; women are not all alike, my dear Pontellier. We've got to consider—"

"I know that; I told you I couldn't explain. Her whole attitude—toward me and everybody and everything—has changed. You know I have a quick temper, but I don't want to quarrel or be rude to a woman, especially my wife; yet I'm driven to it, and feel like ten thousand devils after I've made a fool of myself. She's making it devilishly uncomfortable for me," he went on nervously. "She's got some sort of notion in her head concerning the eternal rights of women; and—you understand—we meet in the morning at the breakfast table."

The old gentleman lifted his shaggy eyebrows, protruded his thick nether lip, and tapped the arms of his chair with his cushioned fingertips.

"What have you been doing to her, Pontellier?"

"Doing! *Parbleu!*"

"Has she," asked the Doctor, with a smile, "has she been associating of late with a circle of pseudo-intellectual women—super-spiritual superior beings? My wife has been telling me about them."

"That's the trouble," broke in Mr. Pontellier, "she hasn't been associating with any one. She has abandoned her Tuesdays at home, has thrown over all her acquaintances, and goes tramping about by herself, moping in the street-cars, getting in after dark. I tell you she's peculiar. I don't like it; I feel a little worried over it."

This was a new aspect for the Doctor. "Nothing hereditary?" he asked, seriously. "Nothing peculiar about her family antecedents, is there?"

"Oh, no, indeed! She comes of sound old Presbyterian Kentucky stock. The old gentleman, her father, I have heard, used to atone for his weekday sins with his Sunday devotions. I know for a fact, that his race horses literally ran away with the prettiest bit of Kentucky farming land I ever laid eyes upon. Margaret—you know Margaret—she has all the Presbyterianism undiluted. And the youngest is something of a vixen. By the way, she gets married in a couple of weeks from now."

"Send your wife up to the wedding," exclaimed the Doctor, foreseeing a happy solution. "Let her stay among her own people for a while; it will do her good."

"That's what I want her to do. She won't go to the marriage. She says a wedding is one of the most lamentable spectacles on earth. Nice thing for a woman to say to her husband!" exclaimed Mr. Pontellier, fuming anew at the recollection.

"Pontellier," said the Doctor, after a moment's reflection, "let your wife alone for a while. Don't bother her, and don't

let her bother you. Woman, my dear friend, is a very peculiar and delicate organism—a sensitive and highly organized woman, such as I know Mrs. Pontellier to be, is
especially peculiar. It would require an inspired psycholo-
gist to deal successfully with them. And when ordinary
fellows like you and me attempt to cope with their idiosyn-
crasies the result is bungling. Most women are moody and
whimsical. This is some passing whim of your wife, due to
some cause or causes which you and I needn't try to
fathom. But it will pass happily over, especially if you let her
alone. Send her around to see me."

"Oh! I couldn't do that; there'd be no reason for it," objected Mr. Pontellier.

"Then I'll go around and see her," said the Doctor. "I'll
drop in to dinner some evening *en bon ami*."

"Do! by all means," urged Mr. Pontellier. "What evening
will you come? Say Thursday. Will you come Thursday?" he
asked, rising to take his leave.

"Very well; Thursday. My wife may possibly have some
engagement for me Thursday. In case she has, I shall let you
know. Otherwise, you may expect me."

Mr. Pontellier turned before leaving to say:

"I am going to New York on business very soon. I have a
big scheme on hand, and want to be on the field proper to
pull the ropes and handle the ribbons. We'll let you in on
the inside if you say so, Doctor," he laughed.

"No, I thank you, my dear sir," returned the Doctor. "I
leave such ventures to you younger men with the fever of
life still in your blood."

"What I wanted to say," continued Mr. Pontellier, with his
hand on the knob; "I may have to be absent a good while.
Would you advise me to take Edna along?"

"By all means, if she wishes to go. If not, leave her here.
Don't contradict her. The mood will pass, I assure you. It

may take a month, two, three months—possibly longer, but it will pass; have patience."

"Well, good-by, *à jeudi,*" said Mr. Pontellier, as he let himself out.

The Doctor would have liked during the course of conversation to ask, "Is there any man in the case?" but he knew his Creole too well to make such a blunder as that.

He did not resume his book immediately, but sat for a while meditatively looking out into the garden.

XXIII

◆

$\mathcal{E}$dna's father was in the city, and had been with them several days. She was not very warmly or deeply attached to him, but they had certain tastes in common, and when together they were companionable. His coming was in the nature of a welcome disturbance; it seemed to furnish a new direction for her emotions.

He had come to purchase a wedding gift for his daughter, Janet, and an outfit for himself in which he might make a creditable appearance at her marriage. Mr. Pontellier had selected the bridal gift, as every one immediately connected with him always deferred to his taste in such matters. And his suggestions on the question of dress—which too often assumes the nature of a problem—were of inestimable value to his father-in-law. But for the past few days the old gentleman had been upon Edna's hands, and in his society she was becoming acquainted with a new set of sensations. He had been a colonel in the Confederate army, and still maintained, with the title, the military bearing which had always accompanied it. His hair and mustache were white and silky, emphasizing the rugged bronze of his face.

He was tall and thin, and wore his coats padded, which gave a fictitious breadth and depth to his shoulders and chest. Edna and her father looked very distinguished together, and excited a good deal of notice during their perambulations. Upon his arrival she began by introducing him to her atelier and making a sketch of him. He took the whole matter very seriously. If her talent had been ten-fold greater than it was, it would not have surprised him, convinced as he was that he had bequeathed to all of his daughters the germs of a masterful capability, which only depended upon their own efforts to be directed toward successful achievement.

Before her pencil he sat rigid and unflinching, as he had faced the cannon's mouth in days gone by. He resented the intrusion of the children, who gaped with wondering eyes at him, sitting so stiff up there in their mother's bright atelier. When they drew near he motioned them away with an expressive action of the foot, loath to disturb the fixed lines of his countenance, his arms, or his rigid shoulders.

Edna, anxious to entertain him, invited Mademoiselle Reisz to meet him, having promised him a treat in her piano playing; but Mademoiselle declined the invitation. So together they attended a *soirée musicale* at the Ratignolle's. Monsieur and Madame Ratignolle made much of the Colonel, installing him as the guest of honor and engaging him at once to dine with them the following Sunday, or any day which he might select. Madame coquetted with him in the most captivating and naïve manner, with eyes, gestures, and a profusion of compliments, till the Colonel's old head felt thirty years younger on his padded shoulders. Edna marveled, not comprehending. She herself was almost devoid of coquetry.

There were one or two men whom she observed at the *soirée musicale;* but she would never have felt moved to any kittenish display to attract their notice—to any feline or feminine wiles to express herself toward them. Their personality attracted her in an agreeable way. Her fancy selected them, and she was glad when a lull in the music gave them an opportunity to meet her and talk with her. Often on the street the glance of strange eyes had lingered in her memory, and sometimes had disturbed her.

Mr. Pontellier did not attend these *soirées musicales*. He considered them *bourgeois,* and found more diversion at the club. To Madame Ratignolle he said the music dispensed at her *soirées* was too "heavy," too far beyond his untrained comprehension. His excuse flattered her. But she disapproved of Mr. Pontellier's club, and she was frank enough to tell Edna so.

"It's a pity Mr. Pontellier doesn't stay home more in the evenings. I think you would be more—well, if you don't mind my saying it—more united, if he did."

"Oh! dear no!" said Edna, with a blank look in her eyes. "What should I do if he stayed home? We wouldn't have anything to say to each other."

She had not much of anything to say to her father, for that matter; but he did not antagonize her. She discovered that he interested her, though she realized that he might not interest her long; and for the first time in her life she felt as if she were thoroughly acquainted with him. He kept her busy serving him and ministering to his wants. It amused her to do so. She would not permit a servant or one of the children to do anything for him which she might do herself. Her husband noticed, and thought it was the expression of a deep filial attachment which he had never suspected.

The Colonel drank numerous "toddies" during the course of the day, which left him, however, imperturbed. He was an expert at concocting strong drinks. He had even invented some, to which he had given fantastic names, and for whose manufacture he required diverse ingredients that it devolved upon Edna to procure for him.

When Doctor Mandelet dined with the Pontelliers on Thursday he could discern in Mrs. Pontellier no trace of that morbid condition which her husband had reported to him. She was excited and in a manner radiant. She and her father had been to the race course, and their thoughts when they seated themselves at table were still occupied with the events of the afternoon, and their talk was still of the track. The Doctor had not kept pace with turf affairs. He had certain recollections of racing in what he called "the good old times" when the Lecompte stables flourished, and he drew upon this fund of memories so that he might not be left out and seem wholly devoid of the modern spirit. But he failed to impose upon the Colonel, and was even far from impressing him with this trumped-up knowledge of bygone days. Edna had staked her father on his last venture, with the most gratifying results to both of them. Besides, they had met some very charming people, according to the Colonel's impressions. Mrs. Mortimer Merriman and Mrs. James Highcamp, who were there with Alcée Arobin, had joined them and had enlivened the hours in a fashion that warmed him to think of.

Mr. Pontellier himself had no particular leaning toward horse-racing, and was even rather inclined to discourage it as a pastime, especially when he considered the fate of that blue-grass farm in Kentucky. He endeavored, in a general way, to express a particular disapproval, and only succeeded in arousing the ire and opposition of his father-in-law. A pretty dispute followed, in which Edna warmly espoused her father's cause and the Doctor remained neutral.

He observed his hostess attentively from under his shaggy brows, and noted a subtle change which had transformed her from the listless woman he had known into a being who, for the moment, seemed palpitant with the forces of life. Her speech was warm and energetic. There was no repression in her glance or gesture. She reminded him of some beautiful, sleek animal waking up in the sun.

The dinner was excellent. The claret was warm and the champagne was cold, and under their beneficent influence the threatened unpleasantness melted and vanished with the fumes of the wine.

Mr. Pontellier warmed up and grew reminiscent. He told some amusing plantation experiences, recollections of old Iberville and his youth, when he hunted 'possum in company with some friendly darky; thrashed the pecan trees, shot the grosbec, and roamed the woods and fields in mischievous idleness.

The Colonel, with little sense of humor and of the fitness of things, related a somber episode of those dark and bitter days, in which he had acted a conspicuous part and always formed a central figure. Nor was the Doctor happier in his selection, when he told the old, ever new and curious story of the waning of a woman's love, seeking strange, new channels, only to return to its legitimate source after days of fierce unrest. It was one of the many little human documents which had been unfolded to him during his long career as a physician. The story did not seem especially to impress Edna. She had one of her own to tell, of a woman who paddled away with her lover one night in a pirogue and never came back. They were lost amid the Baratarian Islands, and no one ever heard of them or found trace of them from that day to this. It was a pure invention. She said that Madame Antoine had related it to her. That, also, was an invention. Perhaps it was a dream she had had. But every glowing word seemed real to those who listened. They could feel the hot breath of the Southern night; they could hear the long sweep of the pirogue through the glistening moonlit water, the beating of birds' wings, rising startled from among the reeds in the salt-water pools; they could see the faces of the lovers, pale, close together, rapt in oblivious forgetfulness, drifting into the unknown.

The champagne was cold, and its subtle fumes played fantastic tricks with Edna's memory that night.

Outside, away from the glow of the fire and the soft lamplight, the night was chill and murky. The Doctor doubled his old-fashioned cloak across his breast as he strode home through the darkness. He knew his fellow-creatures better than most men; knew that inner life which so seldom unfolds itself to unanointed eyes. He was sorry he had accepted Pontellier's invitation. He was growing old, and beginning to need rest and an imperturbed spirit. He did not want the secrets of other lives thrust upon him.

"I hope it isn't Arobin," he muttered to himself as he walked. "I hope to heaven it isn't Alcée Arobin."

XXIV

✦

*E*dna and her father had a warm, and almost violent dispute upon the subject of her refusal to attend her sister's wedding. Mr. Pontellier declined to interfere, to interpose either his influence or his authority. He was following Doctor Mandelet's advice, and letting her do as she liked. The Colonel reproached his daughter for her lack of filial kindness and respect, her want of sisterly affection and womanly consideration. His arguments were labored and unconvincing. He doubted if Janet would accept any excuse—forgetting that Edna had offered none. He doubted if Janet would ever speak to her again, and he was sure Margaret would not.

Edna was glad to be rid of her father when he finally took himself off with his wedding garments and his bridal gifts, with his padded shoulders, his Bible reading, his "toddies" and ponderous oaths.

Mr. Pontellier followed him closely. He meant to stop at the wedding on his way to New York and endeavor by every means which money and love could devise to atone somewhat for Edna's incomprehensible action.

"You are too lenient, too lenient by far, Léonce," asserted the Colonel. "Authority, coercion are what is needed. Put your foot down good and hard; the only way to manage a wife. Take my word for it."

The Colonel was perhaps unaware that he had coerced his own wife into her grave. Mr. Pontellier had a vague suspicion of it which he thought it needless to mention at that late day.

Edna was not so consciously gratified at her husband's leaving home as she had been over the departure of her father. As the day approached when he was to leave her for a comparatively long stay, she grew melting and affectionate, remembering his many acts of consideration and his repeated expressions of an ardent attachment. She was solicitous about his health and his welfare. She bustled around, looking after his clothing, thinking about heavy underwear, quite as Madame Ratignolle would have done under similar circumstances. She cried when he went away, calling him her dear, good friend, and she was quite certain she would grow lonely before very long and go to join him in New York.

But after all, a radiant peace settled upon her when she at last found herself alone. Even the children were gone. Old Madame Pontellier had come herself and carried them off to Iberville with their quadroon. The old madame did not venture to say she was afraid they would be neglected during Léonce's absence; she hardly ventured to think so. She was hungry for them—even a little fierce in her attachment. She did not want them to be wholly "children of the pavement," she always said when begging to have them for a space. She wished them to know the country, with its streams, its fields, its woods, its freedom, so delicious to the young. She wished them to taste something of the life their father had lived and known and loved when he, too, was a little child.

When Edna was at last alone, she breathed a big, genuine sigh of relief. A feeling that was unfamiliar but very delicious came over her. She walked all through the house, from one room to another, as if inspecting it for the first time. She tried the various chairs and lounges, as if she had never sat and reclined upon them before. And she perambulated around the outside of the house, investigating, looking to see if windows and shutters were secure and in order. The flowers were like new acquaintances; she approached them in a familiar spirit, and made herself at home among them. The garden walks were damp, and Edna called to the maid to bring out her rubber sandals. And there she stayed, and stooped, digging around the plants, trimming, picking dead, dry leaves. The children's little dog came out, interfering, getting in her way. She scolded him, laughed at him, played with him. The garden smelled so good and looked so pretty in the afternoon sunlight. Edna plucked all the bright flowers she could find, and went into the house with them, she and the little dog.

Even the kitchen assumed a sudden interesting character which she had never before perceived. She went in to give directions to the cook, to say that the butcher would have to bring much less meat, that they would require only half their usual quantity of bread, of milk and groceries. She told the cook that she herself would be greatly occupied during Mr. Pontellier's absence, and she begged her to take all thought and responsibility of the larder upon her own shoulders.

That night Edna dined alone. The candelabra, with a few candles in the center of the table, gave all the light she needed. Outside the circle of light in which she sat, the large dining-room looked solemn and shadowy. The cook, placed upon her mettle, served a delicious repast—a luscious tenderloin broiled *à point*. The wine tasted good; the *marron glacé* seemed to be just what she wanted. It was so pleasant, too, to dine in a comfortable *peignoir.*

She thought a little sentimentally about Léonce and the children, and wondered what they were doing. As she gave a dainty scrap or two to the doggie, she talked intimately to him about Etienne and Raoul. He was beside himself with astonishment and delight over these companionable advances, and showed his appreciation by his little quick, snappy barks and a lively agitation.

Then Edna sat in the library after dinner and read Emerson until she grew sleepy. She realized that she had neglected her reading, and determined to start anew upon a course of improving studies, now that her time was completely her own to do with as she liked.

After a refreshing bath, Edna went to bed. And as she snuggled comfortably beneath the eiderdown a sense of restfulness invaded her, such as she had not known before.

XXV

✦

When the weather was dark and cloudy Edna could not work. She needed the sun to mellow and temper her mood to the sticking point. She had reached a stage when she seemed to be no longer feeling her way, working, when in the humor, with sureness and ease. And being devoid of ambition, and striving not toward accomplishment, she drew satisfaction from the work in itself.

On rainy or melancholy days Edna went out and sought the society of the friends she had made at Grand Isle. Or else she stayed indoors and nursed a mood with which she was becoming too familiar for her own comfort and peace of mind. It was not despair; but it seemed to her as if life were passing by, leaving its promise broken and unfulfilled. Yet there were other days when she listened, was led on and deceived by fresh promises which her youth held out to her.

She went again to the races, and again. Alcée Arobin and Mrs. Highcamp called for her one bright afternoon in Arobin's drag. Mrs. Highcamp was a worldly but unaffected, intelligent, slim, tall blonde woman in the forties, with an indifferent manner and blue eyes that stared. She had a daughter who served her as a pretext for cultivating the society of young men of fashion. Alcée Arobin was one of them. He was a familiar figure at the race course, the opera, the fashionable clubs. There was a perpetual smile in his eyes, which seldom failed to awaken a corresponding cheerfulness in any one who looked into them and listened to his good-humored voice. His manner was quiet, and at times a little insolent. He possessed a good figure, a pleasing face, not overburdened with depth of thought or feeling; and his dress was that of the conventional man of fashion.

He admired Edna extravagantly, after meeting her at the races with her father. He had met her before on other occasions, but she had seemed to him unapproachable until that day. It was at his instigation that Mrs. Highcamp called to ask her to go with them to the Jockey Club to witness the turf event of the season.

There were possibly a few track men out there who knew the race horse as well as Edna, but there was certainly none who knew it better. She sat between her two companions as one having authority to speak. She laughed at Arobin's pretensions, and deplored Mrs. Highcamp's ignorance. The race horse was a friend and intimate associate of her childhood. The atmosphere of the stables and the breath of the blue grass paddock revived in her memory and lingered in her nostrils. She did not perceive that she was talking like her father as the sleek geldings ambled in review before them. She played for very high stakes, and fortune favored her. The fever of the game flamed in her cheeks and eyes, and it got into her blood and into her brain like an intoxicant. People turned their heads to look at her, and more than one lent an attentive ear to her utterances, hoping thereby to secure the elusive but ever-desired "tip." Arobin caught the contagion of excitement which drew him to

Edna like a magnet. Mrs. Highcamp remained, as usual, un-
moved, with her indifferent stare and uplifted eyebrows.

Edna stayed and dined with Mrs. Highcamp upon being
urged to do so. Arobin also remained and sent away his
drag.

The dinner was quiet and uninteresting, save for the
cheerful efforts of Arobin to enliven things. Mrs. Highcamp
deplored the absence of her daughter from the races, and
tried to convey to her what she had missed by going to the
"Dante reading" instead of joining them. The girl held a
geranium leaf up to her nose and said nothing, but looked
knowing and noncommittal. Mr. Highcamp was a plain,
bald-headed man, who only talked under compulsion. He
was unresponsive. Mrs. Highcamp was full of delicate courtesy and consideration toward her husband. She addressed
most of her conversation to him at table. They sat in the library after dinner and read the evening papers together under the droplight; while the younger people went into the
drawing-room near by and talked. Miss Highcamp played
some selections from Grieg upon the piano. She seemed to
have apprehended all of the composer's coldness and none
of his poetry. While Edna listened she could not help wondering if she had lost her taste for music.

When the time came for her to go home, Mr. Highcamp
grunted a lame offer to escort her, looking down at his slippered feet with tactless concern. It was Arobin who took
her home. The car ride was long, and it was late when they
reached Esplanade Street. Arobin asked permission to enter for a second to light his cigarette—his match safe was
empty. He filled his match safe, but did not light his cigarette until he left her, after she had expressed her willingness to go to the races with him again.

Edna was neither tired nor sleepy. She was hungry again,
for the Highcamp dinner, though of excellent quality, had

lacked abundance. She rummaged in the larder and brought forth a slice of Gruyère and some crackers. She opened a bottle of beer which she found in the ice-box. Edna felt extremely restless and excited. She vacantly hummed a fantastic tune as she poked at the wood embers on the hearth and munched a cracker.

She wanted something to happen—something, anything; she did not know what. She regretted that she had not made Arobin stay a half hour to talk over the horses with her. She counted the money she had won. But there was nothing else to do, so she went to bed, and tossed there for hours in a sort of monotonous agitation.

In the middle of the night she remembered that she had forgotten to write her regular letter to her husband; and she decided to do so next day and tell him about her afternoon at the Jockey Club. She lay wide awake composing a letter which was nothing like the one which she wrote next day. When the maid awoke her in the morning Edna was dreaming of Mr. Highcamp playing the piano at the entrance of a music store on Canal Street, while his wife was saying to Alcée Arobin, as they boarded an Esplanade Street car:

"What a pity that so much talent has been neglected! but I must go."

When, a few days later, Alcée Arobin again called for Edna in his drag, Mrs. Highcamp was not with him. He said they would pick her up. But as that lady had not been apprised of his intention of picking her up, she was not at home. The daughter was just leaving the house to attend the meeting of a branch Folk Lore Society, and regretted that she could not accompany them. Arobin appeared nonplused, and asked Edna if there were any one else she cared to ask.

She did not deem it worth while to go in search of any of

the fashionable acquaintances from whom she had withdrawn herself. She thought of Madame Ratignolle, but knew that her fair friend did not leave the house, except to take a languid walk around the block with her husband after nightfall. Mademoiselle Reisz would have laughed at such a request from Edna. Madame Lebrun might have enjoyed the outing, but for some reason Edna did not want her. So they went alone, she and Arobin.

The afternoon was intensely interesting to her. The excitement came back upon her like a remittent fever. Her talk grew familiar and confidential. It was no labor to become intimate with Arobin. His manner invited easy confidence. The preliminary stage of becoming acquainted was one which he always endeavored to ignore when a pretty and engaging woman was concerned.

He stayed and dined with Edna. He stayed and sat beside the wood fire. They laughed and talked; and before it was time to go he was telling her how different life might have been if he had known her years before. With ingenuous frankness he spoke of what a wicked, ill-disciplined boy he had been, and impulsively drew up his cuff to exhibit upon his wrist the scar from a saber cut which he had received in a duel outside of Paris when he was nineteen. She touched his hand as she scanned the red cicatrice on the inside of his white wrist. A quick impulse that was somewhat spasmodic impelled her fingers to close in a sort of clutch upon his hand. He felt the pressure of her pointed nails in the flesh of his palm.

She arose hastily and walked toward the mantel.

"The sight of a wound or scar always agitates and sickens me," she said. "I shouldn't have looked at it."

"I beg your pardon," he entreated, following her; "it never occurred to me that it might be repulsive."

He stood close to her, and the effrontery in his eyes re-

pelled the old, vanishing self in her, yet drew all her awakening sensuousness. He saw enough in her face to impel
him to take her hand and hold it while he said his lingering
good night.

"Will you go to the races again?" he asked.

"No," she said. "I've had enough of the races. I don't want
to lose all the money I've won, and I've got to work when
the weather is bright, instead of—"

"Yes; work; to be sure. You promised to show me your
work. What morning may I come up to your atelier? To-
morrow?"

"No!"

"Day after?"

"No, no."

"Oh, please don't refuse me! I know something of such
things. I might help you with a stray suggestion or two."

"No. Good night. Why don't you go after you have said
good night? I don't like you," she went on in a high, excited
pitch, attempting to draw away her hand. She felt that her
words lacked dignity and sincerity, and she knew that he
felt it.

"I'm sorry you don't like me. I'm sorry I offended you.
How have I offended you? What have I done? Can't you forgive me?" And he bent and pressed his lips upon her hand as
if he wished never more to withdraw them.

"Mr. Arobin," she complained, "I'm greatly upset by the
excitement of the afternoon; I'm not myself. My manner
must have misled you in some way. I wish you to go,
please." She spoke in a monotonous, dull tone. He took his
hat from the table, and stood with eyes turned from her,
looking into the dying fire. For a moment or two he kept an
impressive silence.

"Your manner has not misled me, Mrs. Pontellier," he said
finally. "My own emotions have done that. I couldn't help it.

When I'm near you, how could I help it? Don't think any-thing of it, don't bother, please. You see, I go when you command me. If you wish me to stay away, I shall do so. If you let me come back, I—oh! you will let me come back?"

He cast one appealing glance at her, to which she made no response. Alcée Arobin's manner was so genuine that it of-ten deceived even himself.

Edna did not care or think whether it were genuine or not. When she was alone she looked mechanically at the back of her hand which he had kissed so warmly. Then she leaned her head down on the mantelpiece. She felt some-what like a woman who in a moment of passion is betrayed into an act of infidelity, and realizes the significance of the act without being wholly awakened from its glamour. The thought was passing vaguely through her mind, "What would he think?"

She did not mean her husband; she was thinking of Robert Lebrun. Her husband seemed to her now like a per-son whom she had married without love as an excuse.

She lit a candle and went up to her room. Alcée Arobin was absolutely nothing to her. Yet his presence, his man-ners, the warmth of his glances, and above all the touch of his lips upon her hand had acted like a narcotic upon her.

She slept a languorous sleep, interwoven with vanishing dreams.

XXVI

✦

$\mathcal{A}$lcée Arobin wrote Edna an elaborate note of apology, palpitant with sincerity. It embarrassed her; for in a cooler, quieter moment it appeared to her absurd that she should have taken his action so seriously, so dramatically. She felt sure that the significance of the whole occurrence had lain in her own self-consciousness. If she ignored his note it would give undue importance to a trivial affair. If she replied to it in a serious spirit it would still leave in his mind the impression that she had in a susceptible moment yielded to his influence. After all, it was no great matter to have one's hand kissed. She was provoked at his having written the apology. She answered in as light and bantering a spirit as she fancied it deserved, and said she would be glad to have him look in upon her at work whenever he felt the inclination and his business gave him the opportunity.

He responded at once by presenting himself at her home with all his disarming naïveté. And then there was scarcely a day which followed that she did not see him or was not reminded of him. He was prolific in pretexts. His attitude became one of good-humored subservience and tacit adoration. He was ready at all times to submit to her moods, which were as often kind as they were cold. She grew accustomed to him. They became intimate and friendly by imperceptible degrees, and then by leaps. He sometimes talked in a way that astonished her at first and brought the crimson into her face; in a way that pleased her at last, appealing to the animalism that stirred impatiently within her.

There was nothing which so quieted the turmoil of Edna's senses as a visit to Mademoiselle Reisz. It was then, in the presence of that personality which was offensive to her, that the woman, by her divine art, seemed to reach Edna's spirit and set it free.

It was misty, with heavy, lowering atmosphere, one afternoon, when Edna climbed the stairs to the pianist's apartments under the roof. Her clothes were dripping with moisture. She felt chilled and pinched as she entered the room. Mademoiselle was poking at a rusty stove that smoked a little and warmed the room indifferently. She was endeavoring to heat a pot of chocolate on the stove. The room looked cheerless and dingy to Edna as she entered. A bust of Beethoven, covered with a hood of dust, scowled at her from the mantelpiece.

"Ah! here comes the sunlight!" exclaimed Mademoiselle, rising from her knees before the stove. "Now it will be warm and bright enough; I can let the fire alone."

She closed the stove door with a bang, and approaching, assisted in removing Edna's dripping mackintosh.

"You are cold; you look miserable. The chocolate will soon be hot. But would you rather have a taste of brandy? I have scarcely touched the bottle which you brought me for my cold." A piece of red flannel was wrapped around Mademoiselle's throat; a stiff neck compelled her to hold her head on one side.

"I will take some brandy," said Edna, shivering as she removed her gloves and overshoes. She drank the liquor from the glass as a man would have done. Then flinging herself upon the uncomfortable sofa she said, "Mademoiselle, I am going to move away from my house on Esplanade Street."

"Ah!" ejaculated the musician, neither surprised nor especially interested. Nothing ever seemed to astonish her very much. She was endeavoring to adjust the bunch of violets which had become loose from its fastening in her hair. Edna drew her down upon the sofa, and taking a pin from her own hair, secured the shabby artificial flowers in their accustomed place.

"Aren't you astonished?"

"Passably. Where are you going? to New York? to Iberville? to your father in Mississippi? where?"

"Just two steps away," laughed Edna, "in a little four-room house around the corner. It looks so cozy, so inviting and restful, whenever I pass by; and it's for rent. I'm tired looking after that big house. It never seemed like mine, anyway—like home. It's too much trouble. I have to keep too many servants. I am tired bothering with them."

"That is not your true reason, *ma belle*. There is no use in telling me lies. I don't know your reason, but you have not told me the truth." Edna did not protest or endeavor to justify herself.

"The house, the money that provides for it, are not mine. Isn't that enough reason?"

"They are your husband's," returned Mademoiselle, with a shrug and a malicious elevation of the eyebrows.

"Oh! I see there is no deceiving you. Then let me tell you: It is a caprice. I have a little money of my own from my mother's estate, which my father sends me by driblets. I won a large sum this winter on the races, and I am beginning to sell my sketches. Laidpore is more and more pleased with my work; he says it grows in force and individuality. I cannot judge of that myself, but I feel that I have gained in ease and confidence. However, as I said, I have sold a good many through Laidpore. I can live in the tiny house for little or nothing, with one servant. Old Celestine, who works occasionally for me, says she will come stay with me and do my work. I know I shall like it, like the feeling of freedom and independence."

"What does your husband say?"

"I have not told him yet. I only thought of it this morning. He will think I am demented, no doubt. Perhaps you think so."

Mademoiselle shook her head slowly. "Your reason is not yet clear to me," she said.

Neither was it quite clear to Edna herself; but it unfolded itself as she sat for a while in silence. Instinct had prompted her to put away her husband's bounty in casting off her allegiance. She did not know how it would be when he returned. There would have to be an understanding, an explanation. Conditions would some way adjust themselves, she felt; but whatever came, she had resolved never again to belong to another than herself.

"I shall give a grand dinner before I leave the old house!" Edna exclaimed. "You will have to come to it, Mademoiselle. I will give you everything that you like to eat and to drink. We shall sing and laugh and be merry for once." And she uttered a sigh that came from the very depths of her being.

If Mademoiselle happened to have received a letter from Robert during the interval of Edna's visits, she would give her the letter unsolicited. And she would seat herself at the piano and play as her humor prompted her while the young woman read the letter.

The little stove was roaring; it was red-hot, and the chocolate in the tin sizzled and sputtered. Edna went forward and opened the stove door, and Mademoiselle rising, took a letter from under the bust of Beethoven and handed it to Edna.

"Another! so soon!" she exclaimed, her eyes filled with delight. "Tell me, Mademoiselle, does he know that I see his letters?"

"Never in the world! He would be angry and would never write to me again if he thought so. Does he write to you? Never a line. Does he send you a message? Never a word. It is because he loves you, poor fool, and is trying to forget you, since you are not free to listen to him or to belong to him."

"Why do you show me his letters, then?"

"Haven't you begged for them? Can I refuse you anything? Oh! you cannot deceive me," and Mademoiselle approached her beloved instrument and began to play. Edna did not at once read the letter. She sat holding it in her hand, while the music penetrated her whole being like an effulgence, warming and brightening the dark places of her soul. It prepared her for joy and exultation.

"Oh!" she exclaimed, letting the letter fall to the floor. "Why did you not tell me?" She went and grasped Mademoiselle's hands up from the keys. "Oh! unkind! malicious! Why did you not tell me?"

"That he was coming back? No great news, *ma foi*. I wonder he did not come long ago."

"But when, when?" cried Edna, impatiently. "He does not say when."

"He says 'very soon.' You know as much about it as I do; it is all in the letter."

"But why? Why is he coming? Oh, if I thought——" and she snatched the letter from the floor and turned the pages this way and that way, looking for the reason, which was left untold.

"If I were young and in love with a man," said Mademoiselle, turning on the stool and pressing her wiry hands between her knees as she looked down at Edna, who sat on the floor holding the letter, "it seems to me he would have to be some *grand esprit;* a man with lofty aims and ability to reach them; one who stood high enough to attract the notice of his fellow-men. It seems to me if I were young and in love I should never deem a man of ordinary caliber worthy of my devotion."

"Now it is you who are telling lies and seeking to deceive me, Mademoiselle; or else you have never been in love, and know nothing about it. Why," went on Edna, clasping her knees and looking up into Mademoiselle's twisted face, "do you suppose a woman knows why she loves? Does she select? Does she say to herself: 'Go to! Here is a distinguished statesman with presidential possibilities; I shall proceed to fall in love with him.' Or, 'I shall set my heart upon this musician, whose fame is on every tongue?' Or, 'This financier, who controls the world's money markets?' "

"You are purposely misunderstanding me, *ma reine.* Are you in love with Robert?"

"Yes," said Edna. It was the first time she had admitted it, and a glow overspread her face, blotching it with red spots.

"Why?" asked her companion. "Why do you love him when you ought not to?"

Edna, with a motion or two, dragged herself on her knees before Mademoiselle Reisz, who took the glowing face between her two hands.

"Why? Because his hair is brown and grows away from his temples; because he opens and shuts his eyes, and his nose is a little out of drawing; because he has two lips and a square chin, and a little finger which he can't straighten from having played baseball too energetically in his youth. Because—"

"Because you do, in short," laughed Mademoiselle. "What will you do when he comes back?" she asked.

"Do? Nothing, except feel glad and happy to be alive."

She was already glad and happy to be alive at the mere thought of his return. The murky, lowering sky, which had depressed her a few hours before, seemed bracing and invigorating as she splashed through the streets on her way home.

She stopped at a confectioner's and ordered a huge box of bonbons for the children in Iberville. She slipped a card in the box, on which she scribbled a tender message and sent an abundance of kisses.

Before dinner in the evening Edna wrote a charming letter to her husband, telling him of her intention to move for a while into the little house around the block, and to give a farewell dinner before leaving, regretting that he was not there to share it, to help her out with the menu and assist her in entertaining the guests. Her letter was brilliant and brimming with cheerfulness.

XXVII

◆

"What is the matter with you?" asked Arobin that evening. "I never found you in such a happy mood." Edna was tired by that time, and was reclining on the lounge before the fire.

"Don't you know the weather prophet has told us we shall see the sun pretty soon?"

"Well, that ought to be reason enough," he acquiesced. "You wouldn't give me another if I sat here all night imploring you." He sat close to her on a low tabouret, and as he spoke his fingers lightly touched the hair that fell a little over her forehead. She liked the touch of his fingers through her hair, and closed her eyes sensitively.

"One of these days," she said, "I'm going to pull myself together for a while and think—try to determine what character of a woman I am; for, candidly, I don't know. By all the codes which I am acquainted with, I am a devilishly wicked specimen of the sex. But some way I can't convince myself that I am. I must think about it."

"Don't. What's the use? Why should you bother thinking about it when I can tell you what manner of woman you are." His fingers strayed occasionally down to her warm, smooth cheeks and firm chin, which was growing a little full and double.

"Oh, yes! You will tell me that I am adorable; everything that is captivating. Spare yourself the effort."

"No; I shan't tell you anything of the sort, though I shouldn't be lying if I did."

"Do you know Mademoiselle Reisz?" she asked irrelevantly.

"The pianist? I know her by sight. I've heard her play."

"She says queer things sometimes in a bantering way that you don't notice at the time and you find yourself thinking about afterward."

"For instance?"

"Well, for instance, when I left her today, she put her arms around me and felt my shoulder blades, to see if my wings were strong, she said. 'The bird that would soar above the level plain of tradition and prejudice must have strong wings. It is a sad spectacle to see the weaklings bruised, exhausted, fluttering back to earth.' "

"Whither would you soar?"

"I'm not thinking of any extraordinary flights. I only half comprehend her."

"I've heard she's partially demented," said Arobin.

"She seems to me wonderfully sane," Edna replied.

"I'm told she's extremely disagreeable and unpleasant. Why have you introduced her at a moment when I desired to talk of you?"

"Oh! talk of me if you like," cried Edna, clasping her hands beneath her head; "but let me think of something else while you do."

"I'm jealous of your thoughts to-night. They're making you a little kinder than usual; but some way I feel as if they were wandering, as if they were not here with me." She only looked at him and smiled. His eyes were very near. He leaned upon the lounge with an arm extended across her, while the other hand still rested upon her hair. They continued silently to look into each other's eyes. When he leaned forward and kissed her, she clasped his head, holding his lips to hers.

It was the first kiss of her life to which her nature had really responded. It was a flaming torch that kindled desire.

XXVIII

✦

*E*dna cried a little that night after Arobin left her. It was only one phase of the multitudinous emotions which had assailed her. There was with her an overwhelming feeling of irresponsibility. There was the shock of the unexpected and the unaccustomed. There was her husband's reproach looking at her from the external things around her which he had provided for her external existence. There was Robert's reproach making itself felt by a quicker, fiercer, more overpowering love, which had awakened within her toward him. Above all, there was understanding. She felt as if a mist had been lifted from her eyes, enabling her to look upon and comprehend the significance of life, that monster made up of beauty and brutality. But among the conflicting sensations which assailed her, there was neither shame nor remorse. There was a dull pang of regret because it was not the kiss of love which had inflamed her, because it was not love which had held this cup of life to her lips.

XXIX

✦

Without even waiting for an answer from her husband regarding his opinion or wishes in the matter, Edna hastened her preparations for quitting her home on Esplanade Street and moving into the little house around the block. A feverish anxiety attended her every action in that direction. There was no moment of deliberation, no interval of repose between the thought and its fulfillment. Early upon the morning following those hours passed in Arobin's society, Edna set about securing her new abode and hurrying her arrangements for occupying it. Within the precincts of her home she felt like one who has entered and lingered within the portals of some forbidden temple in which a thousand muffled voices bade her begone.

Whatever was her own in the house, everything which she had acquired aside from her husband's bounty, she caused to be transported to the other house, supplying simple and meager deficiencies from her own resources.

Arobin found her with rolled sleeves, working in company with the house-maid when he looked in during the afternoon. She was splendid and robust, and had never appeared handsomer than in the old blue gown, with a red silk handkerchief knotted at random around her head to protect her hair from the dust. She was mounted upon a high stepladder, unhooking a picture from the wall when he entered. He had found the front door open, and had followed his ring by walking in unceremoniously.

"Come down!" he said. "Do you want to kill yourself?" She greeted him with affected carelessness, and appeared absorbed in her occupation.

If he had expected to find her languishing, reproachful, or indulging in sentimental tears, he must have been greatly surprised.

He was no doubt prepared for any emergency, ready for any one of the foregoing attitudes, just as he bent himself easily and naturally to the situation which confronted him.

"Please come down," he insisted, holding the ladder and looking up at her.

"No," she answered; "Ellen is afraid to mount the ladder. Joe is working over at the 'pigeon house'—that's the name Ellen gives it, because it's so small and looks like a pigeon house—and some one has to do this."

Arobin pulled off his coat, and expressed himself ready and willing to tempt fate in her place. Ellen brought him one of her dust-caps, and went into contortions of mirth, which she found it impossible to control, when she saw him put it on before the mirror as grotesquely as he could. Edna herself could not refrain from smiling when she fastened it at his request. So it was he who in turn mounted the ladder, unhooking pictures and curtains, and dislodging ornaments as Edna directed. When he had finished he took off his dust-cap and went out to wash his hands.

Edna was sitting on the tabouret, idly brushing the tips of a feather duster along the carpet when he came in again.

"Is there anything more you will let me do?" he asked.

"That is all," she answered. "Ellen can manage the rest." She kept the young woman occupied in the drawing-room, unwilling to be left alone with Arobin.

"What about the dinner?" he asked; "the grand event, the *coup d'état?*"

"It will be day after to-morrow. Why do you call it the '*coup d'état?*' Oh! it will be very fine; all my best of everything—crystal, silver and gold, Sèvres, flowers, music, and champagne to swim in. I'll let Léonce pay the bills. I wonder what he'll say when he sees the bills."

"And you ask me why I call it a *coup d'état?*" Arobin had put on his coat, and he stood before her and asked if his cravat was plumb. She told him it was, looking no higher than the tip of his collar.

"When do you go to the 'pigeon house?'—with all due acknowledgment to Ellen."

"Day after to-morrow, after the dinner. I shall sleep there."

"Ellen, will you very kindly get me a glass of water?" asked Arobin. "The dust in the curtains, if you will pardon me for hinting such a thing, has parched my throat to a crisp."

"While Ellen gets the water," said Edna, rising, "I will say good-by and let you go. I must get rid of this grime, and I have a million things to do and think of."

"When shall I see you?" asked Arobin, seeking to detain her, the maid having left the room.

"At the dinner, of course. You are invited."

"Not before?—not to-night or to-morrow morning or to-morrow noon or night? or the day after morning or noon? Can't you see yourself, without my telling you, what an eternity it is?"

He had followed her into the hall and to the foot of the

stairway, looking up at her as she mounted with her face half turned to him.

"Not an instant sooner," she said. But she laughed and looked at him with eyes that at once gave him courage to wait and made it torture to wait.

XXX

✦

*T*hough Edna had spoken of the dinner as a very grand affair, it was in truth a very small affair and very select, in so much as the guests invited were few and were selected with discrimination. She had counted upon an even dozen seating themselves at her round mahogany board, forgetting for the moment that Madame Ratignolle was to the last degree *souffrante* and unpresentable, and not foreseeing that Madame Lebrun would send a thousand regrets at the last moment. So there were only ten, after all, which made a cozy, comfortable number.

There were Mr. and Mrs. Merriman, a pretty, vivacious little woman in the thirties; her husband, a jovial fellow, something of a shallow-pate, who laughed a good deal at other people's witticisms, and had thereby made himself extremely popular. Mrs. Highcamp had accompanied them. Of course, there was Alcée Arobin; and Mademoiselle Reisz had consented to come. Edna had sent her a fresh bunch of violets with black lace trimmings for her hair. Monsieur Ratignolle brought himself and his wife's excuses. Victor Lebrun, who happened to be in the city, bent upon relaxation, had accepted with alacrity. There was a Miss Mayblunt, no longer in her teens, who looked at the world through lorgnettes and with the keenest interest. It was thought and said that she was intellectual; it was suspected of her that she wrote under a *nom de guerre*. She had come with a gentleman by the name of Gouvernail, connected with one of the daily papers, of whom nothing special could be said, except that he was observant and seemed quiet and inoffensive. Edna herself made the tenth, and at half-past eight they seated themselves at table, Arobin and Monsieur Ratignolle on either side of their hostess.

Mrs. Highcamp sat between Arobin and Victor Lebrun. Then came Mrs. Merriman, Mr. Gouvernail, Miss Mayblunt, Mr. Merriman, and Mademoiselle Reisz next to Monsieur Ratignolle.

There was something extremely gorgeous about the appearance of the table, an effect of splendor conveyed by a cover of pale yellow satin under strips of lace-work. There were wax candles in massive brass candelabra, burning softly under yellow silk shades; full, fragrant roses, yellow and red, abounded. There were silver and gold, as she had said there would be, and crystal which glittered like the gems which the women wore.

The ordinary stiff dining chairs had been discarded for the occasion and replaced by the most commodious and luxurious which could be collected throughout the house. Mademoiselle Reisz, being exceedingly diminutive, was elevated upon cushions, as small children are sometimes hoisted at table upon bulky volumes.

"Something new, Edna?" exclaimed Miss Mayblunt, with lorgnette directed toward a magnificent cluster of diamonds that sparkled, that almost sputtered, in Edna's hair, just over the center of her forehead.

"Quite new; 'brand' new, in fact; a present from my hus-

*There was something in her attitude, in her whole appearance . . .
which suggested the regal woman, the one who rules, who looks on,
who stands alone (page 149).*

band. It arrived this morning from New York. I may as well admit that this is my birthday, and that I am twenty-nine. In good time I expect you to drink my health. Meanwhile, I shall ask you to begin with this cocktail, composed—would you say 'composed?' " with an appeal to Miss Mayblunt— "composed by my father in honor of Sister Janet's wedding."

Before each guest stood a tiny glass that looked and sparkled like a garnet gem.

"Then, all things considered," spoke Arobin, "it might not be amiss to start out by drinking the Colonel's health in the cocktail which he composed, on the birthday of the most charming of women—the daughter whom he invented."

Mr. Merriman's laugh at this sally was such a genuine outburst and so contagious that it started the dinner with an agreeable swing that never slackened.

Miss Mayblunt begged to be allowed to keep her cocktail untouched before her, just to look at. The color was marvelous! She could compare it to nothing she had ever seen, and the garnet lights which it emitted were unspeakably rare. She pronounced the Colonel an artist, and stuck to it.

Monsieur Ratignolle was prepared to take things seriously: the *mets,* the *entre-mets,* the service, the decorations, even the people. He looked up from his pompono and inquired of Arobin if he were related to the gentleman of that name who formed one of the firm of Laitner and Arobin, lawyers. The young man admitted that Laitner was a warm personal friend, who permitted Arobin's name to decorate the firm's letterheads and to appear upon a shingle that graced Perdido Street.

"There are so many inquisitive people and institutions abounding," said Arobin, "that one is really forced as a matter of convenience these days to assume the virtue of an occupation if he has it not."

Monsieur Ratignolle stared a little, and turned to ask

Mademoiselle Reisz if she considered the symphony concerts up to the standard which had been set the previous winter. Mademoiselle Reisz answered Monsieur Ratignolle in French, which Edna thought a little rude, under the circumstances, but characteristic. Mademoiselle had only disagreeable things to say of the symphony concerts, and insulting remarks to make of all the musicians of New Orleans, singly and collectively. All her interest seemed to be centered upon the delicacies placed before her.

Mr. Merriman said that Mr. Arobin's remark about inquisitive people reminded him of a man from Waco the other day at the St. Charles Hotel—but as Mr. Merriman's stories were always lame and lacking point, his wife seldom permitted him to complete them. She interrupted him to ask if he remembered the name of the author whose book she had bought the week before to send to a friend in Geneva. She was talking "books" with Mr. Gouvernail and trying to draw from him his opinion upon current literary topics. Her husband told the story of the Waco man privately to Miss Mayblunt, who pretended to be greatly amused and to think it extremely clever.

Mrs. Highcamp hung with languid but unaffected interest upon the warm and impetuous volubility of her left-hand neighbor, Victor Lebrun. Her attention was never for a moment withdrawn from him after seating herself at table; and when he turned to Mrs. Merriman, who was prettier and more vivacious than Mrs. Highcamp, she waited with easy indifference for an opportunity to reclaim his attention. There was the occasional sound of music, of mandolins, sufficiently removed to be an agreeable accompaniment rather than an interruption to the conversation. Outside the soft, monotonous splash of a fountain could be heard; the sound penetrated into the room with the heavy odor of jessamine that came through the open windows.

The golden shimmer of Edna's satin gown spread in rich folds on either side of her. There was a soft fall of lace encircling her shoulders. It was the color of her skin, without the glow, the myriad living tints that one may sometimes discover in vibrant flesh. There was something in her attitude, in her whole appearance when she leaned her head against the high-backed chair and spread her arms, which suggested the regal woman, the one who rules, who looks on, who stands alone.

But as she sat there amid her guests, she felt the old ennui overtaking her; the hopelessness which so often assailed her, which came upon her like an obsession, like something extraneous, independent of volition. It was something which announced itself; a chill breath that seemed to issue from some vast cavern wherein discords wailed. There came over her the acute longing which always summoned into her spiritual vision the presence of the beloved one, overpowering her at once with a sense of the unattainable.

The moments glided on, while a feeling of good fellowship passed around the circle like a mystic cord, holding and binding these people together with jest and laughter. Monsieur Ratignolle was the first to break the pleasant charm. At ten o'clock he excused himself. Madame Ratignolle was waiting for him at home. She was *bien souffrante,* and she was filled with vague dread, which only her husband's presence could allay.

Mademoiselle Reisz arose with Monsieur Ratignolle, who offered to escort her to the car. She had eaten well; she had tasted the good, rich wines, and they must have turned her head, for she bowed pleasantly to all as she withdrew from table. She kissed Edna upon the shoulder, and whispered: *"Bonne nuit, ma reine; soyez sage."* She had been a little bewildered upon rising, or rather, descending from her cushions, and Monsieur Ratignolle gallantly took her arm and led her away.

Mrs. Highcamp was weaving a garland of roses, yellow and red. When she had finished the garland, she laid it lightly upon Victor's black curls. He was reclining far back in the luxurious chair, holding a glass of champagne to the light.

As if a magician's wand had touched him, the garland of roses transformed him into a vision of Oriental beauty. His cheeks were the color of crushed grapes, and his dusky eyes glowed with a languishing fire.

"Sapristi!" exclaimed Arobin.

But Mrs. Highcamp had one more touch to add to the picture. She took from the back of her chair a white silken scarf, with which she had covered her shoulders in the early part of the evening. She draped it across the boy in graceful folds, and in a way to conceal his black, conventional evening dress. He did not seem to mind what she did to him, only smiled, showing a faint gleam of white teeth, while he continued to gaze with narrowing eyes at the light through his glass of champagne.

"Oh! to be able to paint in color rather than in words!" exclaimed Miss Mayblunt, losing herself in a rhapsodic dream as she looked at him.

> " 'There was a graven image of Desire
>   Painted with red blood on a ground of gold,' "

murmured Gouvernail, under his breath.

The effect of the wine upon Victor was to change his accustomed volubility into silence. He seemed to have abandoned himself to a reverie, and to be seeing pleasing visions in the amber bead.

"Sing," entreated Mrs. Highcamp. "Won't you sing to us?"

"Let him alone," said Arobin.

"He's posing," offered Mr. Merriman; "let him have it out."

"I believe he's paralyzed," laughed Mrs. Merriman. And leaning over the youth's chair, she took the glass from his hand and held it to his lips. He sipped the wine slowly, and when he had drained the glass she laid it upon the table and wiped his lips with her little filmy handkerchief.

"Yes, I'll sing for you," he said, turning in his chair toward Mrs. Highcamp. He clasped his hands behind his head, and looking up at the ceiling began to hum a little, trying his voice like a musician tuning an instrument. Then, looking at Edna, he began to sing:

"Ah! si tu savais!"

"Stop!" she cried, "don't sing that. I don't want you to sing it," and she laid her glass so impetuously and blindly upon the table as to shatter it against a caraffe. The wine spilled over Arobin's legs and some of it trickled down upon Mrs. Highcamp's black gauze gown. Victor had lost all idea of courtesy, or else he thought his hostess was not in earnest, for he laughed and went on:

"Ah! si tu savais
Ce que tes yeux me disent"—

"Oh! you mustn't! you mustn't," exclaimed Edna, and pushing back her chair she got up, and going behind him placed her hand over his mouth. He kissed the soft palm that pressed upon his lips.

"No, no, I won't, Mrs. Pontellier. I didn't know you meant it," looking up at her with caressing eyes. The touch of his lips was like a pleasing sting to her hand. She lifted the garland of roses from his head and flung it across the room.

"Come, Victor; you've posed long enough. Give Mrs. Highcamp her scarf."

Mrs. Highcamp undraped the scarf from about him with her own hands. Miss Mayblunt and Mr. Gouvernail suddenly conceived the notion that it was time to say good night. And Mr. and Mrs. Merriman wondered how it could be so late.

Before parting from Victor, Mrs. Highcamp invited him to call upon her daughter, who she knew would be charmed to meet him and talk French and sing French songs with him. Victor expressed his desire and intention to call upon Miss Highcamp at the first opportunity which presented itself. He asked if Arobin were going his way. Arobin was not.

The mandolin players had long since stolen away. A profound stillness had fallen upon the broad, beautiful street. The voices of Edna's disbanding guests jarred like a discordant note upon the quiet harmony of the night.

XXXI

✦

"**W**ell?" questioned Arobin, who had remained with Edna after the others had departed.

"Well," she reiterated, and stood up, stretching her arms, and feeling the need to relax her muscles after having been so long seated.

"What next?" he asked.

"The servants are all gone. They left when the musicians did. I have dismissed them. The house has to be closed and locked, and I shall trot around to the pigeon house, and shall send Celestine over in the morning to straighten things up."

He looked around, and began to turn out some of the lights.

"What about upstairs?" he inquired.

"I think it is all right; but there may be a window or two unlatched. We had better look; you might take a candle and see. And bring me my wrap and hat on the foot of the bed in the middle room."

He went up with the light, and Edna began closing doors and windows. She hated to shut in the smoke and the fumes of the wine. Arobin found her cape and hat, which he brought down and helped her to put on.

When everything was secured and the lights put out, they left through the front door, Arobin locking it and taking the key, which he carried for Edna. He helped her down the steps.

"Will you have a spray of jessamine?" he asked, breaking off a few blossoms as he passed.

"No; I don't want anything."

She seemed disheartened, and had nothing to say. She took his arm, which he offered her, holding up the weight of her satin train with the other hand. She looked down, noticing the black line of his leg moving in and out so close to her against the yellow shimmer of her gown. There was the whistle of a railway train somewhere in the distance, and the midnight bells were ringing. They met no one in their short walk.

The "pigeon house" stood behind a locked gate, and a shallow *parterre* that had been somewhat neglected. There was a small front porch, upon which a long window and the front door opened. The door opened directly into the parlor; there was no side entry. Back in the yard was a room for servants, in which old Celestine had been ensconced.

Edna had left a lamp burning low upon the table. She had succeeded in making the room look habitable and home-like. There were some books on the table and a lounge near at hand. On the floor was a fresh matting, covered with a rug or two; and on the walls hung a few tasteful pictures. But the room was filled with flowers. These were a surprise to her. Arobin had sent them, and had had Celestine distribute them during Edna's absence. Her bedroom was adjoining, and across a small passage were the dining-room and kitchen.

Edna seated herself with every appearance of discomfort.

"Are you tired?" he asked.

"Yes, and chilled, and miserable. I feel as if I had been wound up to a certain pitch—too tight—and something inside of me had snapped." She rested her head against the table upon her bare arm.

"You want to rest," he said, "and to be quiet. I'll go; I'll leave you and let you rest."

"Yes," she replied.

He stood up beside her and smoothed her hair with his soft, magnetic hand. His touch conveyed to her a certain physical comfort. She could have fallen quietly asleep there if he had continued to pass his hand over her hair. He brushed the hair upward from the nape of her neck.

"I hope you will feel better and happier in the morning," he said. "You have tried to do too much in the past few days. The dinner was the last straw; you might have dispensed with it."

"Yes," she admitted; "it was stupid."

"No, it was delightful; but it has worn you out." His hand had strayed to her beautiful shoulders, and he could feel the response of her flesh to his touch. He seated himself beside her and kissed her lightly upon the shoulder.

"I thought you were going away," she said, in an uneven voice.

"I am, after I have said good night."

"Good night," she murmured.

He did not answer, except to continue to caress her. He did not say good night until she had become supple to his gentle, seductive entreaties.

XXXII

✦

Whom Mr. Pontellier learned of his wife's intention to abandon her home and take up her residence elsewhere, he immediately wrote her a letter of unqualified disapproval and remonstrance. She had given reasons which he was unwilling to acknowledge as adequate. He hoped she had not acted upon her rash impulse; and he begged her to consider first, foremost, and above all else, what people would say. He was not dreaming of scandal when he uttered this warning; that was a thing which would never have entered into his mind to consider in connection with his wife's name or his own. He was simply thinking of his financial integrity. It might get noised about that the Pontelliers had met with reverses, and were forced to conduct their *ménage* on a humbler scale than heretofore. It might do incalculable mischief to his business prospects.

But remembering Edna's whimsical turn of mind of late, and foreseeing that she had immediately acted upon her impetuous determination, he grasped the situation with his usual promptness and handled it with his well-known business tact and cleverness.

The same mail which brought to Edna his letter of disapproval carried instructions—the most minute instructions—to a well-known architect concerning the remodeling of his home, changes which he had long contemplated, and which he desired carried forward during his temporary absence.

Expert and reliable packers and movers were engaged to convey the furniture, carpets, pictures—everything movable, in short—to places of security. And in an incredibly short time the Pontellier house was turned over to the artisans. There was to be an addition—a small snuggery; there was to be frescoing, and hardwood flooring was to be put into such rooms as had not yet been subjected to this improvement.

Furthermore, in one of the daily papers appeared a brief notice to the effect that Mr. and Mrs. Pontellier were contemplating a summer sojourn abroad, and that their handsome residence on Esplanade Street was undergoing sumptuous alterations, and would not be ready for occupancy until their return. Mr. Pontellier had saved appearances!

Edna admired the skill of his maneuver, and avoided any occasion to balk his intentions. When the situation as set forth by Mr. Pontellier was accepted and taken for granted, she was apparently satisfied that it should be so.

The pigeon house pleased her. It at once assumed the intimate character of a home, while she herself invested it with a charm which it reflected like a warm glow. There was with her a feeling of having descended in the social scale, with a corresponding sense of having risen in the spiritual. Every step which she took toward relieving herself from obligations added to her strength and expansion as an individual. She began to look with her own eyes; to see and to apprehend the deeper undercurrents of life. No longer was she content to "feed upon opinion" when her own soul had invited her.

After a little while, a few days, in fact, Edna went up and spent a week with her children in Iberville. They were delicious February days, with all the summer's promise hovering in the air.

How glad she was to see the children! She wept for very pleasure when she felt their little arms clasping her; their hard, ruddy cheeks pressed against her own glowing cheeks. She looked into their faces with hungry eyes that could not be satisfied with looking. And what stories they had to tell their mother! About the pigs, the cows, the mules! About riding to the mill behind Gluglu; fishing back in the lake with their Uncle Jasper; picking pecans with Lidie's little black brood, and hauling chips in their express wagon. It was a thousand times more fun to haul real chips for old lame Susie's real fire than to drag painted blocks along the banquette on Esplanade Street!

She went with them herself to see the pigs and the cows, to look at the darkies laying the cane, to thrash the pecan trees, and catch fish in the back lake. She lived with them a whole week long, giving them all of herself, and gathering and filling herself with their young existence. They listened, breathless, when she told them the house in Esplanade Street was crowded with workmen, hammering, nailing, sawing, and filling the place with clatter. They wanted to know where their bed was; what had been done with their rocking-horse; and where did Joe sleep, and where had Ellen gone, and the cook? But, above all, they were fired with a desire to see the little house around the block. Was there any place to play? Were there any boys next door? Raoul, with pessimistic foreboding, was convinced that there were only girls next door. Where would they sleep, and where would papa sleep? She told them the fairies would fix it all right.

The old Madame was charmed with Edna's visit, and showered all manner of delicate attentions upon her. She was delighted to know that the Esplanade Street house was in a dismantled condition. It gave her the promise and pretext to keep the children indefinitely.

It was with a wrench and a pang that Edna left her children. She carried away with her the sound of their voices and the touch of their cheeks. All along the journey homeward their presence lingered with her like the memory of a delicious song. But by the time she had regained the city the song no longer echoed in her soul. She was again alone.

XXXIII

✦

*I*t happened sometimes when Edna went to see Mademoiselle Reisz that the little musician was absent, giving a lesson or making some small necessary household purchase. The key was always left in a secret hiding-place in the entry, which Edna knew. If Mademoiselle happened to be away, Edna would usually enter and wait for her return.

When she knocked at Mademoiselle Reisz's door one afternoon there was no response; so unlocking the door, as usual, she entered and found the apartment deserted, as she had expected. Her day had been quite filled up, and it was for a rest, for a refuge, and to talk about Robert, that she sought out her friend.

She had worked at her canvas—a young Italian character study—all the morning, completing the work without the model; but there had been many interruptions, some incident to her modest housekeeping, and others of a social nature.

Madame Ratignolle had dragged herself over, avoiding the too public thoroughfares, she said. She complained that Edna had neglected her much of late. Besides, she was consumed with curiosity to see the little house and the manner in which it was conducted. She wanted to hear all about the dinner party; Monsieur Ratignolle had left *so* early. What had happened after he left? The champagne and grapes which Edna sent over were *too* delicious. She had so little appetite; they had refreshed and toned her stomach. Where on earth was she going to put Mr. Pontellier in that little house, and the boys? And then she made Edna promise to go to her when her hour of trial overtook her.

"At any time—any time of the day or night, dear," Edna assured her.

Before leaving Madame Ratignolle said:

"In some way you seem to me like a child, Edna. You seem to act without a certain amount of reflection which is necessary in this life. That is the reason I want to say you mustn't mind if I advise you to be a little careful while you are living here alone. Why don't you have some one come and stay with you? Wouldn't Mademoiselle Reisz come?"

"No; she wouldn't wish to come, and I shouldn't want her always with me."

"Well, the reason—you know how evil-minded the world is—some one was talking of Alcée Arobin visiting you. Of course, it wouldn't matter if Mr. Arobin had not such a dreadful reputation. Monsieur Ratignolle was telling me that his attentions alone are considered enough to ruin a woman's name."

"Does he boast of his successes?" asked Edna, indifferently, squinting at her picture.

"No, I think not. I believe he is a decent fellow as far as that goes. But his character is so well known among the men. I shan't be able to come back and see you; it was very, very imprudent to-day."

"Mind the step!" cried Edna.

"Don't neglect me," entreated Madame Ratignolle; "and

don't mind what I said about Arobin, or having some one to stay with you."

"Of course not," Edna laughed. "You may say anything you like to me." They kissed each other good-by. Madame Ratignolle had not far to go, and Edna stood on the porch a while watching her walk down the street.

Then in the afternoon Mrs. Merriman and Mrs. Highcamp had made their "party call." Edna felt that they might have dispensed with the formality. They had also come to invite her to play *vingt-et-un* one evening at Mrs. Merriman's. She was asked to go early, to dinner, and Mr. Merriman or Mr. Arobin would take her home. Edna accepted in a half-hearted way. She sometimes felt very tired of Mrs. Highcamp and Mrs. Merriman.

Late in the afternoon she sought refuge with Mademoiselle Reisz, and stayed there alone, waiting for her, feeling a kind of repose invade her with the very atmosphere of the shabby, unpretentious little room.

Edna sat at the window, which looked out over the housetops and across the river. The window frame was filled with pots of flowers, and she sat and picked the dry leaves from a rose geranium. The day was warm, and the breeze which blew from the river was very pleasant. She removed her hat and laid it on the piano. She went on picking the leaves and digging around the plants with her hat pin. Once she thought she heard Mademoiselle Reisz approaching. But it was a young black girl, who came in, bringing a small bundle of laundry, which she deposited in the adjoining room, and went away.

Edna seated herself at the piano, and softly picked out with one hand the bars of a piece of music which lay open before her. A half-hour went by. There was the occasional sound of people going and coming in the lower hall. She was growing interested in her occupation of picking out the aria, when there was a second rap at the door. She vaguely wondered what these people did when they found Mademoiselle's door locked.

"Come in," she called, turning her face toward the door. And this time it was Robert Lebrun who presented himself. She attempted to rise; she could not have done so without betraying the agitation which mastered her at sight of him, so she fell back upon the stool, only exclaiming, "Why, Robert!"

He came and clasped her hand, seemingly without knowing what he was saying or doing.

"Mrs. Pontellier! How do you happen—oh! how well you look! Is Mademoiselle Reisz not here? I never expected to see you."

"When did you come back?" asked Edna in an unsteady voice, wiping her face with her handkerchief. She seemed ill at ease on the piano stool, and he begged her to take the chair by the window. She did so, mechanically, while he seated himself on the stool.

"I returned day before yesterday," he answered, while he leaned his arm on the keys, bringing forth a crash of discordant sound.

"Day before yesterday!" she repeated, aloud; and went on thinking to herself, "day before yesterday," in a sort of an uncomprehending way. She had pictured him seeking her at the very first hour, and he had lived under the same sky since day before yesterday; while only by accident had he stumbled upon her. Mademoiselle must have lied when she said, "Poor fool, he loves you."

"Day before yesterday," she repeated, breaking off a spray of Mademoiselle's geranium; "then if you had not met me here to-day you wouldn't—when—that is, didn't you mean to come and see me?"

"Of course, I should have gone to see you. There have

been so many things—" he turned the leaves of Mademoiselle's music nervously. "I started in at once yesterday with the old firm. After all there is as much chance for me here as there was there—that is, I might find it profitable some day. The Mexicans were not very congenial."

So he had come back because the Mexicans were not congenial; because business was as profitable here as there; because of any reason, and not because he cared to be near her. She remembered the day she sat on the floor, turning the pages of his letter, seeking the reason which was left untold.

She had not noticed how he looked—only feeling his presence; but she turned deliberately and observed him. After all, he had been absent but a few months, and was not changed. His hair—the color of hers—waved back from his temples in the same way as before. His skin was not more burned than it had been at Grand Isle. She found in his eyes, when he looked at her for one silent moment, the same tender caress, with an added warmth and entreaty which had not been there before—the same glance which had penetrated to the sleeping places of her soul and awakened them.

A hundred times Edna had pictured Robert's return, and imagined their first meeting. It was usually at her home, whither he had sought her out at once. She always fancied him expressing or betraying in some way his love for her. And here, the reality was that they sat ten feet apart, she at the window, crushing geranium leaves in her hand and smelling them, he twirling around on the piano stool, saying:

"I was very much surprised to hear of Mr. Pontellier's absence; it's a wonder Mademoiselle Reisz did not tell me; and your moving—mother told me yesterday. I should think you would have gone to New York with him, or to

Iberville with the children, rather than be bothered here with housekeeping. And you are going abroad, too, I hear. We shan't have you at Grand Isle next summer; it won't seem—do you see much of Mademoiselle Reisz? She often spoke of you in the few letters she wrote."

"Do you remember that you promised to write to me when you went away?" A flush overspread his whole face.

"I couldn't believe that my letters would be of any interest to you."

"That is an excuse; it isn't the truth." Edna reached for her hat on the piano. She adjusted it, sticking the hat pin through the heavy coil of hair with some deliberation.

"Are you not going to wait for Mademoiselle Reisz?" asked Robert.

"No; I have found when she is absent this long, she is liable not to come back till late." She drew on her gloves, and Robert picked up his hat.

"Won't you wait for her?" asked Edna.

"Not if you think she will not be back till late," adding, as if suddenly aware of some discourtesy in his speech, "and I should miss the pleasure of walking home with you." Edna locked the door and put the key back in its hiding-place.

They went together, picking their way across muddy streets and sidewalks encumbered with the cheap display of small tradesmen. Part of the distance they rode in the car, and after disembarking, passed the Pontellier mansion, which looked broken and half torn asunder. Robert had never known the house, and looked at it with interest.

"I never knew you in your home," he remarked.

"I am glad you did not."

"Why?" She did not answer. They went on around the corner, and it seemed as if her dreams were coming true after all, when he followed her into the little house.

"You must stay and dine with me, Robert. You see I am all

alone, and it is so long since I have seen you. There is so much I want to ask you."

She took off her hat and gloves. He stood irresolute, making some excuse about his mother who expected him; he even muttered something about an engagement. She struck a match and lit the lamp on the table; it was growing dusk. When he saw her face in the lamp-light, looking pained, with all the soft lines gone out of it, he threw his hat aside and seated himself.

"Oh! you know I want to stay if you will let me!" he exclaimed. All the softness came back. She laughed, and went and put her hand on his shoulder.

"This is the first moment you have seemed like the old Robert. I'll go tell Celestine." She hurried away to tell Celestine to set an extra place. She even sent her off in search of some added delicacy which she had not thought of for herself. And she recommended great care in dripping the coffee and having the omelet done to a proper turn.

When she reëntered, Robert was turning over magazines, sketches, and things that lay upon the table in great disorder. He picked up a photograph, and exclaimed:

"Alcée Arobin! What on earth is his picture doing here?"

"I tried to make a sketch of his head one day," answered Edna, "and he thought the photograph might help me. It was at the other house. I thought it had been left there. I must have packed it up with my drawing materials."

"I should think you would give it back to him if you have finished with it."

"Oh! I have a great many such photographs. I never think of returning them. They don't amount to anything." Robert kept on looking at the picture.

"It seems to me—do you think his head worth drawing? Is he a friend of Mr. Pontellier's? You never said you knew him."

"He isn't a friend of Mr. Pontellier's; he's a friend of mine. I always knew him—that is, it is only of late that I know him pretty well. But I'd rather talk about you, and know what you have been seeing and doing and feeling out there in Mexico." Robert threw aside the picture.

"I've been seeing the waves and the white beach of Grand Isle; the quiet, grassy street of the *Chênière;* the old fort at Grande Terre. I've been working like a machine, and feeling like a lost soul. There was nothing interesting."

She leaned her head upon her hand to shade her eyes from the light.

"And what have you been seeing and doing and feeling all these days?" he asked.

"I've been seeing the waves and the white beach of Grand Isle; the quiet, grassy street of the *Chênière Caminada;* the old sunny fort at Grande Terre. I've been working with a little more comprehension than a machine, and still feeling like a lost soul. There was nothing interesting."

"Mrs. Pontellier, you are cruel," he said, with feeling, closing his eyes and resting his head back in his chair. They remained in silence till old Celestine announced dinner.

XXXIV

✦

$\mathcal{T}$he dining-room was very small. Edna's round mahogany would have almost filled it. As it was there was but
a step or two from the little table to the kitchen, to the
mantel, the small buffet, and the side door that opened out
on the narrow brick-paved yard.

A certain degree of ceremony settled upon them with the
announcement of dinner. There was no return to personal-
ities. Robert related incidents of his sojourn in Mexico, and
Edna talked of events likely to interest him, which had occurred during his absence. The dinner was of ordinary
quality, except for the few delicacies which she had sent out
to purchase. Old Celestine, with a bandana *tignon* twisted
about her head, hobbled in and out, taking a personal interest in everything; and she lingered occasionally to talk
patois with Robert, whom she had known as a boy.

He went out to a neighboring cigar stand to purchase cigarette papers, and when he came back he found that Celestine had served the black coffee in the parlor.

"Perhaps I shouldn't have come back," he said. "When you
are tired of me, tell me to go."

"You never tire me. You must have forgotten the hours and hours at Grand Isle in which we grew accustomed to each other and used to being together."

"I have forgotten nothing at Grand Isle," he said, not looking at her, but rolling a cigarette. His tobacco pouch, which he laid upon the table, was a fantastic embroidered silk affair, evidently the handiwork of a woman.

"You used to carry your tobacco in a rubber pouch," said Edna, picking up the pouch and examining the needlework.

"Yes; it was lost."

"Where did you buy this one? In Mexico?"

"It was given to me by a Vera Cruz girl; they are very generous," he replied, striking a match and lighting his cigarette.

"They are very handsome, I suppose, those Mexican women; very picturesque, with their black eyes and their lace scarfs."

"Some are; others are hideous. Just as you find women everywhere."

"What was she like—the one who gave you the pouch? You must have known her very well."

"She was very ordinary. She wasn't of the slightest importance. I knew her well enough."

"Did you visit at her house? Was it interesting? I should like to know and hear about the people you met, and the impressions they made on you."

"There are some people who leave impressions not so lasting as the imprint of an oar upon the water."

"Was she such a one?"

"It would be ungenerous for me to admit that she was of that order and kind." He thrust the pouch back in his pocket, as if to put away the subject with the trifle which had brought it up.

Arobin dropped in with a message from Mrs. Merriman,

to say that the card party was postponed on account of the illness of one of her children.

"How do you do, Arobin?" said Robert, rising from the obscurity.

"Oh! Lebrun. To be sure! I heard yesterday you were back. How did they treat you down in Mexique?"

"Fairly well."

"But not well enough to keep you there. Stunning girls, though, in Mexico. I thought I should never get away from Vera Cruz when I was down there a couple of years ago."

"Did they embroider slippers and tobacco pouches and hat-bands and things for you?" asked Edna.

"Oh! my! no! I didn't get so deep in their regard. I fear they made more impression on me than I made on them."

"You were less fortunate than Robert, then."

"I am always less fortunate than Robert. Has he been imparting tender confidences?"

"I've been imposing myself long enough," said Robert, rising, and shaking hands with Edna. "Please convey my regards to Mr. Pontellier when you write."

He shook hands with Arobin and went away.

"Fine fellow, that Lebrun," said Arobin when Robert had gone. "I never heard you speak of him."

"I knew him last summer at Grand Isle," she replied. "Here is that photograph of yours. Don't you want it?"

"What do I want with it? Throw it away." She threw it back on the table.

"I'm not going to Mrs. Merriman's," she said. "If you see her, tell her so. But perhaps I had better write. I think I shall write now, and say that I am sorry her child is sick, and tell her not to count on me."

"It would be a good scheme," acquiesced Arobin. "I don't blame you; stupid lot!"

Edna opened the blotter, and having procured paper and

pen, began to write the note. Arobin lit a cigar and read the evening paper, which he had in his pocket.

"What is the date?" she asked. He told her.

"Will you mail this for me when you go out?"

"Certainly." He read to her little bits out of the newspaper, while she straightened things on the table.

"What do you want to do?" he asked, throwing aside the paper. "Do you want to go out for a walk or a drive or anything? It would be a fine night to drive."

"No; I don't want to do anything but just be quiet. You go away and amuse yourself. Don't stay."

"I'll go away if I must; but I shan't amuse myself. You know that I only live when I am near you."

He stood up to bid her good night.

"Is that one of the things you always say to women?"

"I have said it before, but I don't think I ever came so near meaning it," he answered with a smile. There were no warm lights in her eyes; only a dreamy, absent look.

"Good night. I adore you. Sleep well," he said, and he kissed her hand and went away.

She stayed alone in a kind of reverie—a sort of stupor. Step by step she lived over every instant of the time she had been with Robert after he had entered Mademoiselle Reisz's door. She recalled his words, his looks. How few and meager they had been for her hungry heart! A vision—a transcendently seductive vision of a Mexican girl arose before her. She writhed with a jealous pang. She wondered when he would come back. He had not said he would come back. She had been with him, had heard his voice and touched his hand. But some way he had seemed nearer to her off there in Mexico.

XXXV

✦

*T*he morning was full of sunlight and hope. Edna could see before her no denial—only the promise of excessive joy. She lay in bed awake, with bright eyes full of speculation. "He loves you, poor fool." If she could but get that conviction firmly fixed in her mind, what mattered about the rest? She felt she had been childish and unwise the night before in giving herself over to despondency. She recapitulated the motives which no doubt explained Robert's reserve. They were not insurmountable; they would not hold if he really loved her; they could not hold against her own passion, which he must come to realize in time. She pictured him going to his business that morning. She even saw how he was dressed; how he walked down one street, and turned the corner of another; saw him bending over his desk, talking to people who entered the office, going to his lunch, and perhaps watching for her on the street. He would come to her in the afternoon or evening, sit and roll his cigarette, talk a little, and go away as he had done the night before. But how delicious it would be to have him there with her! She would have no regrets, nor seek to penetrate his reserve if he still chose to wear it.

Edna ate her breakfast only half dressed. The maid brought her a delicious printed scrawl from Raoul, expressing his love, asking her to send him some bonbons, and telling her they had found that morning ten tiny white pigs all lying in a row beside Lidie's big white pig.

A letter also came from her husband, saying he hoped to be back early in March, and then they would get ready for that journey abroad which he had promised her so long, which he felt now fully able to afford; he felt able to travel as people should, without any thought of small economies—thanks to his recent speculations in Wall Street.

Much to her surprise she received a note from Arobin, written at midnight from the club. It was to say good morning to her, to hope she had slept well, to assure her of his devotion, which he trusted she in some faintest manner returned.

All these letters were pleasing to her. She answered the children in a cheerful frame of mind, promising them bonbons, and congratulating them upon their happy find of the little pigs.

She answered her husband with friendly evasiveness—not with any fixed design to mislead him, only because all sense of reality had gone out of her life; she had abandoned herself to Fate, and awaited the consequences with indifference.

To Arobin's note she made no reply. She put it under Celestine's stove-lid.

Edna worked several hours with much spirit. She saw no one but a picture dealer, who asked her if it were true that she was going abroad to study in Paris.

She said possibly she might, and he negotiated with her

for some Parisian studies to reach him in time for the holiday trade in December.

Robert did not come that day. She was keenly disappointed. He did not come the following day, nor the next. Each morning she awoke with hope, and each night she was a prey to despondency. She was tempted to seek him out. But far from yielding to the impulse, she avoided any occasion which might throw her in his way. She did not go to Mademoiselle Reisz's nor pass by Madame Lebrun's, as she might have done if he had still been in Mexico.

When Arobin, one night, urged her to drive with him, she went—out to the lake, on the Shell Road. His horses were full of mettle, and even a little unmanageable. She liked the rapid gait at which they spun along, and the quick, sharp sound of the horses' hoofs on the hard road. They did not stop anywhere to eat or to drink. Arobin was not needlessly imprudent. But they ate and they drank when they regained Edna's little dining-room—which was comparatively early in the evening.

It was late when he left her. It was getting to be more than a passing whim with Arobin to see her and be with her. He had detected the latent sensuality, which unfolded under his delicate sense of her nature's requirements like a torpid, torrid, sensitive blossom.

There was no despondency when she fell asleep that night; nor was there hope when she awoke in the morning.

XXXVI

✦

*T*here was a garden out in the suburbs; a small, leafy corner, with a few green tables under the orange trees. An old cat slept all day on the stone step in the sun, and an old *mulâtresse* slept her idle hours away in her chair at the open window, till some one happened to knock on one of the green tables. She had milk and cream cheese to sell, and bread and butter. There was no one who could make such excellent coffee or fry a chicken so golden brown as she.

The place was too modest to attract the attention of people of fashion, and so quiet as to have escaped the notice of those in search of pleasure and dissipation. Edna had discovered it accidentally one day when the high-board gate stood ajar. She caught sight of a little green table, blotched with the checkered sunlight that filtered through the quivering leaves overhead. Within she had found the slumbering *mulâtresse,* the drowsy cat, and a glass of milk which reminded her of the milk she had tasted in Iberville.

She often stopped there during her perambulations; sometimes taking a book with her, and sitting an hour or two under the trees when she found the place deserted.

Once or twice she took a quiet dinner there alone, having instructed Celestine beforehand to prepare no dinner at home. It was the last place in the city where she would have expected to meet any one she knew.

Still she was not astonished when, as she was partaking of a modest dinner late in the afternoon, looking into an open book, stroking the cat, which had made friends with her—she was not greatly astonished to see Robert come in at the tall garden gate.

"I am destined to see you only by accident," she said, shoving the cat off the chair beside her. He was surprised, ill at ease, almost embarrassed at meeting her thus so unexpectedly.

"Do you come here often?" he asked.

"I almost live here," she said.

"I used to drop in very often for a cup of Catiche's good coffee. This is the first time since I came back."

"She'll bring you a plate, and you will share my dinner. There's always enough for two—even three." Edna had intended to be indifferent and as reserved as he when she met him; she had reached the determination by a laborious train of reasoning, incident to one of her despondent moods. But her resolve melted when she saw him before her, seated there beside her in the little garden, as if a designing Providence had led him into her path.

"Why have you kept away from me, Robert?" she asked, closing the book that lay open upon the table.

"Why are you so personal, Mrs. Pontellier? Why do you force me to idiotic subterfuges?" he exclaimed with sudden warmth. "I suppose there's no use telling you I've been very busy, or that I've been sick, or that I've been to see you and not found you at home. Please let me off with any one of these excuses."

"You are the embodiment of selfishness," she said. "You

save yourself something—I don't know what—but there is some selfish motive, and in sparing yourself you never consider for a moment what I think, or how I feel your neglect and indifference. I suppose this is what you would call un-womanly; but I have got into a habit of expressing myself. It doesn't matter to me, and you may think me unwomanly if you like."

"No; I only think you cruel, as I said the other day. Maybe not intentionally cruel; but you seem to be forcing me into disclosures which can result in nothing; as if you would have me bare a wound for the pleasure of looking at it, without the intention or power of healing it."

"I'm spoiling your dinner, Robert; never mind what I say. You haven't eaten a morsel."

"I only came in for a cup of coffee." His sensitive face was all disfigured with excitement.

"Isn't this a delightful place?" she remarked. "I am so glad it has never actually been discovered. It is so quiet, so sweet, here. Do you notice there is scarcely a sound to be heard? It's so out of the way; and a good walk from the car. However, I don't mind walking. I always feel so sorry for women who don't like to walk; they miss so much—so many rare little glimpses of life; and we women learn so little of life on the whole.

"Catiche's coffee is always hot. I don't know how she manages it, here in the open air. Celestine's coffee gets cold bringing it from the kitchen to the dining-room. Three lumps! How can you drink it so sweet? Take some of the cress with your chop; it's so biting and crisp. Then there's the advantage of being able to smoke with your coffee out here. Now, in the city—aren't you going to smoke?"

"After a while," he said, laying a cigar on the table.

"Who gave it to you?" she laughed.

"I bought it. I suppose I'm getting reckless; I bought a whole box." She was determined not to be personal again and make him uncomfortable.

The cat made friends with him, and climbed into his lap when he smoked his cigar. He stroked her silky fur, and talked a little about her. He looked at Edna's book, which he had read; and he told her the end, to save her the trouble of wading through it, he said.

Again he accompanied her back to her home; and it was after dusk when they reached the little "pigeon house." She did not ask him to remain, which he was grateful for, as it permitted him to stay without the discomfort of blundering through an excuse which he had no intention of considering. He helped her to light the lamp; then she went into her room to take off her hat and to bathe her face and hands.

When she came back Robert was not examining the pictures and magazines as before; he sat off in the shadow, leaning his head back on the chair as if in a reverie. Edna lingered a moment beside the table, arranging the books there. Then she went across the room to where he sat. She bent over the arm of his chair and called his name.

"Robert," she said, "are you asleep?"

"No," he answered, looking up at her.

She leaned over and kissed him—a soft, cool, delicate kiss, whose voluptuous sting penetrated his whole being—then she moved away from him. He followed, and took her in his arms, just holding her close to him. She put her hand up to his face and pressed his cheek against her own. The action was full of love and tenderness. He sought her lips again. Then he drew her down upon the sofa beside him and held her hand in both of his.

"Now you know," he said, "now you know what I have

She went and sat on the sofa. Then she stretched herself out there, never uttering a sound. She did not sleep. She did not go to bed (page 188).

been fighting against since last summer at Grand Isle; what drove me away and drove me back again."

"Why have you been fighting against it?" she asked. Her face glowed with soft lights.

"Why? Because you were not free; you were Léonce Pontellier's wife. I couldn't help loving you if you were ten times his wife; but so long as I went away from you and kept away I could help telling you so." She put her free hand up to his shoulder, and then against his cheek, rubbing it softly. He kissed her again. His face was warm and flushed.

"There in Mexico I was thinking of you all the time, and longing for you."

"But not writing to me," she interrupted.

"Something put into my head that you cared for me; and I lost my senses. I forgot everything but a wild dream of your some way becoming my wife."

"Your wife!"

"Religion, loyalty, everything would give way if only you cared."

"Then you must have forgotten that I was Léonce Pontellier's wife."

"Oh! I was demented, dreaming of wild, impossible things, recalling men who had set their wives free, we have heard of such things."

"Yes, we have heard of such things."

"I came back full of vague, mad intentions. And when I got here—"

"When you got here you never came near me!" She was still caressing his cheek.

"I realized what a cur I was to dream of such a thing, even if you had been willing."

She took his face between her hands and looked into it as if she would never withdraw her eyes more. She kissed him on the forehead, the eyes, the cheeks, and the lips.

"You have been a very, very foolish boy, wasting your time dreaming of impossible things when you speak of Mr. Pontellier setting me free! I am no longer one of Mr. Pontellier's possessions to dispose of or not. I give myself where I choose. If he were to say, 'Here, Robert, take her and be happy; she is yours,' I should laugh at you both."

His face grew a little white. "What do you mean?" he asked.

There was a knock at the door. Old Celestine came in to say that Madame Ratignolle's servant had come around the back way with a message that Madame had been taken sick and begged Mrs. Pontellier to go to her immediately.

"Yes, yes," said Edna, rising; "I promised. Tell her yes—to wait for me. I'll go back with her."

"Let me walk over with you," offered Robert.

"No," she said; "I will go with the servant." She went into her room to put on her hat, and when she came in again she sat once more upon the sofa beside him. He had not stirred. She put her arms about his neck.

"Good-by, my sweet Robert. Tell me good-by." He kissed her with a degree of passion which had not before entered into his caress, and strained her to him.

"I love you," she whispered, "only you; no one but you. It was you who awoke me last summer out of a life-long, stupid dream. Oh! you have made me so unhappy with your indifference. Oh! I have suffered, suffered! Now you are here we shall love each other, my Robert. We shall be everything to each other. Nothing else in the world is of any consequence. I must go to my friend; but you will wait for me? No matter how late; you will wait for me, Robert?"

"Don't go; don't go! Oh! Edna, stay with me," he pleaded. "Why should you go? Stay with me, stay with me."

"I shall come back as soon as I can; I shall find you here."
She buried her face in his neck, and said good-by again. Her
seductive voice, together with his great love for her, had en-
thralled his senses, had deprived him of every impulse but
the longing to hold her and keep her.

XXXVII

✦

$\mathcal{E}$dna looked in at the drug store. Monsieur Ratignolle was putting up a mixture himself, very carefully, dropping a red liquid into a tiny glass. He was grateful to Edna for having come; her presence would be a comfort to his wife. Madame Ratignolle's sister, who had always been with her at such trying times, had not been able to come up from the plantation, and Adèle had been inconsolable until Mrs. Pontellier so kindly promised to come to her. The nurse had been with them at night for the past week, as she lived a great distance away. And Dr. Mandelet had been coming and going all the afternoon. They were then looking for him any moment.

Edna hastened upstairs by a private stairway that led from the rear of the store to the apartments above. The children were all sleeping in a back room. Madame Ratignolle was in the salon, whither she had strayed in her suffering impatience. She sat on the sofa, clad in an ample white *peignoir,* holding a handkerchief tight in her hand with a nervous clutch. Her face was drawn and pinched, her sweet blue eyes haggard and unnatural. All her beautiful hair had been

drawn back and plaited. It lay in a long braid on the sofa pillow, coiled like a golden serpent. The nurse, a comfortable
looking *Griffe* woman in white apron and cap, was urging
her to return to her bedroom.

"There is no use, there is no use," she said at once to Edna.
"We must get rid of Mandelet; he is getting too old and
careless. He said he would be here at half-past seven; now
it must be eight. See what time it is, Joséphine."

The woman was possessed of a cheerful nature, and refused to take any situation too seriously, especially a situation with which she was so familiar. She urged Madame to
have courage and patience. But Madame only set her teeth
hard into her under lip, and Edna saw the sweat gather in
beads on her white forehead. After a moment or two she
uttered a profound sigh and wiped her face with the handkerchief rolled in a ball. She appeared exhausted. The nurse
gave her a fresh handkerchief, sprinkled with cologne
water.

"This is too much!" she cried. "Mandelet ought to be
killed! Where is Alphonse? Is it possible I am to be abandoned like this—neglected by every one?"

"Neglected, indeed!" exclaimed the nurse. Wasn't she
there? And here was Mrs. Pontellier leaving, no doubt, a
pleasant evening at home to devote to her? And wasn't
Monsieur Ratignolle coming that very instant through the
hall? And Joséphine was quite sure she had heard Doctor
Mandelet's coupé. Yes, there it was, down at the door.

Adèle consented to go back to her room. She sat on the
edge of a little low couch next to her bed.

Doctor Mandelet paid no attention to Madame Ratignolle's upbraidings. He was accustomed to them at such
times, and was too well convinced of her loyalty to doubt
it.

He was glad to see Edna, and wanted her to go with him

into the salon and entertain him. But Madame Ratignolle would not consent that Edna should leave her for an instant. Between agonizing moments, she chatted a little, and said it took her mind off her sufferings.

Edna began to feel uneasy. She was seized with a vague dread. Her own like experiences seemed far away, unreal, and only half remembered. She recalled faintly an ecstasy of pain, the heavy odor of chloroform, a stupor which had deadened sensation, and an awakening to find a little new life to which she had given being, added to the great un-numbered multitude of souls that come and go.

She began to wish she had not come; her presence was not necessary. She might have invented a pretext for staying away; she might even invent a pretext now for going. But Edna did not go. With an inward agony, with a flaming, out-spoken revolt against the ways of Nature, she witnessed the scene of torture.

She was still stunned and speechless with emotion when later she leaned over her friend to kiss her and softly say good-by. Adèle, pressing her cheek, whispered in an ex-hausted voice: "Think of the children, Edna. Oh think of the children! Remember them!"

XXXVIII

✦

*E*dna still felt dazed when she got outside in the open air. The Doctor's coupé had returned for him and stood before the *porte cochère*. She did not wish to enter the coupé, and told Doctor Mandelet she would walk; she was not afraid, and would go alone. He directed his carriage to meet him at Mrs. Pontellier's, and he started to walk home with her.

Up—away up, over the narrow street between the tall houses, the stars were blazing. The air was mild and caressing, but cool with the breath of spring and the night. They walked slowly, the Doctor with a heavy, measured tread and his hands behind him; Edna, in an absent-minded way, as she had walked one night at Grand Isle, as if her thoughts had gone ahead of her and she was striving to overtake them.

"You shouldn't have been there, Mrs. Pontellier," he said. "That was no place for you. Adèle is full of whims at such times. There were a dozen women she might have had with her, unimpressionable women. I felt that it was cruel, cruel. You shouldn't have gone."

"Oh, well!" she answered, indifferently. "I don't know that it matters after all. One has to think of the children some time or other; the sooner the better."

"When is Léonce coming back?"

"Quite soon. Some time in March."

"And you are going abroad?"

"Perhaps—no, I am not going. I'm not going to be forced into doing things. I don't want to go abroad. I want to be let alone. Nobody has any right—except children, perhaps—and even then, it seems to me—or it did seem—" She felt that her speech was voicing the incoherency of her thoughts, and stopped abruptly.

"The trouble is," sighed the Doctor, grasping her meaning intuitively, "that youth is given up to illusions. It seems to be a provision of Nature; a decoy to secure mothers for the race. And Nature takes no account of moral consequences, of arbitrary conditions which we create, and which we feel obliged to maintain at any cost."

"Yes," she said. "The years that are gone seem like dreams—if one might go on sleeping and dreaming—but to wake up and find—oh! well! perhaps it is better to wake up after all, even to suffer, rather than to remain a dupe to illusions all one's life."

"It seems to me, my dear child," said the Doctor at parting, holding her hand, "you seem to me to be in trouble. I am not going to ask for your confidence. I will only say that if ever you feel moved to give it to me, perhaps I might help you. I know I would understand, and I tell you there are not many who would—not many, my dear."

"Some way I don't feel moved to speak of things that trouble me. Don't think I am ungrateful or that I don't appreciate your sympathy. There are periods of despondency and suffering which take possession of me. But I don't want anything but my own way. That is wanting a good deal, of course, when you have to trample upon the lives, the hearts, the prejudices of others—but no matter—still, I shouldn't want to trample upon the little lives. Oh! I don't know what I'm saying, Doctor. Good night. Don't blame me for anything."

"Yes, I will blame you if you don't come and see me soon. We will talk of things you never have dreamt of talking about before. It will do us both good. I don't want you to blame yourself, whatever comes. Good night, my child."

She let herself in at the gate, but instead of entering she sat upon the step of the porch. The night was quiet and soothing. All the tearing emotion of the last few hours seemed to fall away from her like a somber, uncomfortable garment, which she had but to loosen to be rid of. She went back to that hour before Adèle had sent for her; and her senses kindled afresh in thinking of Robert's words, the pressure of his arms, and the feeling of his lips upon her own. She could picture at that moment no greater bliss on earth than possession of the beloved one. His expression of love had already given him to her in part. When she thought that he was there at hand, waiting for her, she grew numb with the intoxication of expectancy. It was so late; he would be asleep perhaps. She would awaken him with a kiss. She hoped he would be asleep that she might arouse him with her caresses.

Still, she remembered Adèle's voice whispering, "Think of the children; think of them." She meant to think of them; that determination had driven into her soul like a death wound—but not to-night. To-morrow would be time to think of everything.

Robert was not waiting for her in the little parlor. He was nowhere at hand. The house was empty. But he had scrawled on a piece of paper that lay in the lamplight:

"I love you. Good-by—because I love you."

Edna grew faint when she read the words. She went and sat on the sofa. Then she stretched herself out there, never uttering a sound. She did not sleep. She did not go to bed. The lamp sputtered and went out. She was still awake in the morning, when Celestine unlocked the kitchen door and came in to light the fire.

XXXIX

✦

Victor, with hammer and nails and scraps of scantling, was patching a corner of one of the galleries. Mariequita sat near by, dangling her legs, watching him work, and handing him nails from the tool-box. The sun was beating down upon them. The girl had covered her head with her apron folded into a square pad. They had been talking for an hour or more. She was never tired of hearing Victor describe the dinner at Mrs. Pontellier's. He exaggerated every detail, making it appear a veritable Lucullean feast. The flowers were in tubs, he said. The champagne was quaffed from huge golden goblets. Venus rising from the foam could have presented no more entrancing a spectacle than Mrs. Pontellier, blazing with beauty and diamonds at the head of the board, while the other women were all of them youthful houris, possessed of incomparable charms.

She got it into her head that Victor was in love with Mrs. Pontellier, and he gave her evasive answers, framed so as to confirm her belief. She grew sullen and cried a little, threatening to go off and leave him to his fine ladies. There were a dozen men crazy about her at the *Chênière;* and since it was the fashion to be in love with married people, why, she could run away any time she liked to New Orleans with Célina's husband.

Célina's husband was a fool, a coward, and a pig, and to prove it to her, Victor intended to hammer his head into a jelly the next time he encountered him. This assurance was very consoling to Mariequita. She dried her eyes, and grew cheerful at the prospect.

They were still talking of the dinner and the allurements of city life when Mrs. Pontellier herself slipped around the corner of the house. The two youngsters stayed dumb with amazement before what they considered to be an apparition. But it was really she in flesh and blood, looking tired and a little travel-stained.

"I walked up from the wharf," she said, "and heard the hammering. I supposed it was you, mending the porch. It's a good thing. I was always tripping over those loose planks last summer. How dreary and deserted everything looks!"

It took Victor some little time to comprehend that she had come in Beaudelet's lugger, that she had come alone, and for no purpose but to rest.

"There's nothing fixed up yet, you see. I'll give you my room; it's the only place."

"Any corner will do," she assured him.

"And if you can stand Philomel's cooking," he went on, "though I might try to get her mother while you are here. Do you think she would come?" turning to Mariequita.

Mariequita thought that perhaps Philomel's mother might come for a few days, and money enough.

Beholding Mrs. Pontellier make her appearance, the girl had at once suspected a lovers' rendezvous. But Victor's as-

tonishment was so genuine, and Mrs. Pontellier's indifference so apparent, that the disturbing notion did not lodge
long in her brain. She contemplated with the greatest interest this woman who gave the most sumptuous dinners in
America, and who had all the men in New Orleans at her
feet.

"What time will you have dinner?" asked Edna. "I'm very
hungry; but don't get anything extra."

"I'll have it ready in little or no time," he said, bustling and
packing away his tools. "You may go to my room to brush
up and rest yourself. Mariequita will show you."

"Thank you," said Edna. "But, do you know, I have a notion to go down to the beach and take a good wash and even
a little swim, before dinner?"

"The water is too cold!" they both exclaimed. "Don't
think of it."

"Well, I might go down and try—dip my toes in. Why, it
seems to me the sun is hot enough to have warmed the very
depths of the ocean. Could you get me a couple of towels?
I'd better go right away, so as to be back in time. It would
be a little too chilly if I waited till this afternoon."

Mariequita ran over to Victor's room, and returned with
some towels, which she gave to Edna.

"I hope you have fish for dinner," said Edna, as she started
to walk away; "but don't do anything extra if you haven't."

"Run and find Philomel's mother," Victor instructed the
girl. "I'll go to the kitchen and see what I can do. By Gim-
miny! Women have no consideration! She might have sent
me word."

Edna walked on down to the beach rather mechanically,
not noticing anything special except that the sun was hot.
She was not dwelling upon any particular train of thought.
She had done all the thinking which was necessary after

Robert went away, when she lay awake upon the sofa till morning.

She had said over and over to herself: "To-day it is Arobin; to-morrow it will be some one else. It makes no difference to me, it doesn't matter about Léonce Pontellier—but Raoul and Etienne!" She understood now clearly what she had meant long ago when she said to Adèle Ratignolle that she would give up the unessential, but she would never sacrifice herself for her children.

Despondency had come upon her there in the wakeful night, and had never lifted. There was no one thing in the world that she desired. There was no human being whom she wanted near her except Robert; and she even realized that the day would come when he, too, and the thought of him would melt out of her existence, leaving her alone. The children appeared before her like antagonists who had overcome her; who had overpowered and sought to drag her into the soul's slavery for the rest of her days. But she knew a way to elude them. She was not thinking of these things when she walked down to the beach.

The water of the Gulf stretched out before her, gleaming with the million lights of the sun. The voice of the sea is seductive, never ceasing, whispering, clamoring, murmuring, inviting the soul to wander in abysses of solitude. All along the white beach, up and down, there was no living thing in sight. A bird with a broken wing was beating the air above, reeling, fluttering, circling disabled down, down to the water.

Edna had found her old bathing suit still hanging, faded, upon its accustomed peg.

She put it on, leaving her clothing in the bath-house. But when she was there beside the sea, absolutely alone, she cast the unpleasant, pricking garments from her, and for the first time in her life she stood naked in the open air, at the mercy of the sun, the breeze that beat upon her, and the waves that invited her.

How strange and awful it seemed to stand naked under the sky! how delicious! She felt like some new-born creature, opening its eyes in a familiar world that it had never known.

The foamy wavelets curled up to her white feet, and coiled like serpents about her ankles. She walked out. The water was chill, but she walked on. The water was deep, but she lifted her white body and reached out with a long, sweeping stroke. The touch of the sea is sensuous, enfolding the body in its soft, close embrace.

She went on and on. She remembered the night she swam far out, and recalled the terror that seized her at the fear of being unable to regain the shore. She did not look back now, but went on and on, thinking of the blue-grass meadow that she had traversed when a little child, believing that it had no beginning and no end.

Her arms and legs were growing tired.

She thought of Léonce and the children. They were a part of her life. But they need not have thought that they could possess her, body and soul. How Mademoiselle Reisz would have laughed, perhaps sneered, if she knew! "And you call yourself an artist! What pretensions, Madame! The artist must possess the courageous soul that dares and defies."

Exhaustion was pressing upon and overpowering her.

"Good-by—because I love you." He did not know; he did not understand. He would never understand. Perhaps Doctor Mandelet would have understood if she had seen him—but it was too late; the shore was far behind her, and her strength was gone.

She looked into the distance, and the old terror flamed up

for an instant, then sank again. Edna heard her father's voice and her sister Margaret's. She heard the barking of an old dog that was chained to the sycamore tree. The spurs of the cavalry officer clanged as he walked across the porch. There was the hum of bees, and the musky odor of pinks filled the air.

Glossary of French Phrases

◆

à jeudi until Thursday

à point done to a turn

accouchement childbirth, delivery

"Allez vous-en! Allez vous-en! Sapristi!" Go away! Go away! For God's sake!

"Au revoir." Until we meet again.

bien souffrante truly indisposed, unwell, ailing

"Blagueur—farceur—gros bête, va!" Joker—buffoon—silly fool, go!

bon garçon good boy

"Bonne nuit, ma reine; soyez sage." Good night, my queen; be good.

bourgeois middle-class, common

camaraderie good friendship

"Ce que tes yeux me disent" What your eyes are telling me

chambres garnies furnished rooms

coup d'état overthrow of government

court bouillon fish broth

en bon ami as a good friend

en bonne ménagère as a good housewife

entre-mets side dishes

friandises delicacies

grand esprit noble soul

Griffe child of a mulatto and a "Negro" according to the Louisiana caste system of the time *la belle dame* the fair lady

les convenances social conventions

ma belle my dear

"Ma foi!" Really!

ma reine my queen

"Mais ce n'est pas mal! Elle s'y connait, elle a de la force, oui." But it's not bad! She knows what she's doing, she has talent, yes.

marron glacé sugared chestnut

ménage household

mets main course

mulâtresse mulatto woman

mules slippers

nom de guerre assumed name

par exemple for goodness' sake

"Parbleu!" By God!

parterre flower bed

"Passez! Adieu! Allez vous-en!" Go! Good-by! Go away!

"Pauvre chérie." Poor darling.

peignoir dressing gown

pension hotel or boardinghouse

porte cochère covered carriage entrance

poudre de riz face powder

Quartier Français French Quarter

"Sapristi!" For God's sake!

"si tu savais" if you only knew

soirée musicale evening party revolving around musical performance

souffrante indisposed, unwell, ailing

tignon variation on "chignon"; hairstyle coiled at the back of the head into a bun

tête montée reckless character

"Tiens! . . . Voilà que Madame Ratignolle est jalouse!" Ah! . . . Perhaps Madame Ratignolle is jealous!

vingt-et-un twenty-one, a card game

APPENDICES

✦

APPENDIX A

✦

Perspectives on
The Awakening

Contemporary Reviews
Pittsburgh Leader
Public Opinion
The Nation

Kate Chopin's Retraction of *The Awakening*

Critical Essays
"A Forgotten Novel: Kate Chopin's *The Awakening*"
KENNETH EBLE

"Tradition and the Female Talent:
The Awakening as a Solitary Book"
ELAINE SHOWALTER

"Characters as Foils to Edna"
BARBARA H. SOLOMON

"A Green and Yellow Parrot . . ."
JOYCE DYER

Contemporary Reviews

✦

Pittsburgh Leader*

A creole "Bovary" is this little novel of Miss Chopin's. Not that the
heroine is a creole exactly, or that Miss Chopin is a Flaubert—save
the mark!—but the theme is similar to that which occupied
Flaubert. There was, indeed, no need that a second "Madame Bovary" should be written, but an author's choice of themes is fre-
quently as inexplicable as his choice of a wife. It is governed by
some innate temperamental bias that cannot be diagrammed. This
is particularly so in women who write, and I shall not attempt to
say why Miss Chopin has devoted so exquisite and sensitive, well-
governed a style to so trite and sordid a theme. She writes much
better than it is ever given to most people to write, and hers is a
genuinely literary style; of no great elegance or solidity; but light,
flexible, subtle and capable of producing telling effects directly and
simply. The story she has to tell in the present instance is new neither in matter nor treatment. "Edna Pontellier," a Kentucky girl,
who, like "Emma Bovary," had been in love with innumerable
dream heroes before she was out of short skirts, married "Leonce
[sic] Pontellier" as a sort of reaction from a vague and visionary passion for a tragedian whose unresponsive picture she used to kiss.
She acquired the habit of liking her husband in time, and even of
liking her children. Though we are not justified in presuming that
she ever threw articles from her dressing table at them, as the
charming "Emma" had a winsome habit of doing, we are told that

* From "Books and Magazines," *Pittsburgh Leader,* July 8, 1899. Signed "Sibert"
[Willa Cather].

"she would sometimes gather them passionately to her heart; she would sometimes forget them." At a creole watering place, which is admirably and deftly sketched by Miss Chopin, "Edna" met "Robert Lebrun," son of the landlady, who dreamed of a fortune awaiting him in Mexico while he occupied a petty clerical position in New Orleans. "Robert" made it his business to be agreeable to his mother's boarders, and "Edna," not being a creole, much against his wish and will, took him seriously. "Robert" went to Mexico, but found that fortunes were no easier to make there than in New Orleans. He returns and does not even call to pay his respects to her. She encounters him at the home of a friend and takes him home with her. She wheedles him into staying for dinner, and we are told she sent the maid off "in search of some delicacy she had not thought of for herself, and she recommended great care in the dripping of the coffee and having the omelet done to a turn."

Only a few pages back we were informed that the husband, "M. Pontellier," had cold soup and burnt fish for his dinner. Such is life. The lover of course disappointed her, was a coward and ran away from his responsibilities before they began. He was afraid to begin a chapter with so serious and limited a woman. She remembered the sea where she had first met "Robert." Perhaps from the same motive which threw "Anna Keraninna" [sic] under the engine wheels, she threw herself into the sea, swam until she was tired and then let go.

> She looked into the distance, and for a moment the old terror flamed up, then sank again. She heard her father's voice, and her sister Margaret's. She heard the barking of an old dog that was chained to the sycamore tree. The spurs of the cavalry officer clanged as he walked across the porch. There was a hum of bees, and the musky odor of pinks filled the air.

"Edna Pontellier" and "Emma Bovary" are studies in the same feminine type; one, a finished and complete portrayal, the other a hasty sketch, but the theme is essentially the same. Both women belong to a class, not large, but forever clamoring in our ears, that demands more romance out of life than God put into it. Mr. G. Barnard [sic] Shaw would say that they are the victims of the

overidealization of love. They are the spoil of the poets, the Iphi-
genias of sentiment. The unfortunate feature of their disease is
that it attacks only women of brains, at least of rudimentary
brains, but whose development is one-sided; women of strong and
fine intuitions, but without the faculty of observation, compari-
son, reasoning about things. Probably, for emotional people, the
most convenient thing about being able to think is that it occasionally gives them a rest from feeling. Now with women of the
"Bovary" type, this relaxation and recreation is impossible. They
are not critics of life, but, in the most personal sense, partakers of
life. They receive impressions through the fancy. With them
everything begins with fancy, and passions rise in the brain rather
than in the blood, the poor, neglected, limited one-sided brain that
might do so much better things than badgering itself into frantic
endeavors to love. For these are the people who pay with their
blood for the fine ideals of the poets, as Marie Delclasse paid for
Dumas' great creation, "Marguerite Gautier." These people really
expect the passion of love to fill and gratify every need of life,
whereas nature only intended that it should meet one of many demands. They insist upon making it stand for all the emotional pleasures of life and art: expecting an individual and self-limited
passion to yield infinite variety, pleasure and distraction, to contribute to their lives what the arts and the pleasurable exercise of
the intellect gives to less limited and less intense idealists. So this
passion, when set up against Shakespeare, Balzac, Wagner,
Raphael, fails them. They have staked everything on one hand, and
they lose. They have driven the blood until it will drive no further,
they have played their nerves up to the point where any relaxation
short of absolute annihilation is impossible. Every idealist abuses
his nerves, and every sentimentalist brutally abuses them. And in
the end, the nerves get even. Nobody ever cheats them, really.
Then "the awakening" comes. Sometimes it comes in the form of
arsenic, as it came to "Emma Bovary," sometimes it is carbolic acid
taken covertly in the police station, a goal to which unbalanced
idealism not infrequently leads. "Edna Pontellier," fanciful and
romantic to the last, chose the sea on a summer night and went
down with the sound of her first lover's spurs in her ears, and

the scent of pinks about her. And next time I hope that Miss Chopin will devote that flexible, iridescent style of hers to a better cause.

✦

$\mathcal{P}$UBLIC $\mathcal{O}$PINION*

"The Awakening," by Kate Chopin, is a feeble reflection of Bourget, theme and manner of treatment both suggesting the French novelist. We very much doubt the possibility of a woman of "solid old Presbyterian Kentucky stock" being at all like Mrs. Edna Pontellier who has a long list of lesser loves, and one absorbing passion, but gives herself only to the man for whom she did not feel the least affection. If the author had secured our sympathy for this unpleasant person it would not have been a small victory, but we are well satisfied when Mrs. Pontellier deliberately swims out to her death in the waters of the gulf.

✦

$\mathcal{T}$HE $\mathcal{N}$ATION†

"The Awakening" is the sad story of a Southern lady who wanted to do what she wanted to. From wanting to, she did, with disastrous consequences; but as she swims out to sea in the end, it is to be hoped that her example may lie for ever undredged. It is with high expectation that we open the volume, remembering the author's agreeable short stories, and with real disappointment that we close it. The recording reviewer drops a tear over one more clever author gone wrong. Mrs. Chopin's accustomed fine workmanship is

* From *Public Opinion,* June 22, 1899.
† From *The Nation,* August 3, 1899.

here, the hinted effects, the well-expended epithet, the pellucid style; and, so far as construction goes, the writer shows herself as competent to write a novel as a sketch. The tint and air of Creole New Orleans and the Louisiana seacoast are conveyed to the reader with subtle skill, and among the secondary characters are several that are lifelike. But we cannot see that literature or the criticism of life is helped by the detailed history of the manifold and contemporary love affairs of a wife and mother. Had she lived by Prof. William James's advice to do one thing a day one does not want to do (in Creole society, two would perhaps be better), flirted less and looked after her children more, or even assisted at more *accouchements*—her *chef d'œuvre* in self-denial—we need not have been put to the unpleasantness of reading about her and the temptations she trumped up for herself.

Kate Chopin's Retraction

OF

*The Awakening**

◆

THE AWAKENING. *By* KATE CHOPIN.

Having a group of people at my disposal, I thought it might be entertaining (to myself) to throw them together and see what would happen. I never dreamed of Mrs. Pontellier making such a mess of things and working out her own damnation as she did. If I had had the slightest intimation of such a thing I would have excluded her from the company. But when I found out what she was up to, the play was half over and it was then too late.

ST. LOUIS, MO., May 28, 1899

Kate Chopin

---

* From "Aims and Autographs of Authors," *Book News* 17 (July 1899): 612.

CRITICAL ESSAYS

✦

A FORGOTTEN NOVEL:
KATE CHOPIN'S *The Awakening**

KENNETH EBLE

When Kate Chopin's novel *The Awakening* was published in 1899, it made its mark on American letters principally in the reactions it provoked among shocked newspaper reviewers. In St. Louis, Mrs. Chopin's native city, the book was taken from circulation at the Mercantile Library, and though by this time she had established herself as one of the city's most talented writers, she was now denied membership in the Fine Arts Club. The St. Louis *Republic* said the novel was, like most of Mrs. Chopin's work, "too strong drink for moral babes and should be labeled 'poison.'" The *Nation* granted its "fine workmanship and pellucid style," but went on, "We cannot see that literature or the criticism of life is helped by the detailed history of the manifold and contemporary love affairs of a wife and mother."

After Mrs. Chopin's death in 1904, a story passed from the *Library of Southern Literature* through F. L. Pattee's *American Literature since 1870* and into the *Dictionary of American Biography* that Kate Chopin's brief writing career came to an abrupt end in her bitter disappointment over the reception of *The Awakening*. The story is false—her manuscript collection shows that she wrote six stories after 1900, three of which were published. But the implications are

* From *Western Humanities Review*, vol. X, no. 3 (Summer 1956): pp. 261–69. Copyright © 1956 by Western Humanities Review. Reprinted by permission of Western Humanities Review.

probably accurate. There is little doubt of the squeamishness of American literary taste in 1900, nor is there much doubt that Kate Chopin was deeply hurt by the attacks on the novel as well as on her own motives and morals. The stories she wrote thereafter lack distinction, and though *The Awakening* was reprinted by Duffield and Company in 1906, it is likely that the author's innocent disregard for contemporary moral delicacies ordained that it should be quickly forgotten.

Today, Kate (O'Flaherty) Chopin is chiefly remembered as a regional writer whose short stories of the Louisiana Creoles are usually compared with the work of George Washington Cable and Grace King. Her writing career is unusual for its brevity: it began in 1889 and ended with her death in 1904. She did not publish until she was thirty-nine, although it is apparent that in the preceding years she read widely and took some pride in her writing as well as in her discriminating tastes in music, art and literature. Given other circumstances, she might have developed into a writer early in her life. As it was, the talent she possessed was quite simply submerged as the result of an early and happy marriage and the raising of a sizable family.

She was born in St. Louis in 1850, educated in a convent school, moved to New Orleans when she married Oscar Chopin in 1870, and there became the mother of six children in the next ten years. She returned to St. Louis after her husband died in 1882, but her life in New Orleans and in Natchitoches Parish, where she lived for two years immediately before her husband's death, gave her most of her fictional material. Her husband's estate was small, and the O'Flaherty family estate had dwindled by the time of her mother's death in 1885. Left alone with a family to support, she may have turned seriously to writing because of a feeling of necessity. From 1889 until her death, her stories and miscellaneous writings appeared in *Vogue, Youth's Companion, Atlantic Monthly, Century, Saturday Evening Post,* and many lesser publications. Her books, in addition to *The Awakening,* are *At Fault* (1890), a novel, and two collections of stories and sketches, *Bayou Folk* (1894) and *A Night in Acadie* (1897).

Her present literary rank is probably somewhere between Oc-

tave Thanet (Alice French) and Sarah Orne Jewett. In the fifty years
after her death, she has provoked two articles and a doctoral dis-
sertation on her life and work.[1] Her own books are long out of
print, and *The Awakening* is particularly hard to find. Their disap-
pearance is not unusual; it is inevitable that much of a minor
writer's work will be lost. What is unfortunate is that *The Awakening,* certainly Mrs. Chopin's best work, has been neglected almost
from its publication.

The claim of the book upon the reader's attention is simple. It is
a first-rate novel. The justification for urging its importance is that
we have few enough novels of its stature. One could add that it is
advanced in theme and technique over the novels of its day, and that
it anticipates in many respects the modern novel. It could be
claimed that it adds to American fiction an example of what Gide
called the *roman pur,* a kind of novel not characteristic of American
writing. One could offer the book as evidence that the regional
writer can go beyond the limitations of regional material. But these
matters aside, what recommends the novel is its general excellence.

It is surprising that the book has not been picked up today by
reprint houses long on lurid covers and short on new talent. The nature of its theme, which had much to do with its adverse reception
in 1899, would offer little offense today. In a way, the novel is an
American *Bovary,* though such a designation is not precisely accurate.
Its central character is similar: the married woman who seeks love
outside a stuffy, middle-class marriage. It is similar too in the defini-
tive way it portrays the mind of a woman trapped in marriage and
seeking fulfillment of what she vaguely recognizes as her essential
nature. The husband, Léonce Pontellier, is a businessman whose nature and preoccupations are not far different from those of Charles
Bovary. There is a Léon Dupuis in Robert Lebrun, a Rodolphe
Boulanger in Alcée Arobin. And too, like *Madame Bovary,* the novel
handles its material superbly well. Kate Chopin herself was probably
more than any other American writer of her time under French influence. Her background was French-Irish; she married a Creole;
she read and spoke French and knew contemporary French literature well; she associated both in St. Louis and Louisiana with families

of French ancestry and disposition. But despite the similarities and the possible influences, the novel, chiefly because of the independent character of its heroine, Edna Pontellier, and because of the intensity of the focus upon her, is not simply a good but derivative work. It has a manner and matter of its own.

Quite frankly, the book is about sex. Not only is it about sex, but the very texture of the writing is sensuous, if not sensual, from the first to the last. Even as late as 1932, Chopin's biographer, Daniel Rankin, seemed somewhat shocked by it. He paid his respects to the artistic excellence of the book, but he was troubled by "that insistent query—*cui bono?*" He called the novel "exotic in setting, morbid in theme, erotic in motivation." One questions the accuracy of these terms, and even more the moral disapproval implied in their usage. One regrets that Mr. Rankin did not emphasize that the book was amazingly honest, perceptive and moving.

The Awakening is a study of Edna Pontellier, a story, as the *Nation* criticized it, "of a Southern lady who wanted to do what she wanted to. From wanting to, she did, with disastrous consequences." Such a succinct statement, blunt but accurate so far as it goes, may suggest that a detailed retelling of the story would convey little of the actual character of the novel. It is, of course, one of those novels a person simply must read to gain any real impression of its excellence. But the compactness of the work in narrative, characterization, setting, symbols and images gives meaning to such an imprecise and overworked expression. Some idea of the style may be conveyed by quoting the opening paragraphs:

> A green and yellow parrot, which hung in a cage outside the door, kept repeating over and over *"Allez vous-en! Allez vous-en! Sapristi!* That's all right."
>
> He could speak a little Spanish, and also a language which nobody understood, unless it was the mocking-bird that hung on the other side of the door, whistling his fluty notes out upon the breeze with maddening persistence.
>
> Mr. Pontellier, unable to read his newspaper with any degree of comfort, arose with an expression and an exclamation of disgust. He walked down the gallery and across the narrow

"bridges" which connected the Lebrun cottages one with the other. He had been seated before the door of the main house. The parrot and the mocking-bird were the property of Madame Lebrun and they had the right to make all the noise they wished. Mr. Pontellier had the privilege of quitting their society when they ceased to be entertaining.

This is Mr. Pontellier. He is a businessman, husband and father, not given to romance, not given to much of anything outside his business. When he comes to Grand Isle, the summer place of the Creoles in the story, he is anxious to get back to his cotton brokerage in Carondelet Street, New Orleans, and he passes his time on Grand Isle at the hotel smoking his cigars and playing cards. When he is on the beach at all, he is not a participant, but a watcher.

He fixed his gaze upon a white sunshade that was advancing at snail's pace from the beach. He could see it plainly between the gaunt trunk of the water-oaks and across the strip of yellow camomile. The gulf looked far away, melting hazily into the blue of the horizon. The sunshade continued to approach slowly. Beneath its pink-lined shelter were their faces, Mrs. Pontellier and young Robert Lebrun.

It is apparent that a triangle has been formed, and going into the details of the subsequent events in a summary fashion would likely destroy the art by which such a sequence becomes significant. Suffice to say that Robert Lebrun is the young man who first awakens, or rather, is present at the awakening of Edna Pontellier into passion, a passion which Mr. Pontellier neither understands nor appreciates. Slowly Edna and Robert fall in love, but once again, the expression is too trite. Edna grows into an awareness of a woman's physical nature, and Robert is actually but a party of the second part. The reader's attention is never allowed to stray from Edna. At the climax of their relationship, young Lebrun recognizes what must follow and goes away. During his absence, Mrs. Pontellier becomes idly amused by a roué, Arobin, and, becoming more than amused, more than tolerates his advances. When Robert returns he

finds that Edna is willing to declare her love and accept the consequences of her passion. But Robert, abiding by the traditional romantic code which separates true love from physical passion,
refuses the offered consummation. When he leaves Mrs. Pontellier,
she turns once again to the scene of her awakening, the sand and sea
of Grand Isle:

> The water of the Gulf stretched out before her, gleaming
> with the million lights of the sun. The voice of the sea is se-
> ductive, never ceasing, whispering, clamoring, murmuring,
> inviting the soul to wander in abysses of solitude. All along the
> white beach, up and down, there was no living thing in sight.
> A bird with a broken wing was beating the air above, reeling,
> fluttering, circling disabled down, down to the water.
>
> Edna had found her old bathing suit still hanging, faded,
> upon its accustomed peg.
>
> She put it on, left her clothing in the bath-house. But when
> she was there beside the sea, absolutely alone, she cast the un-
> pleasant, pricking garments from her, and for the first time in
> her life she stood naked in the open air, at the mercy of the sun,
> the breeze that beat upon her, and the waves that invited her.
>
> How strange and awful it seemed to stand naked under
> the sky! how delicious! She felt like some new-born crea-
> ture, opening its eyes in a familiar world that it had never known.
>
> The foamy wavelets curled up to her white feet, and coiled
> like serpents about her ankles. She walked out. The water was
> chill, but she walked on. The water was deep, but she lifted her
> white body and reached out with a long, sweeping stroke. The
> touch of the sea is sensuous, enfolding the body in its soft,
> close embrace. . . .
>
> She looked into the distance, and the old terror flamed up
> for an instant, then sank again. Edna heard her father's voice
> and her sister Margaret's. She heard the barking of an old
> dog that was chained to the sycamore tree. The spurs of the
> cavalry officer clanged as he walked across the porch. There
> was the hum of bees, and the musky odor of pinks filled
> the air.

Here is the story, its beginning a mature woman's awakening to physical love, its end her walking into the sea. The extracts convey something of the author's style, but much less of the movement of the characters and of human desire against the sensuous background of sea and sand. Looking at the novel analytically, one can say that it excels chiefly in its characterizations and its structure, the use of images and symbols to unify that structure, and the character of Edna Pontellier.

Kate Chopin, almost from her first story, had the ability to capture character, to put the right word in the mouth, to impart the exact gesture, to select the characteristic action. An illustration of her deftness in handling even minor characters is her treatment of Edna's father. When he leaves the Pontelliers' after a short visit, Edna is glad to be rid of him and "his padded shoulders, his Bible reading, his 'toddies' and ponderous oaths." A moment later, it is a side of Edna's nature which is revealed. She felt a sense of relief at her father's absence; she "read Emerson until she grew sleepy."

Characterization was always Mrs. Chopin's talent. Structure was not. Those who knew her working habits say that she seldom revised, and she herself mentions that she did not like reworking her stories. Though her reputation rests upon her short narratives, her collected stories give abundant evidence of the sketch, the outlines of stories which remain unformed. And when she did attempt a tightly organized story, she often turned to Maupassant and was as likely as not to effect a contrived symmetry. Her early novel *At Fault* suffers most from her inability to control her material. In *The Awakening* she is in complete command of structure. She seems to have grasped instinctively the use of the unifying symbol—here the sea, sky and sand—and with it the power of individual images to bind the story together.

The sea, the sand, the sun and sky of the Gulf Coast become almost a presence themselves in the novel. Much of the sensuousness of the book comes from the way the reader is never allowed to stray far from the water's edge. A refrain beginning "The voice of the sea is seductive, never ceasing, clamoring, murmuring, . . ." is used throughout the novel. It appears first at the beginning of Edna Pontellier's awakening, and it appears at the end as the introduction to the long final scene, previously quoted. Looking closely at the final form of this refrain, one can notice the care with which Mrs. Chopin composed this theme and variation. In the initial statement, the sentence does not end with "solitude," but goes on, as it should, "to lose itself in mazes of inward contemplation." Nor is the image of the bird with the broken wing in the earlier passage; rather there is a prefiguring of the final tragedy: "The voice of the sea speaks to the soul. The touch of the sea is sensuous, enfolding the body in its soft, close embrace." The way scene, mood, action and character are fused reminds one not so much of literature as of an impressionist painting, of a Renoir with much of the sweetness missing. Only Stephen Crane, among her American contemporaries, had an equal sensitivity to light and shadow, color and texture, had the painter's eye matched with the writer's perception of character and incident.

The best example of Mrs. Chopin's use of a visual image which is also highly symbolic is the lady in black and the two nameless lovers. They are seen as touches of paint upon the canvas and as indistinct yet evocative figures which accompany Mrs. Pontellier and Robert Lebrun during the course of their intimacy. They appear first early in the novel. "The lady in black was reading her morning devotions on the porch of a neighboring bath-house. Two young lovers were exchanging their hearts' yearnings beneath the children's tent, which they had found unoccupied." Throughout the course of Edna's awakening, these figures appear and reappear, the lovers entering the *pension*, leaning toward each other as the water-oaks bent from the sea, the lady in black, creeping behind them. They accompany Edna and Robert when they first go to the Chênière, "the lovers, shoulder to shoulder, creeping; the lady in black, gaining steadily upon them." When Robert departs for Mexico, the picture changes. Lady and lovers depart together, and Edna finds herself back from the sea and shore, and set among her human acquaintances, her husband; her father; Mme. Reisz, the musician, "a homely woman with a small wizened face and body, and eyes that glowed"; Alcée Arobin; Mme. Ratignolle; and others. One brief scene from this milieu will further illustrate Mrs. Chopin's conscious or unconscious symbolism.

The climax of Edna's relationship with Arobin is the dinner which is to celebrate her last night in her and her husband's house. Edna is ready to move to a small place around the corner where she can escape (though she does not phrase it this way) the feeling that she is one more of Léonce Pontellier's possessions. At the dinner Victor Lebrun, Robert's brother, begins singing, "Ah! si tu savais!" a song which brings back all her memories of Robert. She sets her glass so blindly down that she shatters it against the carafe. "The wine spilled over Arobin's legs and some of it trickled down upon Mrs. Highcamp's black gauze gown." After the other guests have gone, Edna and Arobin walk to the new house. Mrs. Chopin writes of Edna, "She looked down, noticing the black line of his leg moving in and out so close to her against the yellow shimmer of her gown." The chapter concludes:

> His hand had strayed to her beautiful shoulders, and he could feel the response of her flesh to his touch. He seated himself beside her and kissed her lightly upon the shoulder.
>
> "I thought you were going away," she said, in an uneven voice.
>
> "I am, after I have said good night."
>
> "Good night," she murmured.
>
> He did not answer, except to continue to caress her. He did not say good night until she had become supple to his gentle, seductive entreaties.

It is not surprising that the sensuous quality of the book, both from the incidents of the novel and the symbolic implications, would have offended contemporary reviewers. What convinced many critics of the indecency of the book, however, was not simply the sensuous scenes, but rather that the author obviously sympathized with Mrs. Pontellier. More than that, the readers probably found that she aroused their own sympathies.

It is a letter from an English reader which states most clearly, in a matter-of-fact way, the importance of Edna Pontellier. The letter was to Kate Chopin from Lady Janet Scammon Young, and included a more interesting analysis of the novel by Dr. Dunrobin Thomson, a London physician whom Lady Janet said a great editor had called "the soundest critic since Matthew Arnold." "That which makes *The Awakening* legitimate," Dr. Thomson wrote, "is that the author deals with the commonest of human experiences. You fancy *Edna's* case exceptional? Trust an old doctor—most common." He goes on to speak of the "abominable prudishness" masquerading as "modesty or virtue," which makes the woman who marries a victim. For passion is regarded as disgraceful and the self-respecting female assumes she does not possess passion. "In so far as normally constituted womanhood *must* take account of something *sexual*," he points out, "it is called love." But marital love and passion may not be one. The wise husband, Dr. Thomson advises, seeing within his wife the "mysterious affinity" between a married woman and a man who stirs her passions, will help her see the distinction between her heart and her love, which wifely loyalty owes to the husband, and her body, which yearns for awakening. But more than clinically analyzing the discrepancy between Victorian morals and woman's nature, Dr. Thomson testifies that Mrs. Chopin has not been false or sensational to no purpose. He does not feel that she has corrupted, nor does he regard the warring within Edna's self as insignificant.

Greek tragedy—to remove ourselves from Victorian morals— knew well *eros* was not the kind of *love* which can be easily prettified and sentimentalized. Phaedra's struggle with elemental passion in the *Hippolytus* is not generally regarded as being either morally offensive or insignificant. Mrs. Pontellier, too, has the power, the dignity, the self-possession of a tragic heroine. She is not an Emma Bovary, deluded by ideas of "romance," nor is she the sensuous but guilt-ridden woman of the sensational novel. We can find only partial reason for her affair in the kind of romantic desire to escape a middle-class existence which animates Emma Bovary. Edna Pontellier is neither deluded nor deludes. She is woman, the physical woman who, despite her Kentucky Presbyterian upbringing and a comfortable marriage, must struggle with the sensual appeal of physical ripeness itself, with passion of which she is only dimly aware. Her struggle is not melodramatic, nor is it artificial, nor vapid. It is objective, real and moving. And when she walks into the sea, it does not leave a reader with the sense of sin punished, but rather with the sense evoked by Edwin Arlington Robinson's *Eros Turannos:*

> . . . for they
> That with a god have striven
> Not hearing much of what we say,
> Take what the god has given;
> Though like waves breaking it may be,
> Or like a changed familiar tree,
> Or like a stairway to the sea
> Where down the blind are driven.

How wrong to call Edna, as Daniel Rankin does, "a selfish, capricious" woman. Rather, Edna's struggle, the struggle with *eros* itself, is far-thest removed from capriciousness. It is her self-awareness, and her awakening into a greater degree of self-awareness than those around her can comprehend, which gives her story dignity and significance.

Our advocacy of the novel is not meant to obscure its faults. It is not perfect art, but in total effect it provokes few dissatisfactions. A sophisticated modern reader might find something of the derivative about it. Kate Chopin read widely, and a list of novelists she found interesting would include Flaubert, Tolstoy, Turgenev, D'Annunzio, Bourget, Goncourt and Zola. It is doubtful, however, that there was any direct borrowing, and *The Awakening* exists, as do most good nov-els, as a product of the author's literary, real, and imagined life.

How Mrs. Chopin managed to create in ten years the substantial body of work she achieved is no less a mystery than the excellence of *The Awakening* itself. But, having added to American literature a novel uncommon in its kind as in its excellence, she deserves not to be forgotten. *The Awakening* deserves to be restored and to be given its place among novels worthy of preservation.

Notes

1. Daniel S. Rankin, *Kate Chopin and Her Creole Stories* (Philadel-phia, 1932).

◆

$\mathcal{T}$RADITION AND THE $\mathcal{F}$EMALE $\mathcal{T}$ALENT:
The Awakening AS A $\mathcal{S}$OLITARY $\mathcal{B}$OOK*

ELAINE SHOWALTER

***Much of the shock effect of *The Awakening* to the readers of 1899 came from Chopin's rejection of the conventions of women's writing. Despite her name, which echoes two famous heroines of the domestic novel (Edna Earl in Augusta Evans's *St. Elmo* and Edna Kenderdine in Dinah Craik's *The Woman's Kingdom*), Edna Pontellier appears to reject the domestic empire of the mother and the sororal world of women's culture. Seemingly beyond the bonds of womanhood, she has neither mother nor daughter, and even refuses to go to her sister's wedding.

Moreover, whereas the sentimental heroine nurtures others, and the abstemious local color heroine subsists upon meager vegetarian diets, Kate Chopin's heroine is a robust woman who does not deny her appetites. . . . Edna Pontellier eats hearty meals of pâté, pompano, steak, and broiled chicken; bites off chunks of crusty bread; snacks on beer and Gruyère cheese; and sips brandy, wine, and champagne.

Formally, too, the novel has moved away from conventional techniques of realism to an impressionistic rhythm of epiphany and mood. Chopin abandoned the chapter titles she had used in her first novel, *At Fault* (1890), for thirty-nine numbered chapters of uneven length, ranging from the single paragraph of Chapter 28 to the sustained narrative of the dinner party in Chapter 30. The chapters are unified less by their style than by their focus on Edna's consciousness, and by the repetition of key motifs and images: music, the sea, shadows, swimming, eating, sleeping, gambling, the lovers, birth. Chapters of lyri-

* From *New Essays on "The Awakening,"* ed. Wendy Martin (Cambridge and New York: Cambridge University Press, 1988), pp. 42–55. Reprinted with the permission of Cambridge University Press.

cism and fantasy, such as Edna's voyage to the Chênière Caminada, alternate with realistic, even satirical, scenes of Edna's marriage.

Most important, where previous works ignored sexuality or spir-
itualized it through maternity, *The Awakening* is insistently sexual,
explicitly involved with the body and with self-awareness through
physical awareness. Although Edna's actual seduction by Arobin
takes place in the narrative neverland between Chapters 31 and 32,
Chopin brilliantly evokes sexuality through images and details. In
keeping with the novel's emphasis on the self, several scenes suggest Edna's initial autoeroticism. Edna's midnight swim, which
awakens the "first-felt throbbings of desire," takes place in an atmosphere of erotic fragrance, "strange, rare odors . . . a tangle of
the sea-smell and of weeds and damp new-ploughed earth, mingled
with the heavy perfume of a field of white blossoms" (Chap. 10). A
similarly voluptuous scene is her nap at Chênière Caminada, when
she examines her flesh as she lies in a "strange, quaint bed, with its
sweet country odor of laurel" (Chap. 13).

Edna reminds Dr. Mandelet of "some beautiful, sleek animal
waking up in the sun" (Chap. 23), and we recall that among her fantasies in listening to music is the image of a lady stroking a cat. The
image both conveys Edna's sensuality and hints at the self-
contained, almost masturbatory, quality of her sexuality. Her rendezvous with Robert takes place in a sunny garden where both
stroke a drowsy cat's silky fur, and Arobin first seduces her by
smoothing her hair with his "soft, magnetic hand" (Chap. 31).

Yet despite these departures from tradition, there are other respects in which the novel seems very much of its time. As its title
suggests, *The Awakening* is a novel about a process rather than a program, about a passage rather than a destination. Like Edith Whar-
ton's *The House of Mirth* (1905), it is a transitional female fiction of
the *fin-de-siècle,* a narrative of and about the passage from the homosocial women's culture and literature of the nineteenth century
to the heterosexual fiction of modernism. Chopin might have taken
the plot from a notebook entry Henry James made in 1892 about
"the growing divorce between the American woman (with her
comparative leisure, culture, grace, social instincts, artistic ambition) and the male American immersed in the ferocity of business,

with no time for any but the most sordid interests, purely commercial, professional, democratic and political. This divorce is rapidly becoming a gulf."[1] The Gulf where the opening chapters of *The Awakening* are set certainly suggests the "growing divorce" between Edna's interests and desires and Leonce's [sic] obsessions with the stock market, property, and his brokerage business.

Yet in turning away from her marriage, Edna initially looks back to women's culture rather than forward to another man. As Sandra Gilbert has pointed out, Grand Isle is an oasis of women's culture, or a "female colony": "Madame Lebrun's *pension* on Grand Isle is very much a woman's land not only because it is owned and run by a single woman and dominated by 'mother-women' but also because (as in so many summer colonies today) its principal inhabitants are actually women and children whose husbands and fathers visit only on weekends . . . [and it is situated,] like so many places that are significant for women, outside patriarchal culture, beyond the limits and limitations of the city where men make history, on a shore that marks the margin where nature intersects with culture."[2]

Edna's awakening, moreover, begins not with a man, but with Adele [sic] Ratignolle, the empress of the "mother-women" of Grand Isle. A "self-contained" (Chap. 7) woman, Edna has never had any close relationships with members of her own sex. Thus it is Adele who belatedly initiates Edna into the world of female love and ritual on the first step of her sensual voyage of self-discovery. Edna's first attraction to Adele is physical: "The excessive physical charm of the Creole had first attracted her, for Edna had a sensuous susceptibility to beauty" (Chap. 7). At the beach, in the hot sun, she responds to Adele's caresses, the first she has ever known from another woman, as Adele clasps her hand "firmly and warmly" and strokes it fondly. The touch provokes Edna to an unaccustomed candor; leaning her head on Adele's shoulder and confiding some of her secrets, she begins to feel "intoxicated" (Chap. 7). The bond between them goes beyond sympathy, as Chopin notes, to "[what] we might well call love" (Chap. 7).

In some respects, the motherless Edna also seeks a mother surrogate in Adele and looks to her for nurturance. Adele provides maternal encouragement for Edna's painting and tells her that her "talent is immense" (Chap. 18). Characteristically, Adele has rationalized her own "art" as a maternal project: "She was keeping up her music on account of the children . . . a means of brightening the home and making it attractive" (Chap. 9). Edna's responses to Adele's music have been similarly tame and sentimental. Her revealing fantasies as she listens to Adele play her easy pieces suggest the restriction and decorum of the female world: "a dainty young woman . . . taking mincing dancing steps, as she came down a long avenue between tall hedges"; "children at play" (Chap. 9). Women's art, as Adele presents it, is social, pleasant, and undemanding. It does not conflict with her duties as a wife and mother, and can even be seen to enhance them. Edna understands this well; as she retorts when her husband recommends Adele as a model of an artist, "She isn't a musician, and I'm not a painter." (Chap. 19).

Yet the relationship with the conventional Adele educates the immature Edna to respond for the first time both to a different kind of sexuality and to the unconventional and difficult art of Mademoiselle Reisz. In responding to Adele's interest, Edna begins to think about her own past and to analyze her own personality. In textual terms, it is through this relationship that she becomes "Edna" in the narrative rather than "Mrs. Pontellier."

We see the next stage of Edna's awakening in her relationship with Mademoiselle Reisz, who initiates her into the world of art. Significantly, this passage also takes place through a female rather than a male mentor, and, as with Adele, there is something more intense than friendship between the two women. Whereas Adele's fondness for Edna, however, is depicted as maternal and womanly, Mademoiselle Reisz's attraction to Edna suggests something more perverse. The pianist is obsessed with Edna's beauty, raves over her figure in a bathing suit, greets her as "ma belle" and "ma reine," holds her hand, and describes herself as "a foolish old woman whom you have captivated" (Chap. 21). If Adele is a surrogate for Edna's dead mother and the intimate friend she never had as a girl, Mademoiselle Reisz, whose music reduces Edna to passionate sobs, seems to be a surrogate lover. And whereas Adele is a "faultless madonna" who speaks for the values and laws of the Creole community, Mademoiselle Reisz is a renegade, self-assertive and outspoken. She has no patience with petty social rules and violates the most basic expectations of femininity. To a rake like Arobin, she is so unattractive, unpleasant, and unwomanly as to seem "partially demented" (Chap. 27). Even Edna occasionally perceives Mademoiselle Reisz's awkwardness as a kind of deformity, and is sometimes offended by the old woman's candor and is not sure whether she likes her.

Yet despite her eccentricities, Mademoiselle Reisz seems "to reach Edna's spirit and set it free" (Chap. 26). Her voice in the novel seems to speak for the author's view of art and for the artist. It is surely no accident, for example, that it is Chopin's music that Mademoiselle Reisz performs. At the *pension* on Grand Isle, the pianist first plays a Chopin prelude, to which Edna responds with surprising turbulence: "the very passions themselves were aroused within her soul, swaying it, lashing it, as the waves daily beat upon her splendid body. She trembled, she was choking, and the tears blinded her" (Chap. 9). "Chopin" becomes the code word for a world of repressed passion between Edna and Robert that Mademoiselle Reisz controls. Later the pianist plays a Chopin impromptu for Edna that Robert has admired; this time the music is "strange and fantastic—turbulent, plaintive and soft with entreaty" (Chap. 21). These references to "Chopin" in the text are on one level allusions to an intimate, romantic, and poignant musical *oeuvre* that reinforces the novel's sensual atmosphere. But on another level, they function as what Nancy K. Miller has called the "internal female signature" in women's writing, here a literary punning signature that alludes to Kate Chopin's ambitions as an artist and to the emotions she wished her book to arouse in its readers.[3]

Chopin's career represented one important aesthetic model for his literary namesake. As a girl, Kate Chopin had been a talented musician, and her first published story, "Wiser than a God," was about a woman concert pianist who refused to marry. Moreover, Chopin's music both stylistically and thematically influences the language and form of *The Awakening*. The structure of the impromptu, in which there is an opening presentation of a theme, a contrasting middle section, and a modified return to the melodic and rhythmic materials of the opening section, parallels the narrative form of *The Awakening*. The composer's techniques of unifying his work through the repetition of musical phrases, his experiments with harmony and dissonance, his use of folk motifs, his effects of frustration and delayed resolution can also be compared to Kate Chopin's repetition of sentences, her juxtaposition of realism and impressionism, her incorporation of local color elements, and her rejection of conventional closure. Like that of the composer's impromptu, Chopin's style seems spontaneous and improvised, but it is in fact carefully designed and executed.[4]

Madame Ratignolle and Mademoiselle Reisz not only represent important alternative roles and influences for Edna in the world of the novel, but as the proto-heroines of sentimental and local color fiction, they also suggest different plots and conclusions. Adele's story suggests that Edna will give up her rebellion, return to her marriage, have another baby, and by degrees learn to appreciate, love, and even desire her husband. Such was the plot of many late-nineteenth-century sentimental novels about erring young women married to older men, such as Susan Warner's *Diana* (1880) and Louisa May Alcott's *Moods* (1882). Mademoiselle Reisz's story suggests that Edna will lose her beauty, her youth, her husband, and children—everything, in short, but her art and her pride—and become a kind of New Orleans nun.

Chopin wished to reject both of these endings and to escape from the literary traditions they represented; but her own literary solitude, her resistance to allying herself with a specific ideological or aesthetic position, made it impossible for her to work out something different and new. Edna remains very much entangled in her own emotions and moods, rather than moving beyond them to real self-understanding and to an awareness of her relationship to her society. She alternates between two moods of "intoxication" and "languor," expansive states of activity, optimism, and power and passive states of contemplation, despondency, and sexual thralldom. Edna feels intoxicated when she is assertive and in control. She first experiences such exultant feelings when she confides her history to Adele Ratignolle and again when she learns how to swim: "intoxicated with her newly conquered power," she swims out too far. She is excited when she gambles successfully for high stakes at the race track, and finally she feels an "intoxication of expectancy" about awakening Robert with a seductive kiss and playing the dominant role with him. But these emotional peaks are countered by equally intense moods of depression, reverie, or stupor. At the worst, these are states of "indescribable oppression," "vague anguish," or "hopeless ennui." At best, they are moments of passive sensuality in which Edna feels drugged; Arobin's lips and hands, for example, act "like a narcotic upon her" (Chap. 25).

Edna welcomes both kinds of feelings because they are intense, and thus preserve her from the tedium of ordinary existence. They are in fact adolescent emotions, suitable to a heroine who is belatedly awakening; but Edna does not go beyond them to an adulthood that offers new experiences or responsibilities. In her relationships with men, she both longs for complete and romantic fusion with a fantasy lover and is unprepared to share her life with another person.

Chopin's account of the Pontellier marriage, for example, shows Edna's tacit collusion in a sexual bargain that allows her to keep to herself. Although she thinks of her marriage to a paternalistic man twelve years her senior as "purely an accident," the text makes it clear that Edna has married Leonce primarily to secure a fatherly protector who will not make too many domestic, emotional, or sexual demands on her. She is "fond of her husband," with "no trace of passion or excessive and fictitious warmth" (Chap. 7). They do not have an interest in each other's activities or thoughts, and have agreed to a complete separation of their social spheres; Leonce is fully absorbed by the business, social, and sexual activities of the male sphere, the city, Carondelet Street, Klein's Hotel at Grand Isle, where he gambles, and especially the New Orleans world of the clubs and the red-light district. Even Adele Ratignolle warns Edna of the risks of Mr. Pontellier's club life and of the "diversion" he finds there. "It's a pity Mr. Pontellier doesn't stay home more in the evenings," she tells Edna. "I think you would be more—well, if you don't mind my saying it—more united, if he did." "Oh! dear no!" Edna responds, "with a blank look in her eyes. 'What should I do if he stayed home? We wouldn't have anything to say to each other' " (Chap. 23). Edna gets this blank look in her eyes—eyes that are originally described as "quick and bright"—whenever she is confronted with something she does not want to see. When she joins the Ratignolles at home together, Edna does not envy them, although, as the author remarks, "if ever the fusion of two human beings into one has been accomplished on this sphere it was surely in their union" (Chap. 18). Instead, she is moved by pity for Adele's "colorless existence which never uplifted its possessor beyond the region of blind contentment" (Chap. 18).

Nonetheless, Edna does not easily relinquish her fantasy of rhapsodic oneness with a perfect lover. She imagines that such a union will bring permanent ecstasy; it will lead, not simply to "domestic harmony" like that of the Ratignolles, but to "life's delirium" (Chap. 18). In her story of the woman who paddles away with her lover in a pirogue and is never heard of again, Edna elaborates on her vision as she describes the lovers, "close together, rapt in oblivious forgetfulness, drifting into the unknown" (Chap. 23). Although her affair with Arobin shocks her into an awareness of her own sexual passions, it leaves her illusions about love intact. Desire, she understands, can exist independently of love. But love retains its magical aura; indeed, her sexual awakening with Arobin generates an even "fiercer, more overpowering love" for Robert (Chap. 28). And when Robert comes back, Edna has persuaded herself that the force of their love will overwhelm all obstacles: "We shall be everything to each other. Nothing else in the world is of any consequence" (Chap. 36). Her intention seems to be that they will go off together into the unknown, like the lovers in her story. But Robert cannot accept such a role, and when he leaves her, Edna finally realizes "that the day would come when he, too, and the thought of him would melt out of her existence, leaving her alone" (Chap. 39).

The other side of Edna's terror of solitude, however, is the bondage of class as well as gender that keeps her in a prison of the self. She goes blank too whenever she might be expected to notice the double standard of ladylike privilege and oppression of women in southern society. Floating along in her "mazes of inward contemplation," Edna barely notices the silent quadroon nurse who takes care of her children, the little black girl who works the treadles of Madame Lebrun's sewing machine, the laundress who keeps her in frilly white, or the maid who picks up her broken glass. She never makes connections between her lot and theirs.

The scene in which Edna witnesses Adele in childbirth (Chap. 37) is the first time in the novel that she identifies with another woman's pain, and draws some halting conclusions about the female and the human condition, rather than simply about her own ennui. Edna's births have taken place in unconsciousness; when she goes to Adele's childbed, "her own like experiences seemed far away, unreal, and only half remembered. She recalled faintly an ecstasy of pain, the heavy odor of chloroform, a stupor which had deadened sensation" (Chap. 37). The stupor that deadens sensation is an apt metaphor for the real and imaginary narcotics supplied by fantasy, money, and patriarchy, which have protected Edna from pain for most of her life, but which have also kept her from becoming an adult.

But in thinking of nature's trap for women, Edna never moves from her own questioning to the larger social statement that is feminism. Her ineffectuality is partly a product of her time; as a heroine in transition between the homosocial and the heterosexual worlds, Edna has lost some of the sense of connectedness to other women that might help her plan her future. Though she has sojourned in the "female colony" of Grand Isle, it is far from being a feminist utopia, a real community of women, in terms of sisterhood. The novel suggests, in fact, something of the historical loss for women of transferring the sense of self to relationships with men.

Edna's solitude is one of the reasons that her emancipation does not take her very far. Despite her efforts to escape the rituals of femininity, Edna seems fated to reenact them, even though, as Chopin recounts these scenes, she satirizes and revises their conventions. Ironically, considering her determination to discard the trappings of her role as a society matron—her wedding ring, her "reception day," her "charming home"—the high point of Edna's awakening is the dinner party she gives for her twenty-ninth birthday. Edna's birthday party begins like a kind of drawing-room comedy. We are told the guest list, the seating plan, the menu, and the table setting; some of the guests are boring, and some do not like each other; Madame Ratignolle does not show up at the last minute, and Mademoiselle Reisz makes disagreeable remarks in French.

Yet as it proceeds to its bacchanalian climax, the dinner party also has a symbolic intensity and resonance that makes it, as Sandra Gilbert argues, Edna's "most authentic act of self-definition."[5] Not only is the twenty-ninth birthday a feminine threshold, the passage from youth to middle age, but Edna is literally on the threshold of a new life in her little house. The dinner, as Arobin remarks, is a *coup d'état,* an overthrow of her marriage, all the more an act of aggression because Leonce will pay the bills. Moreover, she has created an atmosphere of splendor and luxury that seems to exceed the requirements of the occasion. The table is set with gold satin, Sevres china, crystal, silver, and gold; there is "champagne to swim in" (Chap. 29), and Edna is magnificently dressed in a satin and lace gown, with a cluster of diamonds (a gift from Leonce) in her hair. Presiding at the head of the table, she seems powerful and autonomous: "There was something in her attitude [. . .] which suggested the regal woman, the one who rules, who looks on, who stands alone" (Chap. 30). Edna's moment of mastery thus takes place in the context of a familiar ceremony of women's culture. Indeed, dinner parties are virtual set pieces of feminist aesthetics, suggesting that the hostess is a kind of artist in her own sphere, someone whose creativity is channeled into the production of social and domestic harmony. Like Virginia Woolf's Mrs. Ramsay in *To the Lighthouse,* Edna exhausts herself in creating a sense of fellowship at her table, although in the midst of her guests she still experiences an "acute longing" for "the unattainable" (Chap. 30).

But there is a gap between the intensity of Edna's desire, a desire that by now has gone beyond sexual fulfillment to take in a much vaster range of metaphysical longings, and the means that she has to express herself. Edna may look like a queen, but she is still a housewife. The political and aesthetic weapons she has in her *coup d'état* are only forks and knives, glasses and dresses.

Can Edna, and Kate Chopin, then, escape from confining traditions only in death? Some critics have seen Edna's much-debated suicide as a heroic embrace of independence and a symbolic resurrection into myth, a feminist counterpart of Melville's Bulkington: "Take heart, take heart, O Edna, up from the spray of thy ocean-perishing, up, straight up, leaps thy apotheosis!" But the ending too seems to return Edna to the nineteenth-century female literary tradition, even though Chopin redefines it for her own purpose. Readers of the 1890s were well accustomed to drowning as the fictional punishment for female transgression against morality, and most contemporary critics of *The Awakening* thus automatically interpreted Edna's suicide as the wages of sin.

Drowning itself brings to mind metaphorical analogies between femininity and liquidity. As the female body is prone to wetness, blood, milk, tears, and amniotic fluid, so in drowning the woman is immersed in the feminine organic element. Drowning thus becomes the traditionally feminine literary death.[6] And Edna's last thoughts further recycle significant images of the feminine from her past. As exhaustion overpowers her, "Edna heard her father's voice and her sister Margaret's. She heard the barking of an old dog that was chained to the sycamore tree. The spurs of the cavalry officer clanged as he walked across the porch. There was the hum of bees, and the musky odor of pinks filled the air" (Chap. 39). Edna's memories are those of awakening from the freedom of childhood to the limitations conferred by female sexuality.

The image of the bees and the flowers not only recalls early descriptions of Edna's sexuality as a "sensitive blossom," but also places *The Awakening* firmly within the traditions of American women's writing, where it is a standard trope for the unequal sexual relations between women and men. Margaret Fuller, for example, writes in her journal: "Woman is the flower, man the bee. She sighs out of melodious fragrance, and invites the winged laborer. He drains her cup, and carries off the honey. She dies on the stalk; he returns to the hive, well fed, and praised as an active member of the community."[7] In post–Civil War fiction, the image is a reminder of an elemental power that women's culture must confront. *The Awakening* seems particularly to echo the last lines of Mary Wilkins Freeman's "A New England Nun," in which the heroine, having broken her long-standing engagement, is free to continue her solitary life, and closes her door on "the sounds of the busy harvest of men and birds and bees; there were halloos, metallic clatterings, sweet calls, long hummings."[8] These are the images of a nature that, Edna has learned, decoys women into slavery; yet even in drowning, she cannot escape from their seductiveness, for to ignore their claim is also to cut oneself off from culture, from the "humming" life of creation and achievement.

We can re-create the literary tradition in which Kate Chopin wrote *The Awakening,* but of course, we can never know how the tradition might have changed if her novel had not had to wait half a century to find its audience. Few of Chopin's literary contemporaries came into contact with the book. Chopin's biographer, Per Seyersted, notes that her work "was apparently unknown to Dreiser, even though he began writing *Sister Carrie* just when *The Awakening* was being loudly condemned. Also Ellen Glasgow, who was at this time beginning to describe unsatisfactory marriages, seems to have been unaware of the author's existence. Indeed, we can safely say that though she was so much of an innovator in American literature, she was virtually unknown by those who were now to shape it and that she had no influence on them."[9] Ironically, even Willa Cather, the one woman writer of the *fin-de-siècle* who reviewed *The Awakening,* not only failed to recognize its importance but also dismissed its theme as "trite."[10] It would be decades before another American woman novelist combined Kate Chopin's artistic maturity with her sophisticated outlook on sexuality, and overcame both the sentimental codes of feminine "artlessness" and the sexual codes of feminine "passionlessness."

In terms of Chopin's own literary development, there were signs that *The Awakening* would have been a pivotal work. While it was in press, she wrote one of her finest and most daring short stories, "The Storm," which surpasses even *The Awakening* in terms of its expressive freedom. Chopin was also being drawn back to a rethinking of women's culture. Her last poem, written in 1900, was addressed to Kitty Garesché and spoke of the permanence of emotional bonds between women:

To the Friend of My Youth

It is not all of life
To cling together while the years glide past.
It is not all of love
To walk with clasped hands from the first to last.
That mystic garland which the spring did twine
Of scented lilac and the new-blown rose,
Faster than chains will hold my soul to thine
Thro' joy, and grief, thro' life—unto its close.[11]

We have only these tantalizing fragments to hint at the directions Chopin's work might have taken if *The Awakening* had been a critical success or even a *succès de scandale,* and if her career had not been cut off by her early death. The fate of *The Awakening* shows only too well how a literary tradition may be enabling, even essential, as well as confining. Struggling to escape from tradition, Kate Chopin courageously risked social and literary ostracism. It is up to contemporary readers to restore her solitary book to its place in our literary heritage.

Notes

1. Henry James, November 26, 1892, quoted in Larzer Ziff, *The American 1890s* (New York: Viking, 1966), p. 275.

2. Sandra Gilbert, "Introduction" to *The Awakening and Selected Stories* (Harmondsworth: Penguin, 1984), p. 25.

3. Thanks to Nancy K. Miller of Barnard College for this phrase from her current work on the development of women's writing in France. I am also indebted to the insights of Cheryl Torsney of the University of West Virginia, and to the comments of the other participants of my NEH Seminar on "Women's Writing and Women's Culture," Summer 1984.

4. Thanks to Lynne Rogers, Music Department, Princeton University, for information about Frédéric Chopin.

5. Gilbert, "Introduction," p. 30.

6. See Gaston Bachelard, *L'eau et les rêves* (Paris, 1942), pp. 109–25.

7. Margaret Fuller, "Life Without and Life Within," quoted in Bell G. Chevigny, *The Woman and the Myth* (Old Westbury, N.Y.: Feminist Press, 1976), p. 349. See also Wendy Martin, *An American Triptych: Anne Bradstreet, Emily Dickinson, Adrienne Rich* (Chapel Hill: University of North Carolina Press, 1984), pp. 154–59.

8. "A New England Nun," in Mary Wilkins Freeman, *The Revolt of Mother,* ed. Michele Clark (New York: Feminist Press, 1974), p. 97.

9. Per Seyersted, *Kate Chopin: A Critical Biography* (New York: Octagon Books, 1980), p. 196.

10. "Sibert" [Willa Cather], "Books and Magazines," *Pittsburgh Leader* (July 8, 1899), in Norton Critical Edition, p. 153.

11. Kate Chopin, in *The Complete Works of Kate Chopin,* ed. Per Sey-ersted (Baton Rouge: Louisiana State University Press, 1969), Vol. II, p. 735.

✦

CHARACTERS AS FOILS TO EDNA*

BARBARA H. SOLOMON

***One of the most fertile topics for . . . exploration in Kate Chopin's *The Awakening* is the author's brilliant use of major and mi-nor characters as foils for Edna Pontellier. As Edna undergoes a cri-sis, during her twenty-eighth year, in which her previous identity as Léonce Pontellier's submissive and passionless wife is transformed into that of a rebellious, passionate neophyte artist, she consciously judges the women around her, especially Adèle Ratignolle and Mlle Reisz, as she seeks to understand her own needs and actions. But in addition to the substantial depictions of these two characters, Chopin sketches a series of impressionistic portraits of minor char-acters who dramatize Edna's problems and options. These foils range from the shadowy pair of lovers who are vacationing at Grand Isle and who never speak to any of the other guests to the sensual and provocative Mariequita and, back in New Orleans, the sophisticated Mrs. Highcamp. Though each is very different, all share an important dramatic role. Through their attitudes or be-havior, they illuminate the inevitable results of certain ideas and choices that occur to Edna at various times.

The lovers who appear early in the novel are always pictured by Chopin as backdrop figures. They live for each other, leaving when other characters appear and eschewing the life of the com-munity of families that has grown up around Mrs. Lebrun's hotel.

* From *Approaches to Teaching Chopin's "The Awakening,"* ed. Bernard Koloski (New York: Modern Language Association of America, 1988), pp. 114–17. Reprinted by permission of the Modern Language Association of America.

Chopin emphasizes their isolation with descriptions such as the following:

> The lovers were just entering the grounds of the *pension*. They were leaning toward each other as the water-oaks bent from the sea. There was not a particle of earth beneath their feet. Their heads might have been turned upside-down, so absolutely did they tread upon blue ether. (Chap. 8)

When, late in the novel, Edna declares to Robert that she cares nothing for Léonce Pontellier and suggests that she and Robert will be able to be together, she is, in fact, suggesting that they should turn their backs on the community of family and friends who would be scandalized by such a liaison. Edna believes, or wants to believe, that she and Robert can live for each other without concern for anybody else. Her dream can be summarized by that most romantic phrase, giving up "all for love." But the relationship that Edna proposes must lead to their alienation from the comfortable Creole world to which both now very much belong. They would indeed become like the insubstantial lovers who exclude themselves from the activities of the world.

Next, two portraits of women instruct the reader about the limitations of Edna's choices. The first, Mariequita, is the "young barefooted Spanish girl" who makes the boat trip from Grand Isle to the Chênière Caminada with Edna and Robert on the Sunday when they spend the entire day together. Chopin describes her physical appearance in some detail:

> She had a round, sly, piquant face and pretty black eyes. Her hands were small, and she kept them folded over the handle of her basket. Her feet were broad and coarse. She did not strive to hide them. Edna looked at her feet, and noticed the sand and slime between her brown toes. (Chap. 12)

Edna's obvious curiosity makes Mariequita self-conscious. There is a frankly sensual quality about this girl, who knows Robert and begins to question him. When Mariequita asks whether Edna is Robert's "sweetheart," he responds, "She's a married lady, and has two children." His answer clearly begs the question, one that Robert probably has not yet asked himself. But Mariequita's rejoinder comically prefigures the serious situation that Robert and Edna must face. "Oh! well!" she says, "Francisco ran away with Sylvano's wife, who had four children. They took all his money and one of the children and stole his boat" (Chap. 12). Ironically, only a few minutes later, Robert tells Edna about his plan of patching and trimming his own boat, fantasizing that he and she can go sailing together "some night in the pirogue when the moon shines." But Edna could never adopt Mariequita's casual attitude toward marriage and infidelity, much as she struggles to escape the consequences of her unfortunate marriage to Léonce. Edna may not care whether her behavior hurts her husband, but she is haunted by her fear of the harm she might cause her small sons, Etienne and Raoul.

In the final chapter Mariequita reappears just before Edna's arrival at Grand Isle. Fearing that Victor may be in love with Edna, she attempts to make him jealous. She threatens to abandon him to his fine lady friends and brags about her own attractiveness: "There were a dozen men crazy about her at the Chênière; and since it was the fashion to be in love with married people, why she could run away any time she liked to New Orleans with Célina's husband" (Chap. 39). Mariequita's comments point up the contrast in the two women's attitudes, emphasizing the sense of entrapment that Edna increasingly comes to feel as the novel progresses.

A much more sophisticated woman, Mrs. James Highcamp serves as a second foil who dramatizes the impossibility of a certain kind of future for Edna. Early in the novel, when Léonce notices Mrs. Highcamp's calling card among the other cards of the visitors who had paid a call on one of Edna's Tuesdays at home (only to find her out for the afternoon), he comments, "[T]he less you have to do with Mrs. Highcamp, the better." Significantly, when Léonce is away and Edna has begun to live as she pleases, without regard for her husband's ideas, Edna becomes somewhat friendly with this acquaintance, dining at her house and attending the races with her and Alcée Arobin. Chopin portrays Mrs. Highcamp as a wife and mother who flirts with attractive men and makes a mockery of her marriage: "Mrs. Highcamp was a worldly but unaffected, intelligent, slim, tall blonde in the forties, with an indifferent manner and blue eyes that stared. She had a daughter who served her as a pretext for cultivating the society of young men of fashion" (Chap. 25).

At the birthday dinner that Edna gives just before leaving Léonce's house for her "pigeon house," Mrs. Highcamp is seated next to Victor Lebrun. Chopin describes her demeanor: "Her attention was never for a moment withdrawn from him after seating herself at table; and when he turned to Mrs. Merriman, who was prettier and more vivacious than Mrs. Highcamp, she waited with easy indifference for an opportunity to reclaim his attention" (Chap. 30).

During the course of the evening's festivities, she weaves a garland of yellow and red roses that she places on Victor's head; then she drapes her white silk scarf gracefully around him. When Mrs. Highcamp encourages Victor to sing, he chooses the song that Edna associates with her love for Robert. As Mrs. Highcamp departs, she invites Victor to call on her daughter, ostensibly so that the two young people can enjoy speaking French and singing French songs together. Victor responds that he intends to visit Mrs. Highcamp "at the first opportunity which presented itself." Obviously, under the guise of providing company for her daughter, Mrs. Highcamp intends to pursue this young man for her own needs. Even Edna recognizes the intensity of his physical attractiveness as he apologizes to her for his behavior "with caressing eyes" and a kiss that "was like a pleasing sting to her hand" (Chap. 30).

Edna specifically rejects Mrs. Highcamp's way of life in the closing passages of the novel after she realizes that Robert will not return because of his Creole code of honor concerning infidelity and adultery. Without Robert, she visualizes a pattern for satisfying her sensual needs that the reader recognizes might well parallel Mrs. Highcamp's behavior with men: "[Edna] had said over and over to herself: 'To-day it is Arobin; to-morrow it will be some one else. It makes no difference to me, it doesn't matter about Léonce Pontellier—but Raoul and Etienne!' " (Chap. 39). Having experienced passion and being unwilling to lead a life deprived of such experiences, Edna is also unwilling to lead a life of barely concealed subterfuge such as that of Mrs. Highcamp. . . .

✦

"𝒜 GREEN AND 𝒴ELLOW 𝒫ARROT . . ."*

JOYCE DYER

✳✳✳In the early chapters of *The Awakening* Chopin prepares us symbolically to understand that Edna Pontellier will try to find her own way, will try to abandon the unconscious imitation that has too often, and for too long, determined how she has lived. Edna Pontellier spends the last seasons of her life searching for knowledge of herself. She hopes, she says, "to realize her position in the universe as a human being, and to recognize her relations as an individual to the world within and about her" (p. 23).

Although Edna does not find all the answers some critics have wished she might find, she begins to understand herself in a way that moves us and that predicts future examinations of women's roles in the history and literature of the twentieth century.

A green and yellow parrot appears in the first line of the book. Although Chopin refers to the bird as "he"—perhaps a deliberately ironic touch (Chopin knows from her first sentence that the spirits of men and women are really not so different)—scholars seldom interpret "his" situation as anything but female. Wendy Martin, for example, sees him as a symbol of domesticity, a wild bird "tamed for the amusement of the household."[1] As such a symbol, he becomes part of a symbol pattern that had been historically very common in women's literature. . . .

Ellen Moers discusses the traditional use of bird imagery in the literature of women writers in her *Literary Women: The Great Writers* (1976) and mentions Chopin. She finds a striking absence of references in literature by women of what she calls "the nesting-bird for

* From Joyce Dyer, *The Awakening: A Novel of Beginnings* (New York: Twayne Publishers, 1993), pp. 33–42. Excerpted with permission of Twayne Publishers, an imprint of Simon & Schuster Macmillan. Copyright © 1993 by Twayne Publishers.

motherhood"; modern writers, she contends, know that "birds are frightening and monstrous as well as tiny and sweet." Monstrous or fearsome birds commonly enter "the grotesqueries of modern women's literature," according to Moers.

Moers notices the presence of the nesting-bird in Chopin's description of Adèle Ratignolle, and "the bitterness with which it is used to imply rejection of the maternal role."[2] We ourselves cannot help sensing this "bitterness" as we read through Chopin's description of Adèle: "It was easy to know them, fluttering about with extended, protecting wings when any harm, real or imaginary, threatened their precious brood. They were women who idolized their children, worshiped their husbands, and esteemed it a holy privilege to efface themselves as individuals and grow wings as ministering angels" (pp. 14–15). Women in the Creole community could have wings, but not for flight. Their wings were the holy wings of loving service to husband and children.

Chopin's selection of the parrot to hint at Edna's dilemma has significance beyond its representation of her caged condition, however.[3] First, unlike other caged birds Chopin might have selected, the parrot (probably a yellow-naped Amazon, though the makers of the film *Grand Isle* chose a macaw) imitates what it hears. Seyersted calls the parrot and the mockingbird "caged imitators, the one repeating its master's words, the other echoing the voice of other species."[4] Symbolically, Chopin's parrot emphasizes the force and prevalence of imitation in society. Chopin's parrot speaks the language of the cosmopolitan New Orleans visitors who reside at Grand Isle in the summers. He speaks Spanish and French and English—but also, significantly, "a language which nobody understood" (p. 3).

The parrot's language, then, is important symbolically not only because it represents Edna's tendency to imitate, but also because it hints at the need to discover and form new linguistic (and behavioral) patterns once mimicked speech has been discarded. Michael Gilmore describes the parrot as a "key symbol" in understanding Edna's desire for "authentic language." He observes that as Edna becomes less and less inhibited, less and less a mimic of those around her, she begins "to utter sentiments unintelligible to her companions," sentiments, for example, about a willingness to sacrifice her life for her children—but not to sacrifice herself. Patricia Yaeger, using Jacques Lacan and Michel Foucault, even suggests that the parrot "inhabits a multilingual culture and suggests the babble and lyricism bred by mixing world views."[5]

Like the parrot, most of us live and speak by imitation, as do most of the characters in *The Awakening*. So how will we know how to speak, or what to say, when we have only ourselves to listen to? And should we somehow miraculously be able to find the words and language that are ours, will anyone be able to understand us? Will we ourselves be able to translate our words into meaningful patterns, patterns of both speech and action?

For a parrot, and for a human being, freedom is not an easy matter. Like the domesticated parrot in the novel, Edna is vulnerable when she is free. She has been cared for too long by an owner and taught a language not her own. Also like a parrot, Edna has had her wings clipped so often that she will spend all of her remaining days trying to recover the strength and imagination it takes to soar.

Here, and in her other writing, the unattractive or comic depiction of the parrot reinforces Chopin's belief that imitation in our lives is detestable. The parrot represents Edna before she awakens: had she remained like the parrot, Chopin would undoubtedly have seen her as pathetic rather than sympathetic. . . .

In chapter 1 we are introduced to the Farival twins. The twin motif is another image of imitative behavior that, ironically, is also repeated throughout the book. Immediately after we are told that Léonce Pontellier hears the sound of "the chattering and whistling birds . . . still at it" (p. 4), another noise from the main building is described. "Two young girls," Chopin writes, "the Farival twins, were playing a duet from 'Zampa' upon the piano." Here the juxtaposition between the parrot and the twins, a juxtaposition that will appear again, is first introduced. The twins play two duets over and over: "The Poet and the Peasant" by Franz von Suppé, and "Zampa," an opera by Louis Hérold that, as Culley notes in an annotation, significantly records a romantic death at sea. It is no coincidence that the performances of these pieces by the twins occur in the main building—the building where the summer guests eat and where, very appropriately, the parrot resides outside the door, like a sentinel. The twins soon become tiresome to the residents of the community, and to us.

In chapter 9, in the account of the party that precedes Edna's mystical and dangerous moonlight swim—a party at which the twins again repeat their two pieces—we hear more about them. Chopin describes them always as a pair, never differentiating between them. . . .

Immediately after the twins' program is announced, Chopin ends a paragraph. The first line of her new paragraph registers what appears, very ironically, to be the parrot's own annoyance with the twins: *"Allez vous-en! Sapristi!"* (Go away! For God's sake!) the bird shrieks. "He was the only being present who possessed sufficient candor to admit that he was not listening to these gracious performances for the first time that summer" (p. 40), Chopin humorously tells us.

Later that evening everyone dances except the Farival twins. Their inability to separate from each other has literally immobilized them, keeping them from pleasure, possibility, and promise. "Almost every one danced but the twins, who could not be induced to separate during the brief period when one or the other should be whirling around the room in the arms of a man. They might have danced together, but they did not think of it" (p. 41). Their preference for imitation of each other rather than for individual growth makes them incapable of imagination. It is not surprising that their repertoire consists of only two pieces. . . .

We know early in the novel that Chopin is attempting to show that Edna has potential to be "different" from the crowd. Physically, she lacks the stereotypical, fashion-plate beauty of an Adèle Ratignolle, the quintessential Creole woman. . . .

What seems most important about Edna's face is that it hints at intelligence and depth. The eyebrows are distinctive, but primarily because they "[emphasize] the depth of her eyes" (p. 7). Unlike Adèle's features, Edna's cannot be captured through worn-out and unsurprising similes like sapphires, spun-gold, and cherries. The language that describes her, like the woman herself, is necessarily more complex and abstract: her face displays, for example, "a certain frankness of expression," "a contradictory subtle play of features" (p. 7). We are told in chapter 7 that "a casual and indiscriminating observer, in passing, might not cast a second glance upon the figure. But with more feeling and discernment he would have recognized the noble beauty of its modeling, and the graceful severity of poise and movement, which made Edna Pontellier different from the crowd" (p. 26). . . .

Edna, as we quickly discover, refuses to be a parrot, or a twin, or a representative mother-woman like her friend Adèle Ratignolle. Through the abundant irony Chopin brings to each of these images, we understand that Edna's refusal to imitate is correct and important. She will begin questioning the many assumptions her life has been built upon. She will examine more closely the domestic cage she has occupied. It has been a cage not unlike the one Mary Ryan uses as a prevailing historical metaphor in *Womanhood in America*: "invisible to the untrained eye, disguised by inviting draperies, perhaps even lined with little rewards and comforts."

The image of the cage was present in "Emancipation," Chopin's first story, which was unpublished during her lifetime and in fact bears no date (though it was probably composed, according to Seyersted, in late 1869 or early 1870). The cage houses a large, sleek animal, and it opens one day by accident. The animal is clearly in greater danger outside the boundaries of his narrow world (though, we should notice, his danger is not as great as a parrot's would be), but Chopin applauds the risk of freedom. He rushes ahead, "heedless that he is wounding and tearing his sleek sides—seeing, smelling, touching of all things; even stopping to put his lips to the noxious pool, thinking it may be sweet." She concludes, "So does he live, seeking, finding, joying and suffering. The door which accident had opened is open still, but the cage remains forever empty!"[6]

The cage door in *The Awakening*, however, is a little different from the one in Chopin's very early allegory. It opens not by accident but through the persistence and courage of Edna Pontellier herself.

Notes

1. Wendy Martin, introduction to Martin, *New Essays,* 25; hereafter cited in the text.

2. Ellen Moers, *Literary Women* (New York: Doubleday & Co., 1976), 247.

3. Flaubert uses the parrot image in yet another way in *"Un coeur simple"*: as a symbol of sublimation. As Peter James Petersen points out, Chopin's "The White Eagle" (1900) is "reminiscent of Flaubert's *'un coeur simple,'* in which a woman who is systematically deprived of human contact sublimates all her longings in her relationship to a parrot, which is stuffed after she dies" ("The Fiction of Kate Chopin," Ph.D. diss., The University of New Mexico, 1972, 263). I discuss additional aspects of the eagle's ambiguity in my article, entitled "A Note on Kate Chopin's 'The White Eagle,' " *Arizona Quarterly* 40, no. 2 (Summer 1984), 189–92.

4. Gregory L. Candela discusses elaborate parallels between Chopin's use of the mockingbird and Whitman's in "Walt Whitman and Kate Chopin: A Further Connection," *Walt Whitman Review* 24, no. 4 (December 1978): 163–65.

5. Patricia S. Yaeger, " 'A Language Which Nobody Understood': Emancipatory Strategies in *The Awakening,*" *Novel: A Forum on Fiction* 20, no. 3 (Spring 1987): 203.

6. Kate Chopin, "Emancipation: A Life Fable," in *Complete Works,* vol. 1, 37–38.

Appendix B

✦

Perspectives on Kate Chopin

Chronology and Writings *(compiled by Emily Toth)*
    I. Chronology of Kate Chopin's Life
    II. Kate Chopin's Writings

Kate Chopin on Writing
    "Speaking of Editors"
    "In the Confidence of a Story-Writer"
    "Why Do I Write?"

Biographical Essays
    "An American Pioneer Writer"
    Per Seyersted

    "Kate Chopin: Spanning a Lifetime"
    Susie Mee

Katherine O'Flaherty (Kate Chopin)
CDV photograph by J. J. Scholten, 1869
Courtesy of Missouri Historical Society, St. Louis

Chronology and Writings*

◆

I

Chronology of Kate Chopin's Life

1850—MID-1870—ST. LOUIS

February 8, 1850—birth of Catherine [birth name] O'Flaherty—first home: Eighth Street between Chouteau and Gratiot

Fall 1855—Kate O'Flaherty enrolls in Academy of the Sacred Heart (which she attends sporadically for the next thirteen years), becomes friends with Kitty Garesché

November 1, 1855—death of Thomas O'Flaherty (father) in railroad accident

January 16, 1863—death of Victoire Verdon Charleville (great-grandmother and teacher)

February 17, 1863—death of George O'Flaherty (half-brother), a Confederate soldier

1863—banishment of Kitty Garesché and her family

1865–1866—Kate's family moves to 1118 St. Ange Avenue

Fall 1865—Kate attends the Academy of the Visitation, then returns to Sacred Heart Academy

1867–1870—keeps commonplace book: diary, extracts from authors, original poem ("The Congé"), reactions to flirting and other social obligations

* From Emily Toth, *Kate Chopin: A Life of the Author of The Awakening* (New York: William Morrow and Company, 1990), pp. 409-21. Copyright © 1990 by Emily Toth. All rights reserved. Reprinted by permission of Emily Toth.

June 29, 1868—graduation from Sacred Heart Academy

1869—writes "Emancipation: a Life Fable," unpublished

March–May 1869—visits New Orleans

April 15, 1870—death of Julia Benoist Chopin, Oscar Chopin's mother

June 9, 1870—marriage to Oscar Chopin of Louisiana, Holy Angels Church, St. Louis

June–September 1870—European honeymoon, keeps honeymoon diary in commonplace book

MID-1870–MID-1879——NEW ORLEANS

New Orleans homes: 443 Magazine Street; northeast corner Pitt & Constantinople; 209 (now 1413) Louisiana Avenue

November 14, 1870—death of Dr. J. B. Chopin

May 22, 1871—son Jean Baptiste born in New Orleans, baptized in St. Louis in August

September 24, 1873—son Oscar Charles born in St. Louis, baptized in St. Louis

December 27, 1873—Thomas O'Flaherty (brother) killed in buggy accident, St. Louis

September 14, 1874—Oscar in Battle of Liberty Place, with White League and associated companies, New Orleans

October 28, 1874—son George Francis born in St. Louis, baptized in St. Louis

January 26, 1876—son Frederick born in New Orleans (no baptismal record)

January 8, 1878—son Felix Andrew born in New Orleans (no baptismal record)

LATE 1879–MID-1884——CLOUTIERVILLE ("CLOOCHYVILLE") IN NATCHITOCHES ("NAK-I-TUSH") PARISH, LOUISIANA

December 31, 1879—daughter Lélia born in Cloutierville, baptized Marie Laïza in Cloutierville

December 10, 1882—death of Oscar Chopin

—romance with Albert Sampite

mid-1884—Kate Chopin's return to St. Louis

MID-1884–1904—ST. LOUIS

1884–1885—lives at 1125 St. Ange Avenue, then 1122 St. Ange

June 28, 1885—death of Eliza O'Flaherty

1886—moves to 3317 Morgan Street (now Delmar)

June 1887—first Cloutierville visit since Oscar's death

1888—"Lilia. Polka for Piano" published

1888—writes first draft of what becomes "A No-Account Creole"

May 24, 1888—Loca Sampite leaves Albert Sampite

Sept. 24, 1888—Loca Sampite sues for legal separation from her husband

1888–1889—Chopin works on "Unfinished Story—Grand Isle"

January 10, 1889—first literary publication: "If It Might Be" (poem)

April 24, 1889—Kate brings Oscar's body back to St. Louis from Cloutierville

April 30, 1889—Loca Sampite's suit for separation dismissed

June 1889—Chopin writes "Wiser than a God"

July 5, 1889—begins writing *At Fault*

August 1889—writes "A Point at Issue!"

October 27, 1889—first short-story publication: "A Point at Issue!" *St. Louis Post-Dispatch*

December 1889—"Wiser than a God" published in *Philadelphia Musical Journal*

September 1890—*At Fault* published at Chopin's expense

December 1890—becomes charter member of Wednesday Club

June 1891—John A. Dillon moves to New York

August 19, 1891—Loca Sampite's legal separation from Albert Sampite takes effect

August 20, 1891—"For Marse Chouchoute" (first Louisiana story) published in *Youth's Companion*

March 7, 1892—writes "Miss McEnders"

April 4, 1892—resigns from Wednesday Club

April 9–10, 1892—writes "Loka"

July 15–17, 1892—writes "At the 'Cadian Ball"

August 27, 1892—death of Cora Henry Chopin, sister-in-law

August 27–28, 1892—writes "Ma'ame Pélagie"

Oct. 22, 1892—"At the 'Cadian Ball" published in *Two Tales*

Nov. 24, 1892—writes "Désirée's Baby"

Jan. 14, 1893—*Vogue* publishes "Désirée's Baby"

May 1893—trip to New York and Boston

August 11, 1893—Houghton, Mifflin accepts *Bayou Folk*

October 1, 1893—hurricane of Chênière Caminada destroys much of the Grand Isle area that Chopin knew

October 21–23, 1893—writes "At Chênière Caminada"

March 24, 1894—Houghton, Mifflin publishes *Bayou Folk*

April 19, 1894—Chopin writes "The Story of an Hour" ("Dream of an Hour")

May 4, 1894–October 26, 1896—writes "Impressions" (Diary)

Late June 1894—attends Indiana conference of Western Association of Writers

June 30, 1894—writes "The Western Association of Writers"

July 7, 1894—"Western Association of Writers" published in *Critic*

July 21–28, 1894—hostile responses to Chopin's "Western Association of Writers" in *Minneapolis Journal, Cincinnati Commercial Gazette*

August 1894—first national profile: William Schuyler's article in *The Writer*

December 6, 1894—"Dream of an Hour" published in *Vogue* with note about "Those Who Have Worked With Us"

March 1895—sends Maupassant translation collection to Houghton, Mifflin (rejected)

April 1895—"Cavanelle" published in *The American Jewess*

April 10–28, 1895—writes "Athénaïse"

January 27, 1897—grandmother Athénaïse Charleville Faris dies

February 3, 1897—meets Ruth McEnery Stuart

March 6, 1897—"Miss McEnders" by "La Tour" published in *St. Louis Criterion*

March 11, 1897—Reedy's *Mirror* reveals satirical truth about "Miss McEnders"

Mar. 1897—writes "The Locket," unpublished

June 1897 (?)—begins writing *The Awakening*

June 1897—John A. Dillon makes short trip to St. Louis

June 24–July 1, 1897—Kate Chopin visits Natchitoches Parish

November 1897—Way & Williams (Chicago) publishes *A Night in Acadie*

January 16, 1898—"Is Love Divine?" (*St. Louis Post-Dispatch*) quotes from novel-in-progress

January 21, 1898—finishes *The Awakening*

January 1898—Way & Williams accepts *The Awakening*

February 6, 1898—"Has High Society Struck the Pace That Kills?" (*St. Louis Post-Dispatch*)

March 1898—goes to Chicago, seeking literary agent

Spring–Summer 1898—son Frederick in Spanish-American War

July 19, 1898—writes "The Storm"

November 1898—books transferred from Way & Williams to Herbert S. Stone & Company

December 1898—visits Natchitoches Parish, sells Cloutierville house, visits New Orleans

March 1899—Lucy Monroe's favorable review of *The Awakening* in *Book News*

April 22, 1899—*The Awakening* published (no documentary evidence that it was ever banned)

July 1899—Chopin's statement on *The Awakening* published in *Book News*

October 1899—travels to Wisconsin lake country, where she receives English letters praising *The Awakening*

November 26, 1899—article in *St. Louis Post-Dispatch*: "On certain brisk, bright days," with "A St. Louis Woman Who Has Won Fame in Literature"

November 29, 1899—gives reading at Wednesday Club

1900—John A. Dillon in Chicago

February 1900—Herbert S. Stone returns (declines to publish) "A Vocation and a Voice"

December 9, 1900—publishes "Development of the Literary West: a Review" in *St. Louis Republic*'s Special Book Number

1900—appears in first edition of *Who's Who in America*

1901—is subject of sonnet "To the Author of 'Bayou Folk,' " by R. E. Lee Gibson

June 4, 1902—son Jean marries Emelie Hughes

July 3, 1902—"Polly" published in *Youth's Companion* (last publication)

October 15, 1902—John A. Dillon dies

December 1902—Chopin makes her will

1903—moves to 4232 McPherson Avenue

July 7, 1903—death of Emelie Chopin, Jean's wife

August 20, 1904—Chopin has cerebral hemorrhage after day at the St. Louis World's Fair

August 22, 1904—Chopin dies

August 24, 1904—burial of Kate Chopin

✦

II
$\mathcal{K}$ATE $\mathcal{C}$HOPIN'S $\mathcal{W}$RITINGS

This list, an adaptation and updating of Per Seyersted's bibliography, includes all of Kate Chopin's known writings, both published and unpublished. Also listed here are writings recorded in her manuscript account notebooks, but now destroyed or lost. The items are arranged in order of composition, with final title, date of composition, first appearance in print, and inclusion in collections. Where titles vary, I have listed variations. CW includes information about changes from manuscript to print versions, and KCPP in-

cludes transcriptions of Chopin's manuscript account notebooks.

ABBREVIATIONS

BF = Kate Chopin, *Bayou Folk* (Boston: Houghton, Mifflin,
1894).

CW = Per Seyersted, ed., *The Complete Works of Kate Chopin* (Baton Rouge: Louisiana State University, 1969).

DSR = Daniel S. Rankin, *Kate Chopin and Her Creole Stories*
(Philadelphia: University of Pennsylvania, 1932).

ET = Emily Toth, *Kate Chopin* (New York: William Morrow,
1990).

KCM = Per Seyersted and Emily Toth, eds., *A Kate Chopin Miscel-
lany* (Natchitoches and Oslo: Northwestern State University Press and Universitetsforlaget, 1979).

KCPP = Emily Toth and Per Seyersted, eds., *Kate Chopin's Private
Papers* (Bloomington: Indiana University Press).

NA = Kate Chopin, *A Night in Acadie* (Chicago: Way &
Williams, 1897).

PS1 = Per Seyersted, "Kate Chopin: an Important St. Louis
Writer Reconsidered," *Missouri Historical Society Bulletin*
19 (January 1963), 89–114.

PS2 = Per Seyersted, "Kate Chopin's Wound: Two New Letters," *American Literary Realism* 20:1 (Fall 1987), 71–75.

SCB = Per Seyersted, *Kate Chopin: A Critical Biography* (Oslo and
Baton Rouge: Universitetsforlaget and Louisiana State
University, 1969).

TB = Thomas Bonner, Jr., *The Kate Chopin Companion, with
Chopin's Translations from French Fiction* (Westport, CT:
Greenwood, 1988).

Autograph book (with pictures, poems, brief comments by Kate
O'Flaherty). 1860—.

"Katie O'Flaherty, St. Louis. 1867" (diary and commonplace book).
1867–1870. DSR (in part). KCM (in part). KCPP (in full).

"Emancipation. A Life Fable." Undated: late 1869 or early 1870. PS1. CW.

New Orleans diary. 1870——. Seen by Rankin; later lost.

Letter to Marie Breazeale. June 21, 1887. KCM. KCPP.

"Lilia. Polka for Piano." Undated. Published for the author by H. Rollman & Sons, St. Louis, 1888. KCM. KCPP.

"If It Might Be" (poem). Undated. *America* (Chicago) 1 (January 10, 1889), 9. CW.

("Euphrasie" (story). 1888. See "A No-Account Creole.")

Manuscript Account Books (2). 1888——. KCPP.

"Unfinished Story—Grand Isle." 1888–1889. Destroyed.

"A Poor Girl" (story). May 1889. Destroyed.

"Wiser than a God" (story). June 1889. *Philadelphia Musical Journal* 4 (December 1889), 38–40. CW.

"A Point at Issue!" (story). August 1889. *St. Louis Post-Dispatch*, October 27, 1889. CW.

"Miss Witherwell's Mistake" (story). November 18, 1889. *Fashion and Fancy* (St. Louis) 5 (February 1891), 115–17. CW.

"With the Violin" (story). December 11, 1889. *Spectator* (St. Louis) 11 (December 6, 1890), 196. CW.

At Fault (novel). July 5, 1889–April 20, 1890. Published for the author by Nixon-Jones Printing Co., St. Louis, September 1890. CW.

"Monsieur Pierre" (story; translation from Adrien Vely). April 1890. *St. Louis Post-Dispatch*, August 8, 1892. TB.

"Psyche's Lament" (poem). Undated; probably 1890. DSR. CW.

Letter to the *St. Louis Republic*. October 18, 1890. *St. Louis Republic*, October 25, 1890. KCM. KCPP.

Young Dr. Gosse (novel, also called *Young Dr. Gosse and Théo*). May 4–November 27, 1890. Destroyed.

"A Red Velvet Coat" (story). December 1–8, 1890. Destroyed or lost.

"*At Fault*. A Correction" (letter). December 11, 1890. *Natchitoches Enterprise*, December 18, 1890. ET. KCPP.

"Mrs. Mobry's Reason" (story). January 10, 1891. *New Orleans Times-Democrat*, April 23, 1893. CW.

"The Shape of the Head" (translation of an article listed in Chopin's account book as "A Study in Heads"). Undated. *St. Louis Post-Dispatch*, January 25, 1891. KCPP.

"A No-Account Creole" (story). 1888 (called "Euphrasie"); rewritten January 24, 1891–February 24, 1891. *Century* 47 (January 1894), 382–93. BF. CW.

"Octave Feuillet" (translation?). February 1891. Destroyed or lost.

"Roger and His Majesty" (story). March 1, 1891. Destroyed.

"Revival of Wrestling" (translation). Undated. *St. Louis Post-Dispatch*, March 8, 1891. KCPP.

"For Marse Chouchoute" (story). March 14, 1891. *Youth's Companion* 64 (August 20, 1891), 450–51. BF. CW.

"The Going and Coming of Liza Jane" (story). April 4, 1891. Syndicated, American Press Association, as "The Christ Light." December 1892. CW calls the story "The Going Away of Liza."

"The Maid of Saint Phillippe" (story). April 19, 1891. *Short Stories* (New York) 11 (November 1891), 257–64. CW.

"A Wizard from Gettysburg" (story). May 25, 1891. *Youth's Companion* 65 (July 7, 1892), 346–47. BF. CW.

Letter to the *Century*. May 28, 1891. KCM. KCPP.

"A Shameful Affair" (story). June 5, 7, 1891. *New Orleans Times-Democrat*, April 9, 1893.

Letter to R. W. Gilder. July 12, 1891. KCM. KCPP.

"A Rude Awakening" (story). July 13, 1891. *Youth's Companion* 66 (February 2, 1893), 54–55. BF. CW.

"A Harbinger" (story). September 11, 1891. *St. Louis Magazine* 12 (apparently November 1, 1891: No copies can be found). CW.

"Dr. Chevalier's Lie" (story). September 12, 1891. *Vogue* 2 (October 5, 1893), 174, 178. CW.

"A Very Fine Fiddle" (story). September 13, 1891. *Harper's Young People* 13 (November 24, 1891), 79. BF. CW.

"Boulôt and Boulotte" (story). September 20, 1891. *Harper's Young People* 13 (December 8, 1891), 112. BF. CW.

"Love on the Bon-Dieu" (story). October 3, 1891, as "Love and Easter." *Two Tales* (Boston) 2 (July 23, 1892), 148–56. BF. CW.

"An Embarrassing Position. Comedy in One Act" (play). October 15–22, 1891. *Mirror* (St. Louis) 5 (December 19, 1895), 9–11. CW.

"Beyond the Bayou" (story). November 7, 1891. *Youth's Companion* 66 (June 15, 1893), 302–3. BF. CW.

"Typical Forms of German Music" (essay). Paper read at the Wednesday Club, St. Louis, December 9, 1891. Possibly the same as "Typical German Composers," essay offered in 1899 to the *Atlantic*. Destroyed or lost.

"After the Winter" (story). December 31, 1891. *New Orleans Times-Democrat*, April 5, 1896. NA. CW.

"The Bênitous' Slave" (story). January 7, 1892. *Harper's Young People* 13 (February 16, 1892), 280. BF. CW.

"A Turkey Hunt" (story). January 8, 1892. *Harper's Young People* 13 (February 16, 1892), 287. BF. CW.

"Old Aunt Peggy" (story). January 8, 1892. BF. CW.

"The Lilies" (story). January 27–28, 1892. *Wide Awake* 36 (April 1893), 415–18. NA. CW.

"Mittens" (story). February 25, 1892. Destroyed or lost.

"Ripe Figs" (story). February 26, 1892. *Vogue* 2 (August 19, 1893), 90. NA. CW.

"Croque-Mitaine" (story). February 27, 1892. PS1. CW.

"A Trip to Portuguese Guinea" (translation?). February 27, 1892. Destroyed or lost.

"A Visit to the Planet Mars" (translation?). March 1892. Destroyed or lost.

"Transfusion of Goat's Blood" (translation?). March 1892. Destroyed or lost.

"Miss McEnders" (story). March 7, 1892. *Criterion* (St. Louis) 13 (March 6, 1897), 16–18, signed La Tour. CW.

"Cut Paper Figures" (also called "Manikins" and "How to Make Manikins": translation?). Undated. *St. Louis Post-Dispatch*, April 5, 1892. KCPP.

"Loka" (story). April 9–10, 1892. *Youth's Companion* 65 (December 22, 1892), 670–71. BF. CW.

"Bambo Pellier" (story). May (?) 1892. Destroyed or lost.

"At the 'Cadian Ball" (story). July 15–17, 1892. *Two Tales* (Boston) 3 (October 22, 1892), 145–52. BF. CW.

"A Visit to Avoyelles" (story). August 1, 1892. *Vogue* 1 (January 14, 1893), 74–75. BF. CW.

"Ma'ame Pélagie" (story). August 27–28, 1892. *New Orleans Times-Democrat*, December 24, 1893. BF. CW.

"A Fancy" (poem). Probably 1892. DSR. KCM. KCPP.

"Désirée's Baby" (story). November 24, 1892. *Vogue* 1 (January 14, 1893), 70–71, 74. BF. CW.

"Caline" (story). December 2, 1892. *Vogue* 1 (May 20, 1893), 324–25. NA. CW.

"The Return of Alcibiade" (story). December 5–6, 1892. *St. Louis Life* 7 (December 17, 1892), 6–8. BF. CW.

"In and Out of Old Natchitoches" (story). February 1–3, 1892. *Two Tales* 5 (April 8, 1893), 178–79. NA. CW.

"Mamouche" (story). February 24–25, 1893. *Youth's Companion* 67 (April 19, 1894), 178–79. NA. CW.

Letter to Marion A. Baker. May 4, 1893. KCM. KCPP.

Letter to R. W. Gilder. May 10, 1893. KCM. KCPP.

"Madame Célestin's Divorce" (story). May 24–25, 1893. BF. CW.

"The Song Everlasting" (poem). Before June 1893. Published in the program for the St. Louis Wednesday Club's "Reciprocity Day: An Afternoon with St. Louis Authors." November 29, 1899. CW.

"You and I" (poem). Before June 1893. Published in the program for the St. Louis Wednesday Club's "Reciprocity Day: An Afternoon with St. Louis Authors." November 29, 1899. CW.

"It Matters All" (poem). Before June 1893. DSR. CW.

"If the Woods Could Talk" (poem). Before June 1893. KCM. KCPP.

"A Sentimental Serenade" (poem). Before June 1893. KCM. KCPP.

"A Message" (poem). Before June 1893. KCM. KCPP.

"An Idle Fellow" (story). June 9, 1893. CW.

"A Matter of Prejudice" (story). June 17–18, 1893. *Youth's Companion* 68 (September 25, 1895), 450. NA. CW.

"Azélie" (story). July 22–23, 1893. *Century* 49 (December 1894), 282–87. NA. CW.

"A Lady of Bayou St. John" (story). August 24–25, 1893. *Vogue* 2 (September 21, 1893), 154, 156–58. BF. CW.

"La Belle Zoraïde" (story). September 21, 1893. *Vogue* 3 (January 4, 1894), 2, 4, 8–10. BF. CW.

"At Chênière Caminada" (story). October 21–23, 1893. *New Orleans Times-Democrat*, December 23, 1894. NA. CW.

"A Gentleman of Bayou Têche" (story). November 5–7, 1893. BF. CW.

"In Sabine" (story). November 20–22, 1893. BF. CW.

"A Respectable Woman" (story). January 20, 1894. *Vogue* 3 (February 15, 1894), 68–69, 72. NA. CW.

"Tante Cat'rinette" (story). February 23, 1894. *Atlantic Monthly* 74 (September 1894), 368–73. NA. CW.

"A Dresden Lady in Dixie" (story). March 6, 1894. *Catholic Home Journal* (March 3, 1895). NA. CW.

Bayou Folk (collected stories). Published March 1894, by Houghton, Mifflin (Boston).

"The Story of an Hour" (story). April 19, 1894. *Vogue* 4 (December 6, 1894), 360. Written and first published as "The Dream of an Hour." CW.

"Impressions. 1894" (diary). May 4, 1894–October 26, 1896. Published in part in SCB. KCM (in full). KCPP (in full).

"Lilacs" (story). May 14–16, 1894. *New Orleans Times-Democrat*, December 20, 1896. CW.

"Good Night" (poem). Undated. *New Orleans Times-Democrat*, July 22, 1894. CW.

"The Western Association of Writers" (essay). June 30, 1894. *Critic* 22 (July 7, 1894), 15. CW.

"A Divorce Case" (story; translation from Guy de Maupassant). July 11, 1894. TB.

"A Scrap and a Sketch": "The Night Came Slowly" (story). July 24, 1894; "Juanita" (story). July 26, 1894. *Moods* (Philadelphia) 2 (July 1895), n.p. CW prints the two separately as "The Night Came Slowly" and "Juanita."

"Dorothea" (untitled story, possibly a real-life observation—not listed separately in manuscript account notebook, and not sent out separately for publication). July 25, 1894, in "Impressions. 1894." KCM. KCPP.

"Cavanelle" (story). July 31–August 6, 1894. *American Jewess* 1 (April 1895), 22–25. NA. CW.

"Mad?" (story; translation from Guy de Maupassant). September 4, 1894. TB.

Letter to Stone & Kimball. September 10, 1894. KCM. KCPP.

"Regret" (story). September 17, 1894. *Century* 50 (May 1895), 147–49. NA. CW.

"The Kiss" (story). September 19, 1894. *Vogue* 5 (January 17, 1895), 37. CW.

"Ozème's Holiday" (story). September 23–24, 1894. *Century* 52 (August 1896), 629–31. NA. CW.

" 'Crumbling Idols' by Hamlin Garland" (essay). Undated. *St. Louis Life* 10 (October 6, 1894), 13. CW.

Letter to Waitman Barbe. October 2, 1894. KCM. KCPP.

"The Real Edwin Booth" (essay). Undated. *St. Louis Life* 10 (October 13, 1894), 11. CW.

"Emile Zola's 'Lourdes' " (essay). Undated. *St. Louis Life* 10 (November 17, 1894), 5. CW.

"A Sentimental Soul" (story). November 18–22, 1894. *New Orleans Times-Democrat*, December 22, 1895. NA. CW.

"Her Letters" (story). November 29, 1894. *Vogue* 5 (April 11, 18, 1895), 228–30, 248. CW.

Letters to A. A. Hill. December 26, 1894; January 1, 11, 16, 1895. KCM. KCPP.

"Odalie Misses Mass" (story). January 28, 1895. *Shreveport Times*, July 1, 1895. NA. CW.

"It?" (story; translation from Guy de Maupassant). February 4, 1895. *St. Louis Life* 11 (February 23, 1895), 12–13. TB.

"Polydore" (story). February 17, 1895. *Youth's Companion* 70 (April 23, 1896), 214–15. NA. CW.

"Dead Men's Shoes" (story). February 21–22, 1895. *Independent* (New York) 49 (February 11, 1897), 194–95. NA. CW.

"Solitude" (story; translation from Guy de Maupassant). March 5, 1895. *St. Louis Life* 13 (December 28, 1895), 30. TB.

"Night" (story; translation from Guy de Maupassant). March 8, 1895. TB.

Letter to J. M. Stoddart. March 31, 1895. KCM. KCPP.

"Athénaïse" (story). April 10–28, 1895. *Atlantic Monthly* 78 (August, September 1896), 232–41, 404–13. NA. CW.

"A Lady of Shifting Intentions" (story). May 4, 1895. Destroyed or lost; extant fragment in KCM, KCPP.

"Two Summers and Two Souls" (story). July 14, 1895. *Vogue* 6 (August 7, 1895), 84. CW.

"The Unexpected" (story). July 18, 1895. *Vogue* 6 (September 18, 1895), 180–81. CW.

"Two Portraits" ("The Nun and the Wanton") (story). August 4, 1895. DSR. CW.

"If Some Day" (poem). August 16, 1895. CW.

"Under My Lattice" (poem). August 18, 1895. KCM. KCPP.

"To Carrie B." (poem). Autumn 1895. CW.

"The Falling in Love of Fedora" (story). November 19, 1895. *Criterion* (St. Louis) 13 (February 20, 1897), 9, signed La Tour. Published in CW as "Fedora."

Letter to Cornelia F. Maury. December 3, 1895. KCM. KCPP.

"For Mrs. Ferris(s)" (poem). December 1895. KCM. KCPP.

"To Blanche" (poem). December 1895. KCM. KCPP.

"Vagabonds" (story). December (?) 1895. DSR. CW.

"Suicide" (story; translation from Guy de Maupassant). December 18, 1895. *St. Louis Republic*, June 5, 1898. TB.

"To Hider Schuyler—" (poem). Christmas 1895. CW.

"To 'Billy' with a Box of Cigars" (poem). Christmas 1895. CW.

Letter to Stone & Kimball. January 2, 1896. KCM. KCPP.

"Madame Martel's Christmas Eve" (story). January 16–18, 1896. CW.

"The Recovery" (story). February 1896. *Vogue* 7 (May 21, 1896), 354–55. CW.

"A Night in Acadie" (story). March 1896. NA. CW.

"A Pair of Silk Stockings" (story). April 1896. *Vogue* 10 (September 16, 1897), 191–92. CW.

"Nég Créol" (story). April 1896. *Atlantic Monthly* 80 (July 1897), 135–38. NA. CW.

"Aunt Lympy's Interference" (story). June 1896. *Youth's Companion* 71 (August 12, 1897), 373–74. CW.

"The Blind Man" (story). July 1896. *Vogue* 9 (May 13, 1897), 303. CW.

"In the Confidence of a Story-Writer" (essay). October 1896. *Atlantic Monthly* 83 (January 1899), 137–39, published without an author's name. CW. (An earlier version, written September 1896 and entitled "Confidences," is also published in CW.)

"Ti Frère" (story). September 1896. KCM. KCPP.

"For Sale" (story; translation from Guy de Maupassant). October 26, 1896. TB.

"A Vocation and a Voice" (story). November 1896. *Mirror* (St. Louis) 12 (March 27, 1902), 18–24. CW.

"A Mental Suggestion" (story). December 1896. CW.

"To Mrs. R" (poem). Christmas 1896. CW.

"Let the Night Go" (poem). January 1, 1897. CW.

Letter to the *Century*. January 5, 1897. KCM. KCPP.

Inscription for Ruth McEnery Stuart. February 3, 1897. KCM. KCPP.

"Suzette" (story). February 1897. *Vogue* 10 (October 21, 1897), 262–63. CW.

"As You Like It" (a series of six essays). Undated, individual essay titles supplied by Per Seyersted. *Criterion* (St. Louis), 13:

   I. "I have a young friend . . ." February 13, 1897, 11. CW.

   II. "It has lately been . . ." February 20, 1897, 17. CW.

   III. "Several years ago . . ." February 27, 1897, 11. CW.

   IV. "A while ago . . ." March 13, 1897, 15–16. CW.

   V. "A good many of us . . ." March 20, 1897, 10. CW.

   VI. "We are told . . ." (March 27, 1897), 10. CW.

"The Locket" (story). March 1897. CW.

"A Morning Walk" (story). April 1897. Published as "An Easter Day Conversion." *Criterion* (St. Louis) 15 [sic] (April 17, 1897), 13–14. CW.

"An Egyptian Cigarette" (story). April 1897. *Vogue* 15 (April 19, 1900), 252–54. CW.

A Night in Acadie (collected stories). Published November 1897, by Way & Williams (Chicago).

The Awakening (novel). June (?) 1897–January 21, 1898, listed in Chopin's notebook as "A Solitary Soul." Published April 22, 1899, by Herbert S. Stone & Company (Chicago & New York). CW.

"A Family Affair" (story). December (?) 1897. Syndicated— American Press Association, January 1898. *Saturday Evening Post* 172 (September 9, 1899), 168–69. CW.

" 'Is Love Divine?' The Question Answered by Three Ladies Well Known in St. Louis Society" (interview). *St. Louis Post-Dispatch*, January 16, 1898, 17. ET. KCPP.

"Has High Society Struck the Pace That Kills?" (interview). *St. Louis Post-Dispatch*, February 6, 1898, 12. ET. KCPP.

Letter to Lydia Arms Avery Coonley Ward. March 21, 1898. PS2. KCPP.

"Elizabeth Stock's One Story" (story). March 1898. PS1. CW.

"A Horse Story" (story). Also called "Ti Démon." March 1898. KCM. KCPP.

"Father Amable" (story; translation from Guy de Maupassant). April 21, 1898. TB.

"There's Music Enough" (poem). May 1, 1898. DSR. CW.

"An Ecstasy of Madness" (poem). July 10, 1898. DSR. CW.

"The Roses" (poem). July 11, 1898. KCM. KCPP.

"The Storm" (story). July 19, 1898. CW.

"Lines to Him" (poem). July 31, 1898. KCM. KCPP.

"White Oaks" (poem). August 24, 1898. KCM. KCPP.

"Lines Suggested by Omar" (poem). August 1898. KCM. KCPP.

"The Lull of Summer Time" (poem). Undated, but probably August 1898. KCM. KCPP.

"To Henry One Evening Last Summer" (poem). October 21, 1898. KCM. KCPP.

"By the Meadow Gate" (poem). October 24, 1898. KCM. KCPP.

"Old Natchitoches" (poem). December 1898. KCM. KCPP.

"An Hour" (poem). Undated, but before January 1899. DSR. KCM. KCPP.

"In Spring" (poem). Undated, but before January 1899. *Century* 58 (July 1899), 361. KCM. KCPP.

"I Wanted God" (poem). Undated, but before February 1899. CW.

"My Lady Rose Pouts" (poem). Undated, but before February 1899. KCM. KCPP.

"Come to Me" (poem). Undated, but before February 1899. KCM. KCPP.

"O! Blessed Tavern" (poem). Undated, but before February 1899. KCM. KCPP.

"As Careless As the Summer Breeze" (poem). Undated, but before February 1899. KCM. KCPP.

"One Day" (poem). Undated, but before February 1899. KCM. KCPP.

"Ah! Magic Bird!" (poem). Undated, but before February 1899. KCM. KCPP.

"With a Violet-Wood Paper Knife" (poem). Undated, but before February 1899. KCM. KCPP.

"Because—" (poem). Undated, but probably 1899. CW.

"The Godmother" (story). January–February 6, 1899. *Mirror* (St. Louis) 11 (December 12, 1901), 9–13. CW.

"The Haunted Chamber" (poem). February 1899. CW.

Letter to the *Youth's Companion*. February 11, 1899. KCM. KCPP.

"A Little Country Girl" (story). February 11, 1899. CW.

"Life" (poem). May 10, 1899. DSR. CW.

Letter to Herbert S. Stone. May 21, 1899. KCM. KCPP.

Statement on *The Awakening*. May 28, 1899. *Book News* 17 (July 1899), 612. KCM. KCPP.

Letter to Herbert S. Stone. June 7, 1899. KCM. KCPP.

"A Little Day" (poem). Undated, but probably 1899. KCM. KCPP.

Inscription for Madison Cawein. August 17, 1899. KCM. KCPP.

Letter to Richard B. Shepard. August 24, 1899. KCM. KCPP.

Letter to Richard B. Shepard. November 8, 1899. PS2. KCPP.

"A Reflection" (story). November 1899. DSR. CW.

"On certain brisk, bright days" (untitled essay, title supplied by Per Seyersted). Undated, but undoubtedly November 1899. *St. Louis Post-Dispatch*, November 26, 1899. CW.

"Ti Démon" (story). November 1899. CW.

Letter to the *Century*. December 1, 1899. KCM. KCPP.

"A December Day in Dixie" (story). January 1900. DSR (in part). CW (in full).

"Alexandre's Wonderful Experience" (story). January 23, 1900. KCM. KCPP.

"The Gentleman from New Orleans" (story). February 6, 1900. CW.

Letter to the *Youth's Companion*. February 15, 1900. DSR. KCM. KCPP.

"Charlie" (story). April 1900. CW.

"The White Eagle" (story). May 9, 1900. *Vogue* 16 (July 12, 1900), 20, 22. CW.

"Alone" (poem). July 6, 1900. KCM. KCPP.

"To the Friend of My Youth: To Kitty" (poem). DSR (who dates it August 24, 1900). CW.

"Development of the Literary West: A Review" (essay). Undated. *St. Louis Republic* (December 9, 1900), 1. ET. KCPP.

Letter to R. E. Lee Gibson. October 13, 1901. KCM. KCPP.

"Millie's First Party" (story). Also called "Millie's First Ball." October 16, 1901. Destroyed or lost.

"The Wood-Choppers" (story). October 17, 1901. *Youth's Companion* 76 (May 29, 1902), 270–71. CW.

"Toots' Nurses" (story). October 18, 1901. Destroyed or lost.

"Polly" (story). January 14, 1902, as "Polly's Opportunity." *Youth's Companion* 76 (July 3, 1902), 334–35. CW.

Letter to Marie Breazeale. February 4, 1902. KCM. KCPP.

UNDATABLE MATERIALS

Reminiscences about Kitty Garesché. Undated; 1885? DSR. KCM. KCPP.

"The Impossible Miss Meadows" (story). CW. Possibly a sketch for "The Falling in Love of Fedora."

Letter to Mrs. Tiffany. Undated. KCM. KCPP.

Letter to Professor Otto Heller (Washington University). December 26, no year. KCPP.

Letter to Mrs. Douglas. July 10, year unknown. KCM. KCPP.

KATE CHOPIN ON WRITING

✦

SPEAKING OF EDITORS*

* * * Speaking of editors—though I don't know that I was speaking of them. I must have been thinking of them in connection with Sallie Britton's memoirs, and wondering whether she ever "submitted" them for publication, or how she did it. But editors are really a singular class of men; they have such strange and incomprehensible ways with them.

I once submitted a story to a prominent New York editor, who returned it promptly with the observation that "the public is getting very tired of that sort of thing." I felt very sorry for the public; but I wasn't willing to take one man's word for it, so I clapped the offensive document into an envelope and sent it away again—this time to a well-known Boston editor.

"I am delighted with the story," read the letter of acceptance, which came a few weeks later, "and so, I am sure, will be our readers." (!)

When an editor says a thing like that it is at his own peril. I at once sent him another tale, thinking thereby to increase his delight and add to it ten-fold.

"Can you call this a story, dear madam?" he asked when he sent it back. "Really, there seems to me to be no story at all; what is it all about?" I could see his pale smile.

* From "As You Like It," in *The Complete Works of Kate Chopin,* ed. Per Seyersted (Baton Rouge: Louisiana State University Press, 1969), pp. 717–18. Excerpted from an essay published March 20, 1897, as part of a series of six undated essays, all of which were published in the St. Louis *Criterion.*

It was getting interesting, like playing at battledore and shuttle-cock. Off went the would-be story by the next mail to the New York editor—the one who so considerately gauged the ennui of the public.

"It is a clever and excellent piece of work," he wrote me; "the story is well told." I wonder if the editor, the writer, and the public are ever at one.

✦

In the Confidence of a Story-Writer*

There is registered somewhere in my consciousness a vow that I will never be confidential except for the purpose of misleading. But consistency is a pompous and wearisome burden, and I seek relief by casting it aside; for, like the colored gentleman in the Passemala, I am sometimes—"afraid o' myse'f," but never ashamed.

I have discovered my limitations, and I have saved myself much worry and torment by accepting them as final. I can gain nothing but tribulation by cultivating faculties that are not my own. I cannot reach anything by running after it, but I find that many pleasant and profitable things come to me here in my corner.

Some wise man has promulgated an eleventh commandment, "Thou shalt not preach," which, interpreted, means, "Thou shalt not instruct thy neighbor as to what he should do." But the Preacher is always with us. Said one to me: "Thou shalt parcel off thy day into mathematical sections. So many hours shalt thou abandon thyself to thought, so many to writing; a certain number shalt thou devote to household duties, to social enjoyment, to ministering to thy afflicted fellow creatures." I listened to the voice of the Preacher, and the result was stagnation all along the line of "hours" and unspeakable bitterness of spirit. In brutal revolt I turned to and played solitaire during my "thinking hour," and whist when I should have been ministering to the afflicted. I scribbled a

* From *Atlantic Monthly,* January 1899.

little during my "social enjoyment" period, and shattered the "household duties" into fragments of every conceivable fraction of time, with which I besprinkled the entire day as from a pepper-box. In this way I succeeded in reëstablishing the harmonious discord and confusion which had surrounded me before I listened to the voice, and which seems necessary to my physical and mental well-being.

But there are many voices preaching. Said another one to me: "Go forth and gather wisdom in the intellectual atmosphere of clubs,— in those centres of thought where questions are debated and knowledge is disseminated." Once more giving heed, I hurried to enroll myself among the thinkers, and dispensers of knowledge, and propounders of questions. And very much out of place did I feel in these intellectual gatherings. I escaped by some pretext, and regained my corner, where no "questions" and no fine language can reach me.

There is far too much gratuitous advice bandied about, regardless of personal aptitude and wholly confusing to the individual point of view.

I had heard so often reiterated that "genius is a capacity for taking pains" that the axiom had become lodged in my brain with the fixedness of a fundamental truth. I had never hoped or aspired to be a genius. But one day the thought occurred to me, "I will take pains." Thereupon I proceeded to lie awake at night plotting a tale that should convince my limited circle of readers that I could rise above the commonplace. As to choice of "time," the present century offered too prosaic a setting for a tale intended to stir the heart and the imagination. I selected the last century. It is true I know little of the last century, and have a feeble imagination. I read volumes bearing upon the history of the times and people that I proposed to manipulate, and pored over folios depicting costumes and household utensils then in use, determined to avoid inaccuracy. For the first time in my life I took notes,—copious notes,—and carried them bulging in my jacket pockets, until I felt as if I were wearing Zola's coat. I have never seen a craftsman at work upon a fine piece of mosaic, but I fancy that he must handle the delicate bits much as I handled the words in that story, picking, selecting, grouping, with an eye to color and to artistic effect,—never satisfied. The story completed, I was very, very weary; but I had the satisfaction of feeling that for once in my life I had worked hard. I had achieved something great, I had taken pains.

But the story failed to arouse enthusiasm among the editors. It is at present lying in my desk. Even my best friend declined to listen to it, when I offered to read it to her.

I am more than ever convinced that a writer should be content to use his own faculty, whether it be a faculty for taking pains or a faculty for reaching his effects by the most careless methods. Every writer, I fancy, has his group of readers who understand, who are in sympathy with his thoughts or impressions or whatever he gives them. And he who is content to reach his own group, without ambition to be heard beyond it, attains, in my opinion, somewhat to the dignity of a philosopher. . . .

✦

W_{HY} D_O I W_{RITE}?*

On certain brisk, bright days I like to walk from my home, near Thirty-fourth street, down to the shopping district. After a few such experiments I begin to fancy that I have the walking habit. Doubtless I convey the same impression to acquaintances who see me from the car window "hot-footing" it down Olive street or Washington avenue. But in my sub-consciousness, as my friend Mrs. R— would say, I know that I have not the walking habit.

Eight or nine years ago I began to write stories—short stories which appeared in the magazines, and I forthwith began to suspect I had the writing habit. The public shared this impression, and called me an author. Since then, though I have written many short

* Published as "On Certain Brisk, Bright Days," in *The Complete Works of Kate Chopin,* ed. Per Seyersted (Baton Rouge: Louisiana State University Press, 1969), pp. 721–23. Original essay appeared untitled in the St. Louis *Post-Dispatch,* November 26, 1899.

stories and a novel or two, I am forced to admit that I have not the writing habit. But it is hard to make people with the questioning habit believe this.

"How, where, when, why, what do you write?" are some of the questions that I remember. How do I write? On a lapboard with a block of paper, a stub pen and a bottle of ink bought at the corner grocery, which keeps the best in town.

Where do I write? In a Morris chair beside the window, where I can see a few trees and a patch of sky, more or less blue.

When do I write? I am greatly tempted here to use slang and reply "any old time," but that would lend a tone of levity to this bit of confidence, whose seriousness I want to keep intact if possible. So I shall say I write in the morning, when not too strongly drawn to struggle with the intricacies of a pattern, and in the afternoon, if the temptation to try a new furniture polish on an old table leg is not too powerful to be denied; sometimes at night, though as I grow older I am more and more inclined to believe that night was made for sleep.

"Why do I write?" is a question which I have often asked myself and never very satisfactorily answered. Story-writing—at least with me—is the spontaneous expression of impressions gathered goodness knows where. To seek the source, the impulse of a story is like tearing a flower to pieces for wantonness.

What do I write? Well, not everything that comes into my head, but much of what I have written lies between the covers of my books.

There are stories that seem to write themselves, and others which positively refuse to be written—which no amount of coaxing can bring to anything. I do not believe any writer has ever made a "portrait" in fiction. A trick, a mannerism, a physical trait or mental characteristic go a very short way towards portraying the complete individual in real life who suggests the individual in the writer's imagination. The "material" of a writer is to the last degree uncertain, and I fear not marketable. I have been told stories which were looked upon as veritable gold mines by the generous narrators who placed them at my disposal. I have been taken to spots supposed to be alive with local color. I have been introduced to excruciating characters with frank permission to use them as I liked, but never, in any single instance, has such material been of the slightest service. I am completely at the mercy of unconscious selection. To such an extent is this true, that what is called the polishing up process has always proved disastrous to my work, and I avoid it, preferring the integrity of crudities to artificialities.

How hard it is for one's acquaintances and friends to realize that one's books are to be taken seriously, and that they are subject to the same laws which govern the existence of others' books! I have a son who is growing wroth over the question: "Where can I find your mother's books, or latest book?"

"The very next time any one asks me that question," he exclaimed excitedly, "I am going to tell them to try the stock yards!"

I hope he won't. He might thus offend a possible buyer. Politeness, besides being a virtue, is sometimes an art. I am often met with the same question, and I always try to be polite. "My latest book? Why, you will find it, no doubt, at the bookseller's or the libraries."

"The libraries! Oh, no, they don't keep it." She hadn't thought of the bookseller's. It's real hard to think of everything! Sometimes I feel as if I should like to get a good, remunerative job to do the thinking for some people. This may sound conceited, but it isn't. If I had space (I have plenty of time; time is my own, but space belongs to the *Post-Dispatch*), I should like to demonstrate satisfactorily that it is not conceited.

I trust it will not be giving away professional secrets to say that many readers would be surprised, perhaps shocked, at the questions which some newspaper editors will put to a defenseless woman under the guise of flattery.

For instance: "How many children have you?" This form is subtle and greatly to be commended in dealing with women of shy and retiring propensities. A woman's reluctance to speak of her children has not yet been chronicled. I have a good many, but they'd be simply wild if I dragged them into this. I might say something of those who are at a safe distance—the idol of my soul in Kentucky; the light of my eye off in Colorado; the treasure of his mother's heart in Louisiana—but I mistrust the form of their displeasure, with poisoned candy going through the mails.

"Do you smoke cigarettes?" is a question which I consider impertinent, and I think most women will agree with me. Suppose I do smoke cigarettes? Am I going to tell it out in meeting? Suppose I don't smoke cigarettes. Am I going to admit such a reflection upon my artistic integrity, and thereby bring upon myself the contempt of the guild?

In answering questions in which an editor believes his readers to be interested, the victim cannot take herself too seriously.

BIOGRAPHICAL ESSAYS

✦

AN AMERICAN
PIONEER WRITER*

PER SEYERSTED

*** Had *The Awakening* been tried like a *Lady Chatterley's Lover,* it would no doubt have permanently established the author's fame. As it was, she received support from practically no one. The number of her readers was small. Though she had remarkably little of the provincial, it probably hampered her development that she had no contact with the nationally important writers and critics. While her friends encouraged her, they did not understand or accept what she was really trying to do, not even W. M. Reedy who told Dreiser that *Sister Carrie* was "damned good" and who was later to defend a work like *The Genius.* Whereas Crane, Garland, and Norris all enjoyed the moral support of Howells, and Dreiser was helped by Norris, Kate Chopin stood virtually alone as she became more and more outspoken in her truthful descriptions of life as she saw it.[1]

She took her writing seriously. While she had the commercial instinct and wanted her work to succeed even financially, literary integrity was her paramount concern. She was one of the utterly few who wrote to suit their own taste, and she made practically no concessions to the public and did not aspire to reaching beyond the group who would be in sympathy with her. Partly because she did

* From Per Seyersted, *Kate Chopin: A Critical Biography* (Baton Rouge: Louisiana State University Press, 1969), pp. 196–200. Copyright © 1969, 1980 by Per Seyersted. Reprinted by permission of the author.

not write in self-justification as Mmes. de Staël and Sand had done, she could do away with both their militancy in the portrayals of female emancipation and their protestations that the works were moral. Her courage is even more remarkable when we consider that she did not have her predecessors' influential friends and that she lived in a country where intellectual genius—even in a man— did not count for much.[2]

Kate Chopin had much of the Gaul in her individualism, her frankness and freedom, and her combination of serious thought and subtle humor. Having been exposed to a French skepticism from childhood, she was removed from traditional Yankee optimism. In short, she reflected much of the Creole tradition to which she was born. With Dreiser, she was one of the first writers of a Continental, Catholic background to enter the American literary scene, which was still largely dominated by Anglo-Saxon Protestants; but unlike him, she felt entirely secure with her heritage and was happily free from all need to prove herself for ethnic or social reasons.

As a result of her background, she could also draw fully on the rich French literary traditions. That she had so much of the Gaul and leaned toward the French school in literature did not mean that she had any Gallic bias, however. In a relaxed, unambivalent way she was both a Creole and an American, and though she was foreign to all extreme Yankee nationalism, she shared Howells' feeling that American literature should and could stand on its own.

She agreed with him, for example, that United States authors should employ Americanisms. Terming it "a matter which [touched her] closely concerning the use and misuse of words," she answered a critic who had objected to her speaking in *At Fault* of a "depot" rather than a "railway station" that the latter was an unacceptable Briticism. (Supposing for a moment that Howells had been willing to let "nudities" enter New World fiction, he ought to have applauded Mrs. Chopin who refused to follow the American habit of blurring them by giving them a French garb.) Obviously thinking not only of herself who had a tradition to fall back upon and who, furthermore, was interested in the timeless rather than in her own very usable past, she felt that her country offered its authors enough literary material. This is evident from what she told William Schuyler: "Americans, in their artistic insight and treatment, are," he reports her as saying, "well up with the French; and, with the advantage which they enjoy of a wider and more variegated field for observation, would, perhaps, surpass them," were it not for the bans on free literary expression.[3]

This was thus a major point: To arrive at true art, American authors would have to insist on depicting true life. In this attitude, Kate Chopin did of course reflect the French writers, as she did in her themes and technique. She was also influenced by the general emphasis of the 1890's on sexuality and feminism. But her perspective was wider than that. She drew on both the Greeks and the Bible, on science as well as modern fiction. In a manner combining the ideas of Euripides and Darwin, she had formed her independent and entirely personal view of passion and woman.

Mrs. Chopin had the vision, the originality and independence, and the sense of artistic form which are needed to give us the great novel. She also had remarkable courage. She hid her ambition and her goal somewhat, knowing that men do not readily accept what Mme. de Staël had called "superiority" in a progressive woman. But she was unable to keep her inclinations in check, and the tensions she felt between Paul and Paula, between the dictates of the Biblical male and the urges of the female artist, resulted in unheard of illustrations of woman's spiritual and sensuous self-assertion. No wonder that she was shipwrecked, like another Margaret Fuller, with her cargo of iconoclastic views.

The great achievement of Kate Chopin was that she broke new ground in American literature. She was the first woman writer in her country to accept passion as a legitimate subject for serious, outspoken fiction. Revolting against tradition and authority; with a daring which we can hardly fathom today; with an uncompromising honesty and no trace of sensationalism, she undertook to give the unsparing truth about woman's submerged life. She was something of a pioneer in the amoral treatment of sexuality, of divorce, and of woman's urge for an existential authenticity. She is in many respects a modern writer, particularly in her awareness of the complexities of truth and the complications of freedom. With no desire to reform, but only to understand; with the clear conscience of the rebel, yet unembittered by society's massive lack of understanding, she arrived at her culminating achievements, *The Awakening* and "The Storm."

From "The Poor Girl" to her last novel she was praised for her artistry, but criticized for her subject matter. She obviously does not come near the breadth and stature of Dreiser, but among the American authors of second rank she occupies an important and distinctive position. In her best writings within her particular field, she not only equals Dreiser's courage, but shows an independence, a directness of purpose, a deep understanding, and a sensitive artistry which make them into minor masterpieces. With *The Awakening* and a handful of her stories, such as "Regret," "Athénaïse," and "The Storm," she deserves to be permanently included, not only in her country's literary history, but also in its body of living fiction.

Kate Chopin is a rare, transitional figure in modern literature. In her illustrations of the female condition she forms a link between George Sand and Simone de Beauvoir. In her descriptions of the power of sexuality she reflects the ideas of such a work as *Hippolytus* and foreshadows the forceful 20th-century treatments of Eros.

She was of course too much of a pioneer to be accepted in her time and place. True, Henry Adams asked himself in 1900 whether he knew of any American artist besides Whitman "who had ever insisted on the power of sex, as every classic had always done." Had he looked into *The Awakening,* he would have found more than he may have asked for. D. H. Lawrence would not have accepted Edna, either, since she would not have renounced her sovereignty to achieve his type of man-dictated transcendence. Indeed, in the field of spiritual assertion, Mrs. Pontellier will for a long time to come be faced with male condescension and prejudice—"l'homme que je pourrais aimer n'est pas né, et il ne naîtra peut-être que plusieurs siècles après ma mort," as George Sand lets Lélia observe—and she will also be up against preconceived ideas in a number of women. Most female readers, however, are likely to take to their heart this deeply moving portrait of a woman's growth into self-awareness, just as the author had done with Maupassant's pictures of awakening *Françaises.*[4]

Mrs. Chopin had a daring and a vision all her own, a unique pessimistic realism applied to woman's unchangeable condition. When the storm over *The Awakening* hit her, it showed that she was truly a solitary soul, and indeed, in 1900 she was, with Dreiser, the most isolated, the least recognized of the important American realists of that era. As the old century came to an end, these two writers introduced a belated freedom from all moral preconceptions into American literature. Though they did not openly attack the codes of society, their supreme unconcern with the sacredness of marriage and morals was considered so dangerous that they were forced into silence.

The blow dealt her by the prudish boycott discouraged Kate Chopin from delving as deeply as she could have done into the psychology of her women. She had started out like the animal in "Emancipation," ready to taste and represent life fully. When she finally began to use her literary wings, she reached higher and higher, only to be petrified into the silent, but proud "White Eagle," the final image she created for the public which was not ready for her.

Notes

1. Reedy, as quoted in Max Putzel, "Dreiser, Reedy, and De Maupassant, Junior," *American Literature,* XXXIII (Jan. 1962), 471; Putzel, *Reedy,* p. 261.

2. For an example of such protestations, see George Sand's *Indiana,* I, p. 4.

3. When the St. Louis *Republic* criticized Kate Chopin's use of the words *store* and *depot* instead of *shop* and *railway station,* she replied (St. Louis *Republic,* Oct. 25, 1890) that Howells used *depot* and that she was "hardly ready to believe the value of 'At Fault' marred by following so safe a precedent." This is her only reference to Howells. For an example of the use of French, see George W. Cable, *The Grandissimes* (New York, 1880), p. 182. William Schuyler, "Kate Chopin," *Writer,* VII (Aug. 1894), p. 117.

4. Henry Adams, *The Education of Henry Adams,* Ch. XXV. We might add that Adams felt "unwell," as he termed it, after reading Maupassant (Worthington Chauncey Ford, ed., *Letters of Henry Adams,* I; Boston, 1930, p. 534). George Sand, *Lélia,* p. 529.

✦

$\mathcal{K}$ATE $\mathcal{C}$HOPIN:
$\mathcal{S}$PANNING A $\mathcal{L}$IFETIME

SUSIE MEE

It is now part of literary legend that when Kate Chopin's *The Awakening* first appeared in print in 1899, it was greeted with indignant outcries from critics and public alike. Here was a domestic novel that dared to reject domesticity, a romance that unflinchingly probed relations between the sexes, a brilliant psychological study written during the years when the great Freud himself was poised to startle the world with his theories on female hysteria. Moreover, the heroine of *The Awakening,* Edna Pontellier, was remarkably free of the guilt and sentiment that generally beset her gender (at least in print) and made them fearful of their own sensuality. Even Willa Cather, whom one would have expected to be an ally, attacked Chopin. In reviewing the novel for the *Pittsburgh Leader,* Cather called it "a Creole *Bovary.*" She went on to say that Edna Pontellier belonged to a class of women, "forever clamoring in our ears, that demands more romance out of life than God put into it. . . . They insist upon making it stand for all the emotional pleasures of life and art: expecting an individual and self-limited passion to yield infinite variety, pleasure and distraction, to contribute to their lives what the arts and the pleasurable exercise of the intellect gives to less limited and less intense idealists. . . . They have staked everything on one hand, and they lose."[1] Ironically, years later (in *The Professor's House*), Cather would take up Chopin's same theme—the desire for freedom outside the home—with a male character who, like Edna Pontellier, finds the domestic situation stale, stultifying—and almost impossible to escape.

The legend continues: it was rumored that, depressed by the negative reviews, Kate Chopin virtually gave up writing and, like Keats, died of a broken spirit. This, of course, is only half true. According to Chopin's son Felix, she *was* deeply hurt by the vitriolic tone of many of the critics, but a woman of Chopin's courage would surely have tried to rise above such disappointments, and she did—at least, at first—calling the criticisms "drivel." Sometimes her defensiveness took a witty turn, as in a letter to *Book News*:

> Having a group of people at my disposal, I thought it might be entertaining (to myself) to throw them together and see what would happen. I never dreamed of Mrs. Pontellier making such a mess of things and working out her own damnation as she did. If I had had the slightest intimation of such a thing I would have excluded her from the company. But when I found out what she was up to, the play was half over and it was then too late.[2]

In spite of this show of defiance, the tide of bad reviews kept coming, wave upon wave of relentless animosity, throughout the fall and into the winter: *Public Opinion* felt no sympathy for "this unpleasant person" (Edna Pontellier); the *Chicago Times-Herald* reported that Mrs. Chopin's "many admirers" would be surprised— perhaps disagreeably—by this latest venture; according to the *Providence Sunday Journal,* "The purport of the story can hardly be described in language fit for publication"; to the *Nation,* it was "one more clever author gone wrong," while the *Dial* declared the story "not altogether wholesome."

The real question, however, is not whether Kate Chopin succumbed to despondence—which would be unsurprising, given the circumstances—but whether, in spite of all the criticism, she recognized her own rare genius, a genius so far ahead of its time that the literate public would take half a century to catch up. Since Chopin kept her own counsel, we shall never know. The only available evidence shows that she resumed her varied social life (which included her daughter Lélia's debut), wrote and published a few stories and poems, gave readings around her hometown of St. Louis, Missouri, and even did some reviewing of her own. But eventually there were also murmurings about "not feeling quite well," and her comings and goings grew a bit more circumspect.

Then came an event that captured the imagination of not only

Kate Chopin's personal circle but a good portion of America: the
St. Louis World's Fair of 1904 (which was supposed to have taken
place the year before to mark the centennial of the Louisiana Purchase). Chopin's interest in the fair was intense. She was one of the
first people to buy a season ticket, and indeed attended almost
every day, often by herself. Aside from all the frivolity—the song
"Meet Me in St. Louis" had been composed especially for the occasion and for several months was heard everywhere—the fair had its
serious side: it was meant to be a bridge between the past and the
future. Among the 1,270 acres could be found many extravaganzas:
reenactments of the Galveston Flood, the Boer War, the Hereafter;
reproductions of Greek and Roman temples, of a Philippine "abo-
rigine" village, of Venetian gondolas gliding through artificial
canals; and a miniature railway that (along with camels, burros, ele-
phants, and honking motorcars) transported visitors from one site
to another. In addition, numerous technical innovations were on
display: the wireless radio, X rays, automatic telephones and answering machines, and a Swedish statisticum (a kind of computer).

Kate Chopin was said to have been "enraptured when her eye
caught the Fair ensemble in a certain magical, semi-mystical light." [3]
Perhaps this was the same light that so entranced Edna Pontellier in
The Awakening as she stood by the edge of the ocean, mesmerized by
its beauty and grandeur. There were other resonances between
Chopin and the fair: in creating her heroine in *The Awakening,*
Chopin had also bridged past and future (*Pontellier* means "one who
bridges"). Without breaking entirely with tradition, her innovations looked forward to the time when women could and would
lead independent lives. Did such a thought occur to her, at least un-
consciously, as she traipsed around the huge fairgrounds day after
day (perhaps drinking iced tea or eating an ice-cream cone—both
of which were said to be fair "firsts")? Again, we will never know—
in many ways Chopin remains an enigma. Yet at the very least she
must have looked back in astonishment at the vast changes that had
occurred during the past century, the latter half of which spanned
her lifetime.

* * *

When Kate Chopin (née O'Flaherty) was born in 1850, St. Louis had about 75,000 inhabitants (considerably more than its 1,000 at the time it became part of the United States with the Louisiana Purchase). It was still a frontier town, a place where pioneers could buy provisions for their excursions into wild and often unexplored territory. Her father, Thomas O'Flaherty, had immigrated from County Galway in 1823 and married Kate's mother, Eliza, when she was sixteen (twenty-six years younger than her husband).

Bridges—which would be a motif throughout Chopin's life—figured prominently in one of the two traumas that marked her childhood years. Her father—by this time a well-to-do business-man—had been invited to ride on the ceremonial train making its initial trip over the new Gasconade Bridge that signaled St. Louis's becoming "the gateway to the West." Unfortunately, there was a heavy rainstorm, and just as the locomotive started over the tres-tle, the timbers underneath suddenly gave way, hurling ten of the cars downward into the river. Thirty men drowned, among them Thomas O'Flaherty. Although Eliza O'Flaherty was known as a "pi-ous widow," her daughter, in a story written thirty-nine years later, described a widow's "monstrous joy" upon hearing about her hus-band's reported death in a train wreck. When the husband later walks in, the wife has a sudden attack and dies. We do not know whether the story is based on Chopin's own mother, but in any event, Eliza O'Flaherty never remarried.

The second trauma in Chopin's childhood was the Civil War. Dis-tanced from the East, St. Louis was hopelessly divided on the ma-jor issues: the old aristocratic families (some of whom were French) favored the South, but the newer, German immigrants (who made up the larger number) supported the Union and were adamantly against both secession and slavery. Almost overnight the provincial outpost turned into a potential powder keg seething with unrest and rebellion. Even children were drawn into it: Kate O'Flaherty, in an impulsive gesture, tore down the Union flag that someone had attached to their porch. Instantly Yankee soldiers swarmed through the house, and for a while it looked as though young Kate, now twelve, might be arrested. Only the intervention of a prominent neighbor prevented it; afterward, the story was circulated among Southern sympathizers and Kate was singled out for special admiration.

But the war also brought many changes: schooling (at Sacred Heart Convent) became erratic, as rigid curfews were strictly maintained; a number of friends and acquaintances, including her older stepbrother George, died either in skirmishes or from contagion resulting from poor battlefield conditions. Cherishing her solitude, Kate O'Flaherty continued her reading—Henry Wadsworth Longfellow, Lord Byron, Jane Austen, Sir Walter Scott, popular contemporary novelists such as Dinah Mulock and Catherine Gray, and most especially the novels of Madame de Staël (she read them in the original French), which featured strong-minded, passionate women.

In the meantime Kate O'Flaherty had grown into an "Irish beauty" with abundant dark hair, brown eyes, and a "remarkable self-possession." When the war was over, she made her debut into St. Louis society. But the life of a belle was, as she herself noted, "frantic and all-consuming," requiring a young girl to lace herself up in a tight corset in order to fit into the bustle dress that restricted her even further. It also brought about a deepening discontent with the roles that young women were forced to assume and the effect that these might have on a burgeoning intellect. Already a tension was developing about the disparities between the inner life of the self and outward behavior. Kate reported in her diary about the dizzying round of parties, dances, barbecues, complaining that "my dear reading and writing that I love so well have suffered much neglect." She also wrote disparagingly of the art of social discourse, declaring that it required no intelligence and little energy, except perhaps moving the muscles of one's face.

Then, sometime during this whirl of activities, she met Oscar Chopin, a Frenchman whose family had built a number of plantation houses in Natchitoches Parish in northwest Louisiana. Chopin himself was a fledgling New Orleans cotton broker, a middleman between the cotton growers and the textile buyers. It's not known when Kate O'Flaherty and Oscar Chopin became engaged, because she was unusually discreet about such matters, and his only comment (to a cousin in France) was an offhand remark about St. Louis belles' being "more beautiful than our lovely ladies in Paris," noting in particular their "big fascinating eyes, charming sighs, smiles, which get you, right there in the heart. . . ."[4] At any rate, their betrothal came as a surprise to everyone, even her family.

They were married on June 9, 1870, and as was the custom, set off on a three-month wedding trip abroad. Their honeymoon, however, was not the idyll it might have been—in Paris, Napoleon III was in the process of being deposed and the Second Empire replaced by "la République"; among all the tumult, many tourist attractions were either closed or declared off-limits; also the weather was rainy and dreary. There is no indication that Mrs. Chopin left the Continent with any sense of regret; anyway, by this time she was pregnant and probably yearning to get back home.

The couple visited St. Louis briefly, then continued on to New Orleans, where they began married life in a small house in an unfashionable part of town and where she received, among others, her new father-in-law, Jean Baptiste Chopin. From all accounts the elder Chopin was an unpleasant man who had the reputation of having abused his deceased wife as well as his slaves. However, Kate had little chance to find out whether this was true, for a month later he died. A period of mourning followed, during which she stayed home writing poetry, essays, and occasionally, a story, although in retrospect most of these seem rather crude. The only time she ventured out was to take long, solitary walks around the city.

The Chopins' first child, a son named for Oscar's father, was born in 1871. In rapid succession four more sons followed, and then, on New Year's Eve, 1879, a daughter, Lélia. Kate's time and energies were no longer her own; in contrast to her heroine Edna Pontellier, she (from all appearances) devoted herself to her children, and they returned this devotion by later remaining close to her and supporting her writing endeavors. Sometime during this period, Chopin took up smoking cigarettes, a habit she continued to the end of her life. A New Orleans friend called the Chopin marriage "perfect," although anyone who reads *The Awakening* with a perceptive eye can scarcely believe this to be the whole truth.

In summers, the Chopins moved their menagerie to a nearby resort called Grand Isle, where the children could escape the unhealthy New Orleans heat (a breeding ground for yellow fever, cholera, and typhoid) and where Oscar would spend weekends, returning to the city on Monday morning (like Mr. Pontellier). Then abruptly, their New Orleans life came to a halt. The cotton market had never quite recovered the losses sustained during the war, and from 1878 to 1879, it began to fail miserably. Hoping to avoid financial disaster, Oscar Chopin decided to move the family to Natchitoches Parish, where many of the Chopins had settled after immigrating from France and where Oscar had inherited property.

Whether Kate was distraught about exchanging an urban life for a rural setting, we have no clue. She later described her new home (in a short story titled "For Marse Chouchoute") as a "little French village, which was simply two long rows of very old frame houses, facing one another closely across a dusty roadway." Yet the surrounding landscape was not unpleasant. Aside from the Cane River winding lazily through pine forests, there were substantial plantations of cotton and corn and sugarcane, with silvery green leaves that glittered in the hazy sunlight. Kate Chopin took to riding horseback through the countryside as a substitute for her city walks. (In fact, she was said to have scandalized her neighbors by abruptly jumping astride the horse and galloping off down the road—given her penchant for independence, she may have been deliberately provocative. She also shocked people by ordering her clothes from New Orleans and rolling her own Cuban cigarettes.) Oscar meanwhile had opened a general store and was enjoying being surrounded by a close network of family relations. On Saturdays especially, the store was a beehive, attracting not only customers but also idlers who liked to chew over the local gossip. Kate, who assisted her husband on this day, noted the comings and goings with an astute ear and eye. Years later, much of what she heard and saw would reappear in fictional form, notably in her widely acclaimed book of regional stories, *Cajun Folk,* published under the title *Bayou Folk.*

Both social life and child rearing were much more casual in the

Cane River community than they had been in New Orleans. Cards were a local pastime, and Kate became an avid player. She and Oscar owned a huge gaming table, and often they would invite friends and relatives over for an informal *veillée*. Another kind of amusement could be found at the village dance hall, where on Saturday nights a crowd would stomp, jig, and swirl to the tune of a lone accordion or fiddle. One of Chopin's stories in *Cajun Folk,* " 'Cadian Ball," describes the flirtations and secret trysts that were part of such gatherings. Occasionally a showboat, with its myriad lights and music, would make its way up the river, and local residents, seeing it approach, would gather at the banks.

But, as always, Kate Chopin's favorite entertainment was the musings of her own mind; her solitary nocturnal rides became more and more frequent, reflecting a growing restlessness. Perhaps, like Edna Pontellier, "a certain light was beginning to dawn dimly within her,—the light which, showing the way, forbids it (*The Awakening,* p. 23)." After all, she had been married now for eleven years, had given birth to five children. Her marriage was certainly secure, if no longer exciting; her husband obviously adored her . . . in his way . . . and she loved him, in hers. Still, for a young, beautiful, and curious woman stuck in a provincial backwater, she might be forgiven for having other longings, for wishing to explore the dark paths of forbidden pleasures.

In October 1882, Oscar took sick with a mysterious ailment akin to "swamp fever," an amorphous name for the contagion that rose out of the watery vegetation swarming with mosquitoes and other insects. Under his wife's care, he seemed to be getting better. Then, a month later, he had a relapse; this time, the local doctor was able to make a specific diagnosis—deadly malaria—and ordered a huge dosage of quinine (almost four times the normal amount), but it was too late. Oscar Chopin died on December 10, leaving a multitude of unpaid bills and an estate that was deeply mired in debt. Kate spent much of the next year trying to stave off foreclosure; finally, she was forced to sell a good portion of the land, keeping for herself and her family the plantation house and the store, where she now took Oscar's place. In spite of her enterprising nature, a lone woman's position was particularly precarious in a small village. Years later, neighbors were still talking about the Widow Chopin.

There were many young ladies and young matrons who were sometimes a little jealous of the lovely Kate. When Oscar died, some of the wives felt that their husbands' sympathy for the young widow prompted them to be a little more solicitous in helping her to solve her problems in the store and on the plantation than was necessary.[5]

One married man—Albert Sampite (said to have been the model for Alcée Arobin in *The Awakening*)—was especially attentive. Though six months older than Oscar, Albert was lean, handsome in a roguish way—the typical ladies' man of his day. He and Kate soon took to sharing long rides together. Apparently Chopin's relationship with Albert Sampite was more than mere rumor, since the descendants of neighbors who knew them both remembered hearing about it.

The general talk was that he was in love with the pretty widow, and there were those who believed that she, too, was in love with him. And that may be why she suddenly gave up the store and the plantation and went back to St. Louis.[6]

All this is only surmise, however. No one really knows the reason why Kate Chopin, in 1884, packed up her children and her personal belongings and returned to Missouri—to the house where she had grown up, and where her mother still lived. Some believed that she was exchanging the risk of love for a sedate gentility, although her life in St. Louis would have certain compensations. Instead of the rather confining society of the Cane River community, she now found herself within a circle of liberal-minded and intellectual friends.

Eventually she and her children moved into a smaller bungalow across the street, though she still visited her mother every day. Kate had only been home a year when Mrs. O'Flaherty died. The daughter was, according to an earlier biographer, "prostrate with grief."

In order to avert a possible breakdown, a friend, Dr. Frederick Kolbenheyer, who had admired her long letters from Louisiana, suggested that she begin writing seriously—that is, for publication.

This was not such an unusual thing for a woman to do in 1885. Earlier in the century, a number of women writers had emerged—Hawthorne called them "that damned mob of scribbling women"—who had created a popular literary genre by situating their stories within the home. While male writers concentrated on the ever-expanding frontier, female writers remained fixed on the realm of kin and neighbors, trying to record scenes that would soon disappear forever. These novels, especially geared toward women readers (many of whom were newly literate), dominated the publishing market for fiction before the Civil War. The novels not only showed the vicissitudes of domestic life, but also depicted the local culture in which the heroine lived. As the Chopin scholar Nina Baym has pointed out, these women writers "felt that they had a share in the experiment of the new, democratic nation; they knew that the country was changing rapidly, and they wanted to preserve what they saw."[7] In other words, there was a strong connection between women's writing and regional writing, a connection that persisted—particularly in the South—into the next century.

The postwar period brought a new generation of regional writers who transcended the genre both in craft and subject matter: Sarah Orne Jewett, Mary Wilkins Freeman, Rebecca Harding Davis, Mary Noailles Murfree, Willa Cather. While their themes grew more complex and universal, they continued to root their stories in particular locales. When Kate Chopin began writing, she did it within this regional tradition. Her chosen background, however, was not St. Louis—the place where she had grown up and now lived—but the more colorful Louisiana with its diverse population of Creoles, Acadians, planter-aristocrats, and parvenu entrepreneurs.

Gradually Chopin began to expand her fiction into areas where few authors dared to venture: for instance, the story "Mrs. Mobry's Reason" was about venereal disease—a subject considered off-

limits by most magazines—and was, in fact, Chopin's most rejected story until it was finally published by the *New Orleans Times-
Democrat*. She also started to broaden her literary horizons from
local into national markets: *Vogue* purchased "Ripe Figs," a short
sketch of bayou women; in 1891, after a bit of fawning flattery toward the editor (Richard Watson Gilder), he accepted "A No-Account Creole" for publication in the *Century*, one of the most
prestigious literary magazines in the country, where the fiction of
Mark Twain and George Washington Cable had also appeared. It
was during this period that she came across the writer who would
serve as both an inspiration and a touchstone for her own fictional
experiments. In an essay written several years later (for the *Atlantic*), Chopin described what the discovery of Guy de Maupassant
had meant to her.

> I read his stories and marveled at them. Here was life, not fic-
> tion, for where were the plots, the old-fashioned mechanism
> and stage trapping that in a vague, unthinking way I had fan-
> cied were essential to the art of story making. Here was a man
> who had escaped from tradition and authority, who had en-
> tered into himself and looked out upon life through his own
> being and with his own eyes; and who, in a direct and simple
> way, told us what he saw. When a man does this, he gives us
> the best that he can; something valuable for it is genuine and
> spontaneous.[8]

Maupassant also gave her the courage to move beyond the literary conventions of her time, especially in depicting sex with unusual frankness. One Maupassant story that she translated from the
original French was about a divorce case involving a husband's per-
verted obsession with flowers. Like Maupassant, Chopin wished to
present life realistically, not veiled by innuendo. To achieve this
kind of immediacy, she often wrote an entire story in a single sitting. According to an interview, she did her writing mostly "in the
morning," "on a lapboard with a block of paper, a stub pen and a
bottle of ink bought at the corner grocer, which keeps the best in
town." She also spoke of her distaste for revision.

There are stories that seem to write themselves, and others which positively refuse to be written—which no amount of coaxing can bring to anything. . . . I am completely at the mercy of unconscious selection. To such an extent is this true, that what is called the polishing up process has always proved disastrous to my work, and I avoid it, preferring the integrity of crudities to artificialities.[9]

By 1893, Kate Chopin had published enough stories for a collection, and she traveled to New York and Boston to try and generate some interest in them. Apparently, the trip bore fruit: a few months later, Houghton Mifflin informed her that they wished to publish her collection, now called *Bayou Folk,* and scheduled it for the next March.

When the book appeared, reviews were almost unanimously positive, and Chopin was buoyed up by its reception. In one stroke, the book had raised her from a local writer to one of national stature. In St. Louis, Kate was lionized; several newspapers published articles about her, which noted her personal taste in books (particularly Maupassant and Whitman), as well as her physical characteristics.

In appearance Kate Chopin is a very pretty woman, of medium height, plump, with a mass of beautiful gray hair almost white, regular features, and brown eyes that sparkle with humor. Her five tall sons and pretty young daughter, who have all inherited from some ancestor a height and slenderness that the mother does not possess, make a most attractive family group, the beauty of which is greatly enhanced by the thorough entente cordiale that exists among them.[10]

According to Emily Toth, *Bayou Folk*'s original printing of 1,250 copies sold out and 500 more copies were printed. But when Chopin approached Houghton Mifflin about taking on a second collection (called *A Night in Acadie,* which was finally published by a small press in Chicago), she received a letter alluding to the disappointing sales of *Bayou Folk* and the firm's reluctance to publish another book of short stories. Citing the fact that a longer work had a greater chance of success, the editor did, however, encourage her to write a novel. Within five months, Chopin had embarked upon *The Awakening*.

There has been endless speculation about the extent to which the novel was based on Chopin's own life. It seems safe to declare that, like all fiction, it is an amalgamation of the author's imagination and her experience of the world, whether first-hand or second-hand through newspaper articles and scandalous gossip. Probably both contributed to the characters and the plot; two things are certain: the setting was the same Grand Isle as in Chopin's early marriage, and Edna Pontellier is approximately the same age as Chopin was at that time. More interesting to speculate upon are the taboos that Chopin willfully violated: the description, for instance, of a pregnant woman in the throes of labor; the sensual way that Edna Pontellier expressed her love for Robert Lebrun; her refusal to be a "mother-woman" like her friend Madame Ratignolle; her setting up a separate house from the one where she and her husband lived; and most especially, Chopin's refusal to settle for a "happy ending." These violations precipitated the equally violent reactions when the book was published.

Five years passed between publication of *The Awakening* and the opening of the World's Fair. Though Chopin continued writing, some of her confidence seems to have ebbed away. Perhaps the fair afforded her not only an escape from the ill will and doubts that continued to plague her, but also an intimation of other possibilities. The fairgrounds were not far from where she lived, and as noted before, she went often. Her last visit was on August 20—said to have been "the hottest day since the Fair opened." She arrived home exhausted, and with a splitting headache, which grew worse during the night. By the next day, she was dead, apparently of a brain hemorrhage.

The Awakening appeared to have died with her. For many decades—through the early 1900s and on through the '20s, '30s, and '40s—the novel remained virtually unread; whenever Chopin's name was mentioned in some obscure literary journal or other, it was as a regional writer of local-color stories. It took a French critic to "awaken" this "sleeping beauty."

In 1953, Cyrille Arnavon published a French translation of *The Awakening* (retitled *Edna*), which in turn captured the attention of a few American critics: Van Wyck Brooks called *The Awakening* the "one novel of the nineties in the South that should be remembered, one small perfect book that matters more than the whole life-work of many a prolific writer." In a landmark article published in *Western Humanities Review,* Kenneth Eble termed *The Awakening* "a first-rate novel" and ended his piece with a plea for it to be "given its place among novels worthy of preservation."[11] However, this restoration did not happen overnight. In spite of some renewed interest by prominent men of letters, such as Edmund Wilson and Stanley Kauffman—and also a Norwegian scholar named Per Seyersted (a student of Arnavon's), who published a two-volume edition of Chopin's work—it took the feminist movement of the late '60s and early '70s to hoist the book into national prominence.

Today *The Awakening*—still thought-provoking, challenging, engaging, inspiring—is one of the most widely discussed novels in the American canon. The inconclusiveness of the ending, which so outraged earlier critics, is now considered salutary, even ambiguously postmodern. At the same time, the pertinence of its theme—the struggle to create and nourish an inner self—remains undiminished. On the cusp of yet another century, Edna Pontellier continues swimming toward the future.

Notes

1. "Sibert" [Willa Cather], *Pittsburgh Leader,* July 8, 1899.

2. *Book News,* July 1899.

3. Per Seyersted, *Kate Chopin: A Critical Biography* (The American Institute, University of Oslo; Baton Rouge: Louisiana State University Press, 1969), p. 185.

4. Emily Toth, *Kate Chopin* (New York: William Morrow, 1990), p. 93.

5. Ibid., p. 164.

6. Ibid., p. 172.

7. Nina Baym, ed., *The Awakening and Selected Stories* (New York: Modern Library, 1993), p. xiii.

8. Seyersted, *Kate Chopin,* p. 51.

9. Ibid., p. 117.

10. Sue V. Moore, "Mrs. Kate Chopin," *St. Louis Life,* July 9, 1894.

11. Reprinted in this edition of *The Awakening.* See pp. 207–17.

Colophon

✦

*T*he text of this edition is from Louisiana State University Press's *The Complete Works of Kate Chopin* edited by Per Seyersted. It is set in 13-point Perpetua, 15.5 point leaded. The display face is Bellevue.

This volume was composed by Digital Composition of Berryville, Virginia, and printed and bound by Quebecor Printing Book Group. The color illustrations were printed by Disc Graphics, Inc. The text stock is Lyons Falls' Lucida Book with a laid texture. It is acid-free for archival durability and is milled using a chlorine-free process. The case cover and jacket were printed by Disc Graphics, Inc.

John Collier's pastel and gouache illustrations were filmset by Oceanic Graphics. The typography and binding design are by Charles J. Ziga of Ziga Design.